SARAH MARINE
LESSONS IN DRY DROWNING

Published in the United States of America by AVANTHAM, an imprint of Book Biz Hub, LLC

avantham.com

For permissions or information on bulk orders:
contact@bookbizhub.com

ISBNs:
979-8-9929691-0-8 (e-Book)
979-8-9929691-1-5 (Paperback)
9979-8-9929691-2-2 (Hardback)

Library of Congress No. 2025910670

First Edition

"'Dry drowning'...refers to complications that can arise after a person takes in water through their nose and/or mouth, but not into their lungs, causing a spasm that closes the airway."

parents.com

"The existence of secondary/delayed/dry drowning has been debunked by multiple organizations; it continues to be presented to the public by the media and their consultants. It has terrified parents into believing their child could die following any submersion or exposure to in-water activities."

The American Red Cross

Contents

Prologue   1

PART I
OVERWHELM   7

PART II
CONVULSIONS   77

PART III
DEATH   195

Epilogue   312

Resources   317
Acknowledgments   321
About the Author   325

Prologue

Ten Years Ago

"I've got them!" Lucy called from the pool shed. She was carrying two pink foam noodles.

"These are perfect!" I said, examining one in my hand. The pool had only opened for the summer a week ago, so the noodles hadn't had a chance to get sprinkled with bite marks from the little kids—or crushed by the town's Senior Water Aerobics classes.

"Ready? One, two,..." Lucy started to count off.

"Wait! I need my goggles!" I shouted, running back into the pool shed to retrieve a pair from the community bin. I strapped the SpongeBob-themed goggles over my knotted brown ponytail and pulled the straps until my head hurt. I used to tighten them to the last possible notch, but after seeing one of those watermelon rubber band explosion videos, I figured the second-tightest option would do. I didn't need my brain splattered like watermelon pieces all over the deck to the Little Kid Pool.

"Okay, I'm ready."

We mounted our foam horses, lined up on the edge, and with a one, two, and three, we jumped into the deep end.

"What'd you name your seahorse, Lucy?"

"Whaley," she said with a smile, stroking the foam mane between her legs.

"But she's not a whale. That doesn't make any sense." I liked things to make sense.

"It doesn't need to."

"Well, I named mine Seabiscuit," I said proudly. I'd seen the movie a week ago. It was a good name for a horse. Especially a seahorse.

"Cool. Hey, look at this!" Lucy yelled.

I watched as Lucy dipped the front end of her hollow noodle into the water and then pulled it up after a few seconds. Making sure the back end of the noodle was still above water, Lucy pulled the front to her mouth, and with a big breath, blew into it. It sounded like my grandpa when he would blow raspberries on my cheek. The water sprayed out the other end of the noodle in a marvelous shower that left me covered in seahorse pee.

"Hey, it IS kinda like a whale, because they spray water from their blowholes!"

"I guess." Lucy blew another raspberry.

I tried one too. I blew as hard as I could, and most of the water sprayed out the other end, but a bit of it came back into my mouth, the chlorine stinging one of my canker sores. It was still worth it, though, because I could tell that all the little kids playing Mermaids in the pool were eyeing us with jealousy.

"Girls!" the lifeguard called, "just make sure you're not breathing in any of that water."

"Okay, we won't!" Lucy yelled back with her signature, dimpled smile.

I smiled too, but I wondered how someone would know for sure if the water went down the wrong pipe. I didn't blow any more fountains after that.

As I started to get out of the pool, I noticed Brian. He was watching me as I awkwardly pushed myself up on the side of the pool with my hands, my weak, skinny arms shaking as I brought my right knee up and then the left, and then tried to stand on my stick-skinny legs without slipping or pitching forward onto my face. There's no graceful way to pull yourself out of a pool, especially when you're a top-heavy seven-year-old kid. I looked like a baby giraffe learning to walk as I regained my balance on the slippery pool deck.

I usually preferred to use the ladder, but there was a group of older kids hanging out in the corner by the ladder, and I wasn't about to ask them to move. No one ever seemed to pay any attention to Brian, and I usually ignored him too, but he still had a way of making me feel self-conscious. He was a know-it-all and hung around the pool a lot, minding other people's business. Lucy called him "Bossy Pants" when I told her how he acted like a teacher sometimes. But really, I think he just loved to give advice. Like that old wise turtle in Kung Fu Panda, except that no one ever cared to listen to him. I felt bad for people like that.

"You know why the lifeguard doesn't want you to breathe in the water?" he asked, almost mysteriously.

"Why?" I asked, even though I wasn't sure I wanted to hear the answer. Normally, I feel like I need to know the answer to everything. I think I'm the only kid in the whole school that the teachers told to stop asking questions. Usually, they want you to be curious. Except in Bible Study class. We're only supposed to have our "listening ears" on when we are in the chapel.

"Have you ever heard of 'dry drowning'?" For a third grader, Brian was a walking encyclopedia of information on potential disasters and worst-case scenarios. I bet someone had given him one of those "How to Survive ____" books and he just took it upon himself to memorize the whole thing. My grandparents had a book, something like the "Worst-Case Scenario Survival Handbook" that they kept in the upstairs bathroom instead of the regular old magazine tray they kept in the downstairs one. I got in big trouble once when I tried to flush it down the toilet. In my defense, it probably was full of germs anyway.

Dry drowning hadn't made it into the survival handbook

between shark attacks and quicksand, but I vaguely remembered my mother warning me about this when I was younger. She read some article on Facebook about a kid who swallowed too much water in the pool and then died the next day in his sleep or something like that. It scared me at the time, but then I think I sort of forgot about it until now.

Without waiting for me to answer, which was very rude, Brian said, "It's when you get water in your airway, but it doesn't make it all the way to your lungs. Instead, your vocal cords just spasm and they try to cough up the water, but you can't get it all out, no matter how hard you try. And then you die. It can happen minutes or hours later. You're just tempting fate every time you jump in."

He sounded like Mom whenever she said I was "tempting fate" by riding a skateboard on the big-kid ramp. "Just because you've done it before, doesn't mean you won't fall and get hurt this time." I did it every day for a year after she said that, just to show her the statistics. Only I can never pronounce that word right.

"All I'm saying, Liz, is don't take breathing for granted." I didn't even know what that expression meant: "for granted." I feel like my dad may have said it to me once though.

"Cool, thanks, Dr. Brian," I said sarcastically, but I was trying to hide that building, icky feeling in my stomach. I didn't think I had inhaled any water, but I did start quietly coughing just in case there was any pool water lingering in my throat making its way to my vocal cords, whatever those are. I would be able to feel it, right? Dry drowning sounded like it was up there with being buried alive as one of the worst ways to die. The scariest part was, you could be drowning and not know it until it was too late.

There was no way to know. I coughed again to clear my throat just to be safe.

Thinking about it more, I wasn't sure which was more horrifying: that you could be drowning and not know it, or that your own body could be tricked into killing you. I wanted to ask Brian more, but he had already disappeared.

OVERWHELM

Chapter 1

HIGH TIDES

[Present Day]

The last day of high school rolled around quicker than I ever could have imagined. Probably because I had anticipated it being in June, rather than April. And because I likely pictured myself having a diploma on that day too. But shit happens. It was a miracle I'd made it all the way to senior year, to be honest. I don't know how I went back to school after the Big Breakup with Brian; though to be fair, I only lasted about a week before I lost my shit, and my high school career abruptly ended. Brian and I had been together since freshman year, and by junior year we were practically inseparable. But if I really think about it, he'd been a big part of my life since grade school, back when I thought he was a helpful, albeit sometimes annoying, friend. It's almost like something horrible has to happen when a relationship like that falls apart. Like the universe has to acknowledge it in some way or else it never really happened.

I just wish the universe could have waited until after I graduated high school to send that asteroid, just for the sake of my future and all. Even more annoying is the fact that Mom still thinks I have one: a future. She's all "GED" this and "community college" that and "keep the cap and gown for the Christmas card." I'm not sure she gets it. This whole high school dropout thing. It's not something she can just wish away with her stupid motivational Instagram reels she sends me every day. I'm not saying she won't force me into getting my degree one day, but it's not the same. There will always be that one big stain on my life. It's the kind of stain that stays with you, even when you've used up a whole Tide pen trying to dab it out. The smell still lingers; it follows you.

I know people who never went to college or ended up flunking out. My dad's brother being one of those people that looked at the ground when the conversation turned to alma maters and what frat were you in? It was all kind of messed up in my opinion. I mean, when was it normalized to just casually ask where someone went to college? It wasn't fair to anyone. First off, when the person tells you they didn't go, it's gotta be one of the most uncomfortable moments in your life. And second, it makes the other guy feel like absolute shit. And for what? Not going to some fancy school to get some fancy certificate to frame above your desk at your 9-5 job that you hate? And yet that's the truth. Because guys like my Uncle Jim end up spending their whole lives trying to prove themselves to guys like my dad, who has his Cornell license plate to do it for him. He'd probably be overjoyed that I was the one dropping out of high school. Like I said before, stains like these don't just fade away. If anything, you pass them on.

I mean, seriously, how did I get here? It wasn't too long ago that I had everything together: a straight-A student (and well on my way in battling out Mia Davis in the pursuit for valedictorian), heading off to an Ivy League-adjacent college, a best friend I could be my total weirdo self with, a toned, fit body, clear(-ish) skin and silky blond hair (fake, of course), and Brian, who was more than any boyfriend you could imagine. Now, the only clothes that fit me are sweatpants, and I couldn't even tell you the name of my colorist anymore—it's been a long, long time since I've stepped inside a salon. My dark brown, nearly black roots reached my chin, with my damaged bleached blond ends extending six inches below my shoulders. My college acceptance offer was rescinded when I couldn't complete my senior year, but worst of all, my best friend Lucy is gone and never coming back. And Brian? Well, I wish I could say the same.

The only thing I have to put forth now is a lousy "please-don't-sue-us" honorary diploma my high school finally handed over in July, two months after Mom came barging through those rusty doors, demanding my extra summer courses supplemented my "mental health leave" (AKA dropout). If I let her, she probably would have threatened Principal Louis into letting me attend graduation too. That woman had a mind of her own when it came to proving how far she would go for her kid. There wasn't a single thing in the world she wouldn't do for me—except listen.

If I had anyone to thank for getting that belated diploma, though, it wasn't her. It was Brian. He was the one that forced me into taking all those summer courses every year of high school, always telling me I'd be glad I did it in the future. He was right: lake parties and summer barbecues weren't worth being a loser for the rest of your life. Except I'd skipped most of those parties and still ended up a loser.

As for my dad, I'm still not sure if he thought the whole "I'm dropping out of school" call was serious or not. With him, nothing was. My first pet goldfish died? Let's go get ice cream. You're scared about dying now? Here's a dog. You want to talk about Grandpa's funeral? Sorry, football's on at five. The man just couldn't handle life. Which was ironic, because he single-handedly managed a multi-million-dollar company. But then again, the executives probably had their own people to run the crisis management department. For as long as I could remember, that was Mom.

Speaking of the devil, a text from her appeared on my phone. "Lucy said hi to me in line at CVS this morning."

She doesn't understand. My mom loves Lucy, but she doesn't

understand her. Lucy would never be the kind of girl to lose her good manners just because your daughter ruined her life. Clearly Mom thought that there was a chance to repair everything that went down at Lucy's house that night, or at least whatever she thought went down. For all she knew, it was probably just another petty bitch fight about who stole whose earrings, and all I had to do was return those cheap gold hoops of Lucy's that made my ears green anyway. She'd even bought me a graduation dress, probably thinking I'd go back to school before the end of senior year. Not like I would have even wanted to go to graduation if I could. Not after the night I fucked it all up. Not after everything I did to Lucy.

"Liz, what the hell! You still haven't cleaned your room?" Mom posed it like a question, but it was plain as day that I hadn't done shit.

Her eyes went from the pile of leaking soda cans on the carpet to my greasy rat's nest of hair.

"You haven't showered either?! God, for one day can't you just make my life a little easier!?" Apparently, it was my job to make her life easier.

I stared back at her blankly.

"Liz!!! C'mon, what are you doing? I told you your dad is coming over!"

"Thanks for the reminder."

Mom sighed as she started collecting the stray socks that littered the floor and the half-eaten ice cream cartons that had begun seeping into the wet carpet. "Aren't you going to help me?" she said it like it should've been my first instinct.

I sighed, a deep, exhausted sigh like I hadn't just spent the better half of the day hibernating in my bed. It wasn't that I didn't want to help, I just didn't want to do anything. There's a difference, I think. "I can't" was the best I could make out. Just getting out of bed to pee felt like enough activity to justify going back to sleep after I flushed. And I only bothered at all because I'd seen that episode of Euphoria and kidney stones seemed like the worst pain in the world, next to losing your best friend. The combination of the two would've been lethal.

"What do you mean, you can't? Did your legs stop working?"

"I'm just too tired." She couldn't be mad at the truth, it's all she was ever asking for.

"You've been in bed all day!" Well, on second thought, I guess truths are subjective.

I laid my head back on my pillow, staring up at the ceiling. My eyes traced the cracks that ran along the white paint like little, intertwining rivers, finally landing on the spot where the star had fallen off.

I was expecting a fight, but I was more terrified by Mom's

silence. I watched as her eyes searched for a meaning behind my words and in my own face, and I watched as they realized there was nothing there to find. There was a darkness in my eyes that one could only look at directly for so long: it left your eyes darting in circles, looking for somewhere to focus. When I was born, instead of having light eyes like most babies, Mom said mine looked like two black coals. She said it meant I'd be a diamond one day. I think we'd both given up on that hope by now.

Mom shook her head, let out a sigh of exhaustion, and ascended the stairs with the overpacked laundry bin at her hip.

"Just don't feel bad when your dad blames all of this on me, Liz," she called from the doorway.

I rolled my black coal eyes. It seemed to keep the tears in.

"And come upstairs for breakfast," she added as she reached the kitchen. Maybe I'm just bitter or maybe I'm just trying to defy Brian's obsession with success and status, but there's a real part of me that just doesn't care about anything anymore. There's a reason why the same word used to describe one's hopes and dreams also means inhaling foreign matter into the lungs: either one can kill you.

Mom says I'm just overreacting to this whole breakup, and that I'm purposely swinging to the opposite extreme just to piss Brian off. And maybe I am. So what? She was the one who got a bob after she and my dad split, which was a real commitment in my opinion, judging that she and my dad had always agreed that such a haircut should be reserved for children under five only.

"Liz! Breakfast!" Mom called down the banister. She hated that I wasn't on the same floor as her, but I couldn't stay in my old room after all the shit went down. The basement was my new little safe haven.

"Eli-za-beth!!! You're eighteen years old; I shouldn't have to call you up like this!!!"

Partly because I wasn't in the mood to fight and partly because I actually was starving, I grudgingly sulked up the stairs, passing by the mountains of dishes left for the next "tomorrow" to put away.

My mother, or Margaret as Brian had always referred to her, was standing by the table in her Target sweater and faded jeans, glasses readily perched at the tip of her nose. She had a letter in her hand. Oh god.

"I've got something that I think will make you happy!" she said in an overly cheerful voice.

I winced. There was that word again. I heard it from everyone, in the form of a question, concern, offer, anything that would remind me I wasn't it. Happy.

"Mom, tell me you didn't do something?" For once I wish she actually hadn't.

She stared at me, all of her chins sinking further into her green turtleneck.

"Listen, your father made some calls…" She took another deep breath in and her whole shell rose with it. "Franklin College had an open spot, and they think you're great. They're expecting you in September!"

Hearing those words leave her mouth made my blood boil to the point steam was probably rolling out of my ears. The whole room physically felt hotter. Maybe I wasn't living in an ocean, but a big old pot of turtle soup. I'd been played like the damn frog that thought he was getting a free bath.

"Mom, you guys have no right to go behind my back and try to do these things for me. I didn't ask for it, I don't want it, and I'm not doing it. I'm a grown adult; I don't need your help!" I practically screamed.

"Yeah, a grown adult that has tantrums because she can't decide which color Post-it notes she wants!" Mom blurted out.

I dropped my gaze to the ground as a coldness ran through my blood, numbing every part of me. I had expected that coming from anyone else, even if my dad had made the comment, it would not have come as big of a shock as hearing Mom say it. But how could I blame her and not myself?

"Liz, I'm just trying to help. I guess I just don't understand why you're not taking it. Honey, I'm giving you a lifeline here. We just gotta ride this wave, we can do it together."

It took everything in me not to roll my eyes. God did that woman love her analogies.

"Mhm."

"I just feel like you're headed down a dangerous road, Liz."

"Dangerous?"

"No, that's not the right word..." She looked at the floor like it was the dictionary she needed.

"If you think I'm planning on killing myself, I hate to break it to you, but it's not on my agenda."

Honestly, I'd been to so many therapists who all seemed so preoccupied with whether I had suicidal thoughts or plans or ideations that they didn't seem interested in anything else I had to say. No one gives a shit as long as you aren't suicidal and therefore a potential lawsuit that could take down their practice. Or in Mom's case, her reputation as the most progressive neighbor "any kid could turn to"—except her own apparently.

I could only imagine the shit people were talking about me dropping out of high school and living in the basement. I could already picture Mrs. Donahue from across the street in her big ugly mansion whispering "that's what you get for being snowflakes" like she didn't still have some lingering around her nose. Everyone says high schoolers are the judgiest, but really, it's their parents you better watch out for. I guess the Donahue brothers would've been in school with me if they hadn't been shipped off to military school the second they hit puberty. If only Mrs. Donahue knew I'd watched her little Tommy "propose" to another boy back at All Saints. We were always putting on weddings in that kindergarten. Something about going to school in a church just sort of established it. Of course, we weren't allowed to do it anymore after the whole Tommy and Nathan scandal. I sure did wonder how he was liking the military.

"Liz, you know that's not what I meant. I'm just scared." I'll admit it, I liked being an asshole.

"Scared about what?" I asked.

"That you're going to miss out on things."

"Like what? Attending a stupid party school a five-year-old could get into?"

"Like following your dreams?" Mom offered. "You'll have to leave the house for that."

"This house has nothing to do with it."

Chapter 2

FUEL UP

[Six Years Ago]

"What'd you get for summer reading?"

"I'm stuck with this stupid book about a teacher! Like why would I want to read about school in summer?!" Lucy exclaimed. "Why are you bringing up school anyway, Liz? I don't want to think about it."

Lucy and I were sitting on the hot plastic chairs overlooking the pool, the vinyl stripes leaving white lines across our sunburnt bottoms. My skin had only two tones: ghostly pale or bright red sunburnt. No shades of tan in between, unless you count the smattering of freckles across my nose and cheekbones.

We were 11 now: one more year until we could walk to the pool alone. And only 47 days until we'd be walking through the big doors of Maple Brook Middle.

"Oof. At least you don't have to read Wonder for like the 3rd time in a row!" I complained.

"Just watch the movie. I wish Mr. Terupt had one." Lucy sighed. "I don't know..."

"Well, don't complain to me about it and then don't take my advice."

"No, it's just that I think that'd kind of be cheating," I mumbled, playing with the blades of grass at my feet.

"It's not cheating. I did the same thing for Bridge to Terabithia," Lucy said, her voice taking on a sterner tone. I could already predict the "You think you're better than me?" on the way. I wanted to tell Lucy that it was the other way around. That I just felt like I owed it to myself to meet certain standards. The tedious work, not the pride. Instead, I told her, "Yeah, I guess I'll watch it," even though my TV hadn't been working all summer. Lucy had spent enough sleepovers putting on reenactments of our favorite Jessie episodes to know that.

"Liz?"

"Mhm."

"Speaking of movies, what should we watch tonight?" Lucy and I loved to watch scary movies together, it was kind of our thing.

My answer was the one I always gave, no matter the question. Two hands up with a shoulder shrug. I swore that emoji was based on me. Lucy didn't mind though because she liked to have her way. She only asked me sometimes to be polite.

"Oh wait," Lucy interjected, "they're about to call Adult Swim. We gotta be first in line at the Shack!" She grabbed my arm and practically pulled me out of my chair. We'd sat out most of the regular swim because Lucy could tell I was getting overwhelmed by all the kids splashing around me; I wasn't good with crowds, especially if water was involved. She was a good friend like that. And she had good ideas too, like how to make sure we didn't spend the entire 20 minutes of Adult Swim standing in a slippery wet line at the Snack Shack, shivering in our wet bathing suits and damp towels.

I loved summer. It was nothing like school, where you had homework and had to worry about following rules and wearing the right clothes and taking tests and about whether your teacher likes you or thinks you're smart, and you're scared of missing one single lesson in case you get behind and will never catch up no matter how hard you try. And I always tried really hard. No, summers were for splashing, swimming, and snacking at the Snack Shack. I'm pretty sure I loved summer even more than Lucy did, but that's only because every day was probably like summer vacation for her.

"Quick!" Lucy yelled as we approached the Snack Shack, just as the loudspeaker announced it was time for Adult Swim. "Ok great, only three people ahead of us. You stand in line, I gotta go pee," Lucy ordered. I was happy to oblige. I was always happy to follow orders. We worked well like that; she liked being a boss and I liked having someone else make the decisions.

"Wait!" I panicked, realizing she wouldn't be back from the bathroom before I had to order. "What should I get you?"

Lucy was already halfway out the door running towards the restrooms and she yelled back, "Whatever you're getting!"

This was going to be a problem. I usually just ordered whatever Lucy did, it was easier that way. Lucy didn't seem to mind, she said imitation was a form of flattery. I didn't tell her she had no cause to be flattered; it had nothing to do with her.

I stood frozen like the ice pop the little girl at the front of the line ordered. She looked like she was five years old—I was more than double her age. How did she know what to order? The snot-nosed little girl left the Snack Shack, licking her ice pop from the top while the bottom melted onto her tiny, grubby hands. Terrible technique. Now there were only two people in front of me. Behind me, a long twisting line was growing. Soggy, cold, hungry and impatient kids all waiting for their frozen treats.

Suddenly I had a flashback to my fifth birthday party. It was princess-themed and in the backyard of my old house. The house with the pirate ship (aka jungle gym) and the golden sea (aka dead, yellow grass). I could see it all so clearly, like I was looking out of that plastic spyglass mounted above the tire swing. A five-year-old Cinderella ran past me to climb up the slide, a ginger Elsa twirled around with an Ariel who kept tripping over her tail. Snow White had peed her pants already, and I heard her mom say something like "yellow snow" to the other parents and they were all laughing.

I was Rapunzel, I had the long yellow braided wig and everything, it was my birthday party after all. Most of the kids had cake frosting for lipstick, but my mom had made sure to also serve ice cream: my favorite. Back when I could choose favorites.

Mom rang the dinner bell so we could all pretend we were getting called to the ball racing in our flats, and Ariel face planting in the dry grass of course. But when I got to the porch, and saw the two cartons: chocolate and vanilla, the corset of my costume began to feel real.

Mom asked me which flavor I wanted, but they had both seemed delicious. I remembered saying, "I don't know?" and Mom replied, "Just tell me which one you want, you'll know." I had run into the bathroom then. I started to cry on the toilet seat as my little legs dangled above the tile floor. I thought something was wrong with me, that I was born wrong. All the other kids knew which flavor to choose, they didn't even think twice. I remembered thinking about my favorite show at the time, "Dora the Explorer," and the way the objects had a golden ring around them, the one you were supposed to pick. But neither ice cream carton had a golden halo. All the other kids must have seen that halo. All the other kids got to eat ice cream that day.

I never dressed up as a princess again after that.

The kid in front of me was ordering now and I was running out of time. My heart was racing. How long did it take to pee? There was probably just as big of a line in the bathroom, it didn't matter that Lucy washed her hands in only 22 seconds (I counted.) My body was shaking, and I was grateful for the fact that I was in a bathing suit so it looked like I was shivering from the cold rather than the fear that was racing through my body. How was I supposed to choose just one thing? And what if I ordered something and Lucy didn't like it? So much for the lazy carefree summer pool day.

That's when Brian tapped me on the shoulder. Brian, whose

description of dry drowning had haunted me for the past four summers, always seemed to be lurking around, whether you noticed him or not. That summer before middle school started, he was hanging around me more than usual, like he'd sort of latched onto me. Except when Lucy was around, he tried to keep his distance; I think he was sort of scared of her. Who wouldn't be?

"Trouble deciding?" he asked like it was written on my face. Was it?

"Uh, no. Um, I'm just thinking," I said, embarrassed.

"Don't worry, I get it," he said reassuringly. "There are just SO many choices you can make, and there is no way to tell whether you are making the 'right' one."

"Exactly!" I said excitedly. Finally, someone who understood the severity of the situation.

"I'll tell you a trick that I use, it works every time." Brian spoke so matter-of-factly, he instantly put me at ease. "Just look at the menu and go down in order, reciting 'eenie-meenie-miney-moe,' and whatever you land on, is the one you order."

"But what if it lands on something I don't like, or Lucy doesn't like?" I asked.

"Well then," Brian said, "it wasn't your fault, it was the universe's fault."

I didn't think about it, I just did what he said and counted my finger down the various ice cream flavors down to the popsicles and then back up to ice cream while reciting this childhood rhyme until I landed on Rocket Pop. Not bad.

"Two Rocket Pops, please!" I said confidently to the pimply cashier, trying to hide my excitement at my new trick. Maybe this Brian kid wasn't so bad after all.

Chapter 3

GOING SWIMMING

The first day of middle school was finally here, but I wasn't sure I was going to make it there.

My anxiety was already at high tide. I looked through my drawers, hangers, and hampers, but both the magnitude of my options and of my first day of middle school's importance made it difficult to choose an outfit without immediately questioning myself after. Sometimes the shirts would be too tight, or the pants were itchy, or sometimes it just didn't feel right.

I worried that if I wore white, I would spill food on it, that red was too provocative, that beige was too plain. I had no clue what colors went best with pale white skin, dark brown hair, and brown eyes. If only I had inherited my father's blue eyes, I could wear blue shirts to show off my eyes, the last thing I wanted to bring out was my boring brown.

A skirt or shorts would accentuate my knobby knees and pale gangling legs, but jeans would highlight my lack of a butt. I wished I had a friend to call, anyone that I trusted, to help me decide, to reassure me that my taste wasn't hideous or at least to confirm that it was. I would've called Lucy, but she was never up this early before school because she literally lived next door to the school.

"Liz! We are leaving in 5 minutes!!" Mom called from downstairs.

I stared into the great abyss of my closet. I knew it really didn't matter which outfit I chose, I doubted anyone would really care, but the pressure I felt on my shoulders was weighing me down, more than all the hundreds of sweaters I had tried on.

"Liz, I already pulled out an outfit in the car for you, you can change in the car on the way there!"

Thank God. The waves submerged back into the water, leaving only ripples in the new tide.

But as we made our way to the car, I took a pause in the driveway, my hand quickly falling on the left of my chest. My breath came in and out so fast that I felt more air would come through my nose if I just stopped trying to breathe. Memories of this sensation, stronger than the events actually causing them, came crashing back to me, and I imagined my knees buckling down to the pavement. I wished desperately to bring my body down to the cement, to curl up in a fetal position, pressing my closed eyelids against my knees, because I needed them to feel the calm of utter darkness rather than just see it. Every part of me yearned to run back into the house, slam the door and disappear under the covers where I was safe from the what ifs of the outside world. Sometimes I really did feel like Rapunzel. Suddenly my vision started to blur, and Mom's face was distorted in my eyes until I felt our foreheads meet.

"Liz! You've got to snap out of it! Lizz!"

I felt like I was underwater, sinking with an arm outstretched and fingertips just inches below the surface as muffled voices called me back from above. Mom's words sounded like my voice when I sang in the bathtub, with my ears submerged in water. But slowly I felt myself being carried out of the depths of the ocean, and warm, dry hands were placed on my own heaving shoulders as they shook my whole body, trying to get the water out of my lungs. Mom's face again appeared in front of me, and I felt myself being guided to the car, then placed into the back seat. As my mother pulled out of the driveway, I felt myself slowly becoming more used to the air around me, as if with each breath I took, I was getting farther and farther from the ocean.

I picked up the outfit Mom had chosen for me, and I immediately wished I had stayed home. I knew my mother didn't have much of a taste in fashion and sometimes preferred the more "Tomboy" look, but this was one of the most unflattering outfits I'd ever seen. The pants were black velvet and wrinkled from being thrown in the car, and the shirt looked like it belonged to an 8-year-old—probably mine from four years ago. But whatever the clothes were, they would at least be a bit more school appropriate than the pajamas I was wearing.

When I finally fit myself into the velvet trousers and striped, pink shirt, I looked at myself in the rear-view mirror. Normally I wouldn't care if I looked bad, or ugly, or like I hadn't put any effort into my appearance, and normally I hadn't. But middle school was different, I felt a new obligation to present myself more fashionably, more 'put together' in a way I never felt in elementary school or in the summer.

"Ok Liz, we're here. Let's just move on from this morning, start a clean slate. Just do your best."

I rolled my eyes. What was it with these hippy parents and millennial teachers always saying that phrase "do your best." As if there was some magic magnitude of effort like the flags along a pool lane that when you've reached the threshold, ding ding ding, you've done your best, and you're done. It was the worst when teachers would tell me to do my best on writing assignments. You can always add one more word, the best authors know their work is never done. I think that's why poets are always calling themselves "tortured." They weren't exaggerating. They were just doing their best.

"Go get 'em, tiger."

She must have seen other parents calling their kids nicknames and figured it was never too late to start. But it was too late.

"Yeah, I got it, you can stop being cheesy now, jeez."

Mom's expression immediately softened at my remark, and I realized why humor made a good mask. Maybe I was more like my dad than I thought.

I eventually made my way out of the car and took a number of slow steps, testing the waters, I imagined, until I reached the sidewalk in front of the big brick building.

I realized Mom was right behind me. How embarrassing. "It's fine, just leave," I could see the concern in her eyes. She was about to turn away when she pulled out her phone and asked to take a picture of me outside the school.

The camera flashed and her smile returned. I was relieved to watch as she turned around in her heels and clicked down the pavement and into the car. I never understood why Mom was dressed up for such a small thing, but I guessed today was as big of a day for her as it was for me.

The second her car drove away from the parking lot, I was dumped right back into the water, and the drowning sensation continued. I hadn't realized how much of a lifeline Mom really had been.

The doors to the Maple Brook Middle School were so big they made giant shadows the size of elephants on the main stairs. Mom told me the school wasn't really that big and that I was just small and one day the boys would get so tall in my grade that they would be able to jump up and slap the top of the doorway. I asked her why on Earth they would want to do that, and she told me it was one of the greatest mysteries in life. I really hope I find out sometime, because I like to understand things.

"Liz! Over here!" I heard Lucy's voice call out to me. She was standing at the top of the stairs already holding a blackboard that said "Today's my first day of middle school" on it. I wondered why her mom hadn't just taken the picture outside the front door of her house like a normal person, because this was sort of embarrassing. But I guess Lucy wasn't the type to be easily embarrassed, not by her family at least. I walked over to her; she was hard to miss with her neon pink JoJo Siwa backpack.

"Here, stand next to me!" she said, grabbing me by the tail of my own Jansport and reeling me in for a photo. She moved the blackboard sign so that it was in the middle of both of us.

"Hold on," her mom said, "let's wait for this group to move out of the way."

I looked over my shoulder, and then I wished I hadn't. Huge herds of kids of all different heights and weird smells were piling into the school like it was an escape exit, and the fire was on the outside. All the screaming coming from the building must have been the kids realizing it was hell they'd just shoved their way into. Some of their faces were covered with zits the size of pepperoni and I wondered what would happen if they tripped on those stairs. Would they just pop all over the place? What about the short kids, how were they supposed to squeeze through that stampede? Or did they just get trampled, and growth spurts in puberty were really just a form of natural selection? We waited five more minutes. The doorway somehow just got more and more crowded. I looked back at Lucy, she was still holding her picture-perfect smile for the camera. I squeezed her hand; I know it's not how it works, but I was kind of hoping she could transmit some kind of wave of confidence into my body, to make it a little less terrifying.

I guess Lucy's mom must have realized that there was never going to be a free spot for a picture, so she just counted down to three and then flash, it was done. I looked at Lucy, she was still smiling.

The first thing we did when we walked into the zoo was get our lockers. They handed each of us a slip of paper with a number on it and a lock. 302. That was my locker number. There hadn't even been 300 kids in my entire elementary school last year. But that was the thing, all the elementary schools from around town merged into one single, massive, middle school. It was straight out of a horror movie.

"My dad told me that the 8th graders used to wedgy any kid

that stood in front of their locker for too long, isn't that silly?" Lucy said, giggling.

I cleared my throat and placed my shaky hands on the fake belt loops of my jeggings, just in case.

"Why would you tell me that?!"

"Relax, Liz. That was like in the 1900s, things have changed." She looked around at the zoo of kids, smiling in awe. I'm not sure what kind of magic those new contacts of hers were doing but there was no way we were seeing the same hallway. Everywhere I looked there were kids shrieking and jumping about and giving each other bear hugs I felt uncomfortable just witnessing. And then there was the smell of the place, some concoction of paper supplies, bleach, body odor, and something nasty that was wafting out of the cafeteria, wherever that was.

Lucy and I didn't have many classes together, but we were in the same homeroom. Unfortunately, Aubrey's entire clan was in it too. All of them were wearing black leggings with their Nike socks pulled up over them and a few of them had matching white tops on. Lucy said they looked like zebras. It was true though, if you stared at them long enough and squinted, you just saw one big black and white blob. Suddenly a few fluffy heads started to mix like lions coming to feast. The zebra neighs went up an octave and combined with the sound of shuffling paws. I could already tell that the middle school air had contaminated my classmates: boys and girls mixed now. It's like all the cages were broken down, just as I'd gotten used to them. The bell rang and it was time to go to my first class, all on my own, with a whole new teacher. What kind of zoo just lets all the animals roam free?

I had math on my schedule, but sense of direction was one thing my dad and I had in common, in that we had none of it. I was about to run into the bathroom and wait out the tide for a bit when Brian appeared at my side. He had math first period too.

"Our biggest hope is finding some kid to latch onto who's going the same way," he said, reading my mind. Clearly, he didn't know the way to math either.

I was too shy to ask anyone, so we just ended up just shuffling around the halls, eavesdropping on conversations until I heard: "We can't be late for Mr. Streight." I looked down at my schedule paper. Bingo. The crowd these kids were in was so big that they couldn't all be best friends, so I figured I could walk next to them, and they'd assume I knew someone who knew someone in this hallway blob.

I quickly learned that if you wanted to survive in middle school, you had to learn to swim. You also have to be swimming at the same speed as all the other fish so that you can start trailing in their whirlpool and eventually, you'll arrive at the right classroom. There's a reason they call it a school of fish.

Chapter 4

SPLASHING

When I got home after my first day of middle school, I planned on relaxing. I was indulging myself in a big bowl of popcorn and a shirtless Logan Huntzburger on my laptop when I suddenly realized the deep, deep trouble I was in. I was prepared to lock myself in my room and never leave. I was ready to start bargaining with God: I hadn't done my summer reading. After all the crap I gave Lucy about just watching the movie instead, here I was now. No Wonder. I called Mom as soon as I realized, but the town library was all out of copies. There wasn't a single Wonder book I could get my hands on before 8:00 am tomorrow and I was panicking. I knew that book from cover to cover but the assignment hadn't been to recite Wonder, it had been to read it. Not last summer, not for the last two summers and third grade too, but this summer. The one before middle school.

"I have to go to the library," I said it like I was about to pee my pants.

"Liz, it's closed. Look outside, it's already dark out."

I thought maybe it was just my eyes making it look like that at first. They played tricks like that sometimes.

"But this is middle school!" She didn't seem to be grasping the importance of this stage in my life. "I can't just goof around anymore, it matters now."

"Relax, it's not high school, and even if you were, it's not the worst thing in the world to have a bad grade or two. In the grand scheme of the universe, we live on a floating pebble, so God forbid you forget to do your summer reading, it's not the end of the world. I'm sure most kids didn't do it, Liz."

"And that makes it okay?" Sometimes it felt like I had to be the parent for both of us.

"It makes it not as big of a deal as you're acting like."

But it was a big deal. Your performance in middle school dictates what sort of high school you'll get into, and what track you'll be put on. Then college. Then a job. It does matter.

"Here, if you really wanted to, you could just watch the movie. We already own it."

"But that's cheating!" I blurted out instinctively.

"Says who??"

"If it's not following the rules it's cheating, Mom!"

She just rolled her eyes at me and started blasting the TV like a true teenager. The first scene appears on the screen, and it is Auggie with his big astronaut mask jumping on his bed. I think he pretends to be in space because things like the way your face looks or the grade you get in 6th grade doesn't matter there. No oxygen and no judgement kind of go together. Next, he's getting ready to go to school, where kids like Julian are going to pick him apart. I want to tell him just to stay home. He's gonna see soon that it's not just in the movies, that some kids are just plain brutal. They'll throw rocks at you because you're different. And if they throw them hard enough, they might just put another planet like this shithole into orbit. And there's nothing he can do about it. Because nothing is ever gonna change on this stupid floating rock. How can it, when apparently nothing matters on its surface?

The wifi buffered for a second and that's when I noticed a new book on the table beside the TV. It was still wrapped up with the price tag and all. "How to Parent a Worrier."

I made a frown at Mom but didn't dare take my eyes off of Owen Wilson's dazzling blue ones. What a cheat I was, eating a TV dinner in my pajamas and listening to the hottest accent alive instead of doing my work. And even worse, I liked the movie. Well, I had been liking it until I recognized a pale snooping face in the window: Brian. I forgot I'd invited him over to help me deal with all my First Week of School jitters. He said he got them too. I tried to turn off the TV before he could see what was playing but I reached the remote too late. Without even looking at him I could sense he was disappointed.

"Oh, I thought we were supposed to read that book?" he said when I let him in.

He knew I knew we were too.

"I didn't know there was a movie option, or else I would—"

"There isn't a movie option, Brian, you know that."

"Well, I'm glad you're admitting it."

I wanted to tell him to shut up, but I bit my tongue. It was better than the hand that was feeding me in this zoo of a middle school.

"I mean it's your responsibility to get the book and read it."

"Well, yeah, it was my fault in the past but there's nothing I can do now."

"Well, that's simply not true."

"What, you think I should go run around town knocking on every single door until someone can lend me a copy?" I was just trying to predict the worst of what he could suggest.

"I'm not saying you should do that, I'm just saying don't say 'there's nothing I can do' when you literally thought of an alternative in .2 seconds."

The kid had a point.

"Well, realistically, what can I do here?"

He threw his head up like a seal balancing a circus ball on his nose. "'Realistic-ness' is a useless measurement but that's a lecture for another day." I swore this kid was autistic sometimes.

"But what you could do, in your perception of 'being realistic,' would be to tell your teacher."

"You mean, like tell Mr. Garner I didn't do the reading because I'd already read Wonder?"

"Ermm," he shifted on his feet, "I feel like that might come off as you making excuses. Why don't you just confess to watching the movie instead?" He asked it like I'd committed a crime. But then again, laws were just rules made by Mr. Government instead of Mr. Garner. I promised to go to school early the next day so I could catch him in his office. I hoped that would make the icky feeling in my stomach go away.

Mr. Garner's office had a glass wall facing the hallway, and I could see him grading papers, stamping away with his rubber stamp like a machine. I decided I better take a quick detour to the bathroom, just so he could finish his work. It was the polite thing to do.

I sat on that toilet for a good ten minutes just looking at the dirty linoleum tiles beneath my bouncing feet. There comes a time in every kid's life where you've got to make a decision. A decision of greatness: whether you're going to be it or watch someone else be it from the couch. But if you're going to choose greatness, you've got to commit to it. No excuses, no "I'll do it tomorrows" or buts. You've got to stick to your truth and never doubt it. If you can remind yourself where you're headed and why you're going there then the going gets easier. I wanted to be successful, brilliant, impressive—someone your mom told you to be like and you said, "but I bet I have more fun than her." And you probably do, but that's not the point. I'm in it for the long run: Maple Brook Middle School Valedictorian...Liz Rosenthal. It had a ring to it. Brian told me it did. And he knew how to get there. All I had to do was trust the process. Work hard now and enjoy the harvest later. Besides, I heard high school parties are way better than bat mitzvahs. I'll have fun then. I looked down at my Swatch. Homeroom started in 10 minutes.

~

"I'm really sorry," I added, after I blurted out my confession about watching the movie instead.

"Well, I'm glad you regret your choices, but I can't let this be a precedent in my classroom. This is middle school now, Liz, you have to be more responsible."

I nodded, my eyes searching for somewhere to look behind him. I was in trouble. My legs began to bounce, my fingers started to shake, that heavy anchor sunk in my stomach. But maybe this was what I needed to do better next summer.

"You cut enough corners and pretty soon you fall miles behind."

"What?"

"I'll let you think about that one," he said, opening the door so I could leave.

Chapter 5

FUN AND GAMES

I honestly don't know how anyone could sit through any other kind of movie. Horrors are just the best. Dalia would tell you the acting is bad, and Andy would say you could predict the storyline in the first five minutes and then end up peeing her pants by the last five. But Lucy loved them. We loved them. Every Friday, we called them our Freaky Fridays, she'd come over and we'd pick out a movie to watch. When we were younger, we liked to cleanse our palates with the silly old stuff like the Alfred Hitchcock classics. We mainly just mocked them. But we'd matured since the "Birds" and the "It's Alive" days. Some of our favorites now were the "Sixth Sense," "Sleeping with the Enemy," "Fatal Attraction," just to name a few. We drew the line at whack stuff like "Midsommar."

The doorbell rang just as the microwave started beeping. Lucy always arrived when the popcorn was ready; she said she could smell that bag twirling around in the microwave from down the street.

"You ready?" she said with a creepy smile plastered on her face.

"Oh please, I don't get scared," I said, opening the door wide for her to come in.

Lucy was still laughing as she reached for a bowl for our popcorn. It was true though, I mean not for the real world, I was definitely an anxious kid. But movies, they just didn't really scare me. I guess it was because in the back of my mind I always knew they weren't real, that these sort of things just didn't happen to people. I'd also only watched them with Lucy, and being around her always gave me confidence. Sometimes it was her reaction that made me squeal more than the actual jump-scare.

We carried our sleeping bags up to the third floor where the big TV was. She handed me the popcorn bowl and I set it down in between us on the carpet. I handed her the remote. I watched with my legs crisscrossed as Lucy clicked through the prospective titles in the thriller section. It hurt my eyes when she would switch from title to title so fast on the screen, especially when it had anything to do with the devil. We had an unspoken agreement not to watch those kinds of movies. We had a lot of those kinds of agreements. Eventually Lucy settled on one with a teenage girl holding a flip phone.

"This good with you?"

I read the title. "When a Stranger Calls." I nodded but she'd already clicked play.

The movie started like any other horror, with the pretty girl touring this big house where she was babysitting.

"There's definitely going to be something in that window later," Lucy predicted. The camera lingered on the large windows that framed the back side of the house. It was easy to scout for these things. The parents' car finally left the driveway.

"About time," Lucy interrupted again.

"Shhh!" I said.

A good horror will make the set-up the creepiest part. It's boring in the beginning if you're expecting ghosts and guts, but it's the little details that remind you something bad is going to happen. There will be signs. If the movie's any good, it won't just be the music that clues you in.

I watched in suspense as the girl lounged on the couch with

her blonde friend who would soon be dead. They both seemed like the most unbothered people in the world. I don't think there's anything scarier than something that seems perfect like that.

Sure enough, Tiffany—that's her friend's name—can't get her car to start. She's rattling the keys and the engine's making all sorts of weird sounds.

"Just go back to the house! Your friend will let you back in, you big dummy!" Lucy yelled at the screen.

I told her it was too late for that. Tiffany was done for the moment she left her car again to try and move the branch that just so happened to be blocking her way. That wasn't the scary part though, it was the scene after that gave me chills.

The babysitter girl starts to hear this knocking, this loud obnoxious knocking on the door. It gets louder and louder, and I almost have to put my head in my hands because I hate that noise so much. I don't get scared but certain sounds can trigger my body to panic.

It didn't take long for the first call to come through. The voice was soft but strained, like the speaker was trying to catch their breath but couldn't. I looked over at Lucy; I think she was feeling the same way.

"Why did she pick it up?" Lucy whispered, her voice taking on a more earnest tone.

"She didn't know who it was going to be," I replied.

After the second creepy call, it didn't take a rocket scientist to figure out, they were just going to keep coming. Lucy couldn't seem to wrap her head around why the girl kept answering. I could. If someone's ringing that much, they must have something important to tell you, it isn't just for fun. Besides, it's not like you can just ignore the calls and hope they go away. It's not going to solve the problem.

All of a sudden, the door bursts open and Lucy screamed so loud I thought my eardrum was gonna burst.

"Oh my gosh, I'm so sorry girls. I didn't mean to scare you! I brought some water for you guys."

Lucy said thank you and I grabbed the water glass.

"What are you watching?" Mom asked, hovering at my side.

I paused the movie so she could read the title.

"Ooh, that's from my time. Scary, isn't it?"

We nodded.

"Ok, I'll be downstairs if you girls have nightmares. Don't be afraid to bother me, I don't mind."

I nodded and gently pushed her out of the room. Lucy gave me a look. I know she thought it was weird how I could boss my mom around like that. When we were at her house, Lucy never dared talk back to her parents, which was hard for her, because she was a sassy type of girl. Normally we just stayed out of her parents' hair, it was easier that way since I didn't know proper manners anyway.

I pressed play on the movie.

"If I were her, I'd just ditch the kids and get the hell out of there."

I laughed but that was a stupid plan. The girl wound up leaving the house to search the guest house for the stranger and the calls started coming there too.

"Told you they'd follow her."

Lucy didn't say anything. We'd reached the part of the movie where there's no way for the character to escape, no trying to come up with getaway plans now. We just had to sit back and watch.

The music started to mount, and the girl was now running all over the house like a madwoman and trying to figure out why this stranger was so intent on torturing her. I hoped it was one of those movies where we'd get to find out.

The next call was from the police.

The calls were coming from inside the house.

Lucy told me she knew it all along, but I didn't believe her.

She would've said something. She wouldn't have waited that long to say something.

Chapter 6

STAYING ABOVE WATER

I should have known something was coming the minute my parents called a "family meeting" in the dining room. I was an only child. Normally they'd just call my name. I guess they were trying to jump back on that "we're still a family" train right as the tracks forked.

The two of them were standing up opposite the couch, so my dad could only watch the football game playing behind him on the TV by turning his back to me.

"We know this is probably going to be hard for you, Liz," Mom started, "but I promise, nothing's going to be any different than how things used to be." I watched her left hand nudge my dad on his back. He turned back towards me.

"Yep, your mother's right, we are still a family." Why did they keep saying that word? I know they were saying nothing would change but my dad had never agreed with Mom like that. I didn't like any of this.

"And none of this is your fault, Liz. It has nothing to do with you."

I thought that was a little bit of a weird thing to say. I'd never even suggested that.

"We're gonna be taking turns staying in the house while your dad looks for an apartment. So, for now, nothing will be different. Same bed, same house, same everything. We can cross the bridge of taking turns and packing suitcases and whatnot when we get there."

I hadn't really been listening to anything she said after she said, "your dad," instead of Dad. I had always thought it was weird that she referred to her husband as "Dad" in front of me, but now it felt even stranger to hear "your dad." I guess that's what they would be to each other from now on: strangers.

If it weren't for my pesky ass they wouldn't be connected to each other at all. I wonder if that would've been less painful. For everyone.

~

"So, they're just up and leaving you like that?"

I stared up above my bed at the glow-in-the-dark stars stuck on my ceiling. I couldn't tell if I liked them better or worse now that there was a crack in the ceiling paint. I guess they sort of looked like constellations.

"No one's leaving anyone, Brian. We're still a family, just like, separately now."

"Let me guess, that's what your mom told you?"

I was glad the lights were off because my cheeks felt like hot tamales. "No," I lied.

"Interesting."

Everything always was to him.

"No offense, but like was it your fault in any way?"

I waited a second to process if I was hearing him correctly. This was not at all how Lucy had reacted when I told her. She just asked if I'd be getting double presents for my birthday and Christmas.

"You can't ask me that!"

"Why not?" Brian asked innocently.

"Well," I paused, "I think it's bad manners. Not like you ever have any though." I nodded on my pillow, determined I had settled that discussion.

"You know what having manners makes you?" he asked. "A good person."

"A liar."

I rolled my eyes, but not before clarifying that, "No, it wasn't my fault my parents are not in love anymore."

"Whose parents are?"

"Literally all my friends' parents are still together and say I love you and smile when they're in the same room and everything," I said, thinking of all the times I'd seen Lucy's parents kiss each other on the cheek before leaving for work.

"Remember what I said about manners, Liz."

"Oh, c'mon you're being unrealistic."

"No, I agree with you that most children don't grow up with separated parents, but that's only because the parents are pretending to love each other for the sake of the kid. They don't want to compromise seeing their little ball of sunshine only every other week. That's why everyone hires a divorce lawyer the second their kids are off to college."

"They do?"

"Yep."

"But I'm not in college yet. I'm still here."

"Physically, yes, but have you really been here for your dad?"

"Huh?"

"Look at those stars on the ceiling. There used to be ten, right?"

I looked up at one of the silicon stars, five points pulling in all five directions, somehow staying put. That's five different forces that have to cancel each other out, perfectly.

"Yeah, I got ten for my tenth birthday," I said. "But there's only nine now."

I counted them in my head. I still saw 10 but I probably miscounted somewhere.

"I guess one must have fallen down," I told him.

"And tell me, Liz: is it the star's fault for falling, or the person who put them up there's fault, for not sticking them with enough glue?"

I didn't feel like answering him. He knew I'd been the one to decorate my room.

Then I remembered my dad had offered to help me, but as usual I turned him down. I also turned him down to watch the Madagascar movies he loved because I was ten now and watching animated movies was below my maturity level. I told him he wasn't allowed to call me "kiddo" anymore either. I didn't mean I still couldn't be his kid though.

But maybe kids were like puppies. No one wants them when they're grown up and not cute anymore. Maybe that's what I'd done: grown up. I grew out my little bob cut my dad had loved. I was too old for him now and he thought I didn't need him anymore. When I thought about it, I didn't like growing up either, I just liked impressing the waiters by ordering the veggie quinoa salad instead of the mac-n-cheese all the other 10-year-olds got to enjoy.

※

"Yes! It's Pasta Day!" Lucy exclaimed as we got in line in the cafeteria. Pasta day was the day where the food counter was filled with every pasta shape and sauce you could think of. The Maple Brook cafeteria was way more stressful than the lunchroom at the elementary school had been. If middle school was a zoo, the cafeteria was feeding time in the pigsty, with more germs. That's not even what I was worried about though. It was the food that had me tranquilized. There were just too many choices. Luckily, I had lunch period with Lucy, so I just filled my tray with whatever she got. And if Lucy was ever absent, I followed the rule Brian taught me over the summer—good old eenie meenie-minie-moe.

"I'm getting two garlic breadsticks today, I'm starving. But don't worry, I brought breath mints," Lucy explained as she placed a second breadstick on top of her spaghetti Bolognese.

"Oh goodie, me too, I love the breadsticks," I said as I reached for the tongs to follow Lucy's lead. It was good to have a friend with such excellent taste.

"I wouldn't do that if I were you," I heard a voice from behind. I didn't need to turn around to look where it was coming from, I knew it was Brian. He always had a way of sneaking up on me like that. What did he want now?

"Why not?" I asked. "The breadsticks are the best food in this whole wide cafeteria," I said, though I started to doubt myself. Brian was such a know-it-all he had a way of making me doubt everything.

"Because they're extra calories and extra carbs. You're already getting pasta which is more carbs than you need for the entire day anyway. No offense, but I noticed your jeans are looking a little tight and I'm just looking out for you. Swap the breadstick for a carrot stick. Two carrot sticks even. You'll thank me later."

I would?

"Shut up and mind your own business," I returned, though I replaced the empty tongs as I said it, and sheepishly grabbed a couple carrot sticks as I passed the salad bar. It couldn't hurt. Besides, this kid seemed to know a thing or two about what the universe had in store for us. He predicted that Lucy wouldn't be in my reading level this year because she watched Nickelodeon after school every day. He probably always knew my dad would get bored of me too.

Chapter 7

BOBBING FOR AIR

I would have forgotten about it if Lucy hadn't asked what I was going to wear. Apparently, the middle school dance was a big deal, kind of like the first official treaty where we could all agree no one had cooties anymore. Technically we were supposed to bring a date. Lucy was just going solo though, and I would have gone with Brian, if he hadn't been so scared of an undistracted Lucy.

I ran to my closet. I had an hour to get ready and I was still wearing my fuzzy pink bathrobe, so I started rummaging through my dresses and skirts. Within minutes the floor was covered in clothes, heaping piles with no sense of organization. In what felt like another five minutes, I put half the clothes away—thrown into the closet rather than placed. It wasn't that I didn't like my clothes, or didn't like myself in them, but more so that I did, and that made it impossible to choose between.

I tried on a blue dress, the kind that had fringe along the bottom and the sleeves. I put on a white cardigan, tucked it up in the back and let it hang down in the front like all the girls always did in high school; the way you could show off your ass without looking like you were trying to show off your ass. But then again, there was also a purple dress; one that would also go with the cardigan, maybe even go better.

I tried on that dress too; I would pair a necklace with the low-cut neckline. But then there was always another necklace to go with that dress; perhaps it would even go better.

The cycle continued as I tried on outfits, and retried them on, and rearranged them. I got so flustered and sweaty from all the changes that I almost wished I had only one dress in my whole wardrobe, regardless of how ugly it was or how unflattering it looked on me. Mom used to actually do that back in pre-K—back before she'd read about "accommodating"—empty out my entire closet except for one dress just so I could tell all the other kids I got dressed all on my own too. I think I've always felt like an imposter.

With piles of clothes everywhere, my room looked more like a minefield than a carpet and with every step there was a chance it may all be blown to bits. I wished miraculously that an enormous tide would come and wash everything away, eliminating choice and bringing me to shore.

Suddenly, a loud knock interrupted my thoughts: Brian. I looked down at my current outfit. I had on one sleeve of a purple bodysuit unclipped at the bottom, two different skirts, three necklaces, and two different shoes. I felt homeless in my own home: poor and surrounded by hundreds of dollars' worth of clothes. I wasn't in the mood for his critical opinions.

I started to pace again, debating whether I should just stay home. The house stood in a loud silence as if it was mimicking my own thoughts and the air felt harder to inhale, running away from my waiting lungs.

"Liz?" Brian called, entering my bedroom without waiting for me to let him in.

Panic began to build in my body and the butterflies seemed to be multiplying in my stomach, and soon I worried they would run out of space and burst right through my skin.

"Hey Liz, Liz?" Brian's voice was gentle as he took in the mess of clothing to my dismay.

"What are you doing here?" I snapped.

"I thought I'd come a few minutes early to help you get ready. I know how much trouble you have making decisions. And, well, I think I can tell what's going on here."

"You do?" I asked.

"Sure, I do. It's a big dance with tons of people you barely know—talk about stress. Don't worry, I got you."

I paused, it was weird how something as small as having a right-sized life jacket could make you feel safe, even if you were stranded in the middle of the Atlantic.

"Picking out your outfit is a big decision, especially tonight. What if you just didn't have to make it?"

"What do you mean? I can't keep having my mom pick out my clothes every day, I'm not a toddler."

Brian moved to the center of the room, surrounded by the clothing mines. "Ok, so here we have six piles, correct?"

I nodded. "Yeah, but some of them have—"

Brian cut me off. "Ba-ba-ba, let me handle this." I couldn't help laughing, I loved it when Brian got all fake bossy with me.

"So, we have six piles of clothes, I would say the average girl goes out with approximately five garments, correct?"

I had to think about this one, taking out my fingers to imagine what I often saw girls dressing in: dress, cardigan, socks, underwear, bra. I nodded.

"Well, in that case, why don't we pick out one item from each pile."

I considered this. "But I'll still have to sort through all the items and pair them and rethink my choices and—"

"Ba-ba-ba, let me finish." I sighed.

"When you pick the clothes, you'll have your eyes closed," Brian finished, sounding proud of his new scheme.

"So, it's random?"

"So, it's random."

I thought of my famous "bum seat" where I'd scavenge together all the toys at Farbrook Day Care and sit on them until one fell out of the pile and that would be the one I played with that day. I liked how every day could be new and exciting. When the other kids started complaining that the Woody toy didn't talk anymore, I was glad to snag it from them. When you've played with a decapitated Barbie for three weekends in a row (her head came off the first time I sat on her), you get to appreciate the mute cowboys.

I considered Brian's idea. "But the piles aren't really organized properly—and what if I pick five dresses? Am I supposed to walk around with five dresses and no underwear!" Sitting on a bum seat with such high stakes felt a little risky. I hated heights.

"No, no, no, don't be stupid. If you pick a garment that you already have, then you can pick again."

"But..." I struggled for another point to protest. "But what happens if the clothes don't match, and I look hideous?"

Brian paused for a moment, seeming to ponder my question. "Well tell me this, Liz: wouldn't you rather look bad than make the bad choice?"

Brian was right, if I ended up looking like a clown, it was my fate—not my fault.

"Ok, so let's start here." He pointed to the pile closest to them.

I turned around so I could see the clothes. If I squinted hard enough, they looked like a bunch of melted rocket pops at the snack shack.

"Hey! No looking, close your eyes!"

I knew he was just being silly, but I had the feeling it would be better to just play along with this game of his.

"Okay, they're closed."

Reaching into the first pile, I pulled out a pair of gray Puma socks—score! Those were some of my favorites.

"Okay, well we have the start to your outfit."

"Yeah, I guess we do," I laughed as I shifted over to the next pile. Out of the corner of my eye I spotted a Hello Kitty swimsuit top that Mom had forgotten to donate already—I crossed my fingers for the black sweater next to it. Instead of either garment, however, when I pulled up my hand, a singular black sock was in my face—and it must have been a dirty one because it smelled horrid.

"Ewww, can I pick again?" I pleaded.

"I'm going to pretend like you didn't just say that. But, since you already picked out a pair of socks—if you really want to, you can keep picking until you get another garment."

I felt like I was on a reality show, that with one random pick I could get it all or lose it all. "What do you mean if I really want to?"

"Well, you could pick again, but if you're really dedicated to trusting the process, if I were you, I'd keep the sock," Brian replied, emphasizing the dedicated part. Sometimes it feels like Brian had listened to that first grade Storytime in the chapel too, where the glorious God asks the Abraham dude to murder his son and he's like "bet."

Sometimes I wonder how far Brian will let me go. Hell, poor Isaac was two seconds away from getting a blade rammed through his neck.

I again shifted to the next pile, with only three socks in my basket I was really hoping for the jackpot. Bending down, I felt a fluffy material, possibly pajamas, and some blue jeans next to them; thankfully I ended up pulling out leggings. They were the black ones from Lulu, and they were always collecting lint and other fuzz balls on them that drove me crazy, but considering that a rainbow tutu was also in the mix, I was feeling pretty lucky. The next pile was not so fortunate, and we both burst out laughing as we admired the green and pink polka dot shirt I'd gotten as a 2000s kid hand-me-down. It had orange ruffles on the sleeves, and it made you kind of dizzy if you looked at the pattern for too long. In any other circumstance, I would've been having a panic attack over the idea of wearing such an embarrassing dress in public, but with Brian it felt like I was doing the right thing.

"Well, now that's done. I'm glad that you aren't worried about your clothes anymore."

I smiled; I figured I would be getting a lot of compliments that night—the kind where someone is wearing something so crazy that everyone they talk to can't help but say something about it. I figured that out when Mom came home from work bragging about all the praise she got for her leopard print earrings.

"Even if people think you're a little strange," Brian began, seemingly reading my thoughts, "it's not a diss on you, it's not like you picked it out."

"Yeah, well I think the universe needs some lessons in the fashion department then…"

"Ah, you never know, maybe there'll be some polka dot fans out there waiting just for you—trust the process."

Brian was right, I concluded, because if it was up to me, I'd probably end up wearing some beige, boring white dress and a black cardigan. The universe doesn't give miracles to people that blend into the wall behind them, it probably can't even see them.

❧

"Are you nervous?" Lucy asked as we got out of her mom's car outside the school.

I saw her side-eye my attire. She was used to my quirks by now, and it didn't take a genius to figure out they got quirkier the more anxious I was.

"I'm gonna take that as a yes," Lucy chimed after a few moments of awkward silence had passed.

"What, no, I'm not!" I blurted out defensively, and upon further thought I revised, "Well, not about my outfit at least."

"Hmmm," Lucy hummed with a smirk plastered across her pale face.

We got to the dance five minutes early, on her insistence; she probably figured I'd chicken out if I saw how many kids would be in that gym. Lucy was wearing a pretty lilac dress that was trimmed just above her knees, and it had a cute collar at the top. She had on white ballet flats, and it looked like her mom had even straightened her hair. I would've said she'd taken this whole thing a little bit too seriously, but that was before I saw all the other girls.

Aubrey and her clan walked in with kitten heels, teeny pastel dresses, and a nauseating amount of Sol de Janeiro. You could practically see the perfume's fruity mist framing overhead like an orangey smoke out for a concert, except that the glam squad was walking into a gymnasium with disco lights and there were mom chaperones instead of groupies eager to pamper them.

"How many bottles of hairspray do you think went into that production?" Lucy asked.

"I don't know, but if we were in the '90s, the ozone layer would be holding on for dear life."

I looked at Lucy to see if she got the joke. "Okay, nerd."

She hadn't.

I looked back over at Aubrey, and I guess it must've been that instinct you get when someone's looking at you, because the whole group of them was staring at me. It was like when the sunlight left a cave and all the bat eyes were staring at you, or at least that was how I imagined it would happen. I'd never technically been inside a cave before, and I didn't plan to after seeing what happened to that soccer team in Thailand.

I knew they thought my outfit was out of place, and that I wasn't pretty enough or popular enough to wear something out-of-the-norm as a "statement," so I was just a plain freak to them.

"You know," Lucy began, admiring a red velvet cupcake she'd picked up from the snacks table, "I bet if I threw one of these cupcakes into that crowd they'd run away." She was staring back at them, and whether she knew it or not, I was thankful because her eagle eye was drawing their attention away from me, who they were actually laughing at.

"I'm not so sure about that plan though. Some of those girls haven't seen carbs since 4th grade. It might have a deer-in-head-lights effect."

We both laughed so hard I thought we were going to end up on the floor. I couldn't catch my breath, but for once in my life I was smiling while I gasped for air.

No one in the entire world could make us laugh more than each other. It was freeing, having a shared humor with Lucy. I guess you can't overthink when you're on the ground like a roly-poly. I think part of it was just the thrill of her. The risks she took that would've had me peeing my pants. Lucy was kind of like my lighthouse in the ocean. I told Brian that once and he said I had better be careful, because sometimes the light distracts the captain.

～

"So how was it?" Mom asked as I opened the front door. "Oh god, please don't tell me you wore that in public!"

I looked down at my outfit, I had almost forgotten, and a smile formed at my lips. "Sorry, I guess I won't tell you anything then," I responded with a smirk, and before my mother could ask any more pestering questions, I hurried upstairs.

Chapter 8

CALLING FOR HELP

I didn't understand why Mom was making me go to the doctor again; I felt totally fine. Besides, the lady sitting in the blue armchair wasn't even a real doctor; she was the "special kind of doctor"—the kind that didn't even have to go to medical school. The kind of doctor that visited our preschool class when Mr. Johnston took a "forever type of nap" right in the middle of Show & Tell time. They made us all sit in one big circle on that nasty rug filled with boogers and protruding butt-cracks and talk to the woman in the suit who could "make you feel better." Some of the kids were crying and a few were sleeping. I was just mad I never got to present my toy elephant to the class; his sparkling silver tusks were way cooler than feelings and whatever else Dr-who-makes-you-feel-better was babbling on about.

"Liz?"

"Mhm."

The woman, this time dressed in a purple suit, took a few moments to write something down on her clipboard before looking back up. I didn't understand what kind of earth-shattering insight she could have possibly gotten without me opening my mouth, but I sat quietly as she scratched away.

"Tell me. Why do you think you are here today?"

What a stupid question. "Because my mom brought me here," I told her.

"And why do you think your mom did that?"

"I don't know, why don't you ask her?"

I genuinely was curious too. Maybe it was the tank top in 2-degree weather that really made her stop and look at me for a second. Except she wouldn't really be seeing me. It's easy to look at the mismatched clothes and the stacks of extra work piled on my desk and say I was having a breakdown. But this is the first time in my life I felt like I was actually improving something, like each day I was actively becoming smarter, more diligent, more prepared for life now that Brian was coaching me through it. Now that I wasn't wasting brain space on outfit decisions and friend drama, I had the capacity to really become brilliant. I think people often mistake breakdowns and breakthroughs.

More likely though, Mom had probably sent me here to "process the divorce." She'd told me in the car ride here that my dad wasn't exactly moving into his own apartment and that actually he was moving into his girlfriend's house. His girlfriend had a six-year-old daughter. I guess she just wanted to load me up with some nerve-wracking information so we could all get our money's worth from this "doctor."

"Well, I'm going to have a session with your mom after this. But today I want to focus on you."

"Oh, and don't worry, what we talk about here stays in here," she said, staring at me with a smile as fake as her blonde hair stemming from her grown out black roots.

After she said that, I was pretty much certain I was about to either get molested or sucked into one of those slumber party truth circles; I wasn't sure which one would be worse. In second grade, Aubrey had come up with the spectacular idea of going around and having everyone say one thing they didn't like about another one of the girls in the circle. It was my first one of these, and of course I was the one sitting closest to Aubrey. Everyone's jaws practically fell to their sleeping bags when I said she looked like an ostrich when she smiled. I guess what they were looking for was more along the lines of "annoying" or "drama queen." Talking about a girl's appearance like that was "not cool" and most certainly did not stay in that circle. Like I mentioned before, sitting in circles was never a good idea.

"Do you want to tell me how you're feeling right now?"

I was tempted to roll my eyes at her, or just not respond at all, but I knew how these things went. I didn't want Defiance Disorder landing up on that clipboard. Dylan, the punky kid who always interrupted and refused to pull down his hood in science class, got branded with that. His parents shipped him off to the woods for three months before the Spring semester even started. He didn't talk at all after that.

"I feel fine."

"Fine isn't an emotion."

You've got to be kidding me. "Alright, fine. I feel content," I told her.

The lady nodded, squinting her eyes like she was seeing right through mine.

"And what about anxiety? Do you ever feel anxious, Liz?"

"Yeah, sometimes."

I watched as the woman bent toward the clipboard again.

"I don't worry about weird things though. Everyone gets nervous sometimes," I tried to tell her, hoping she could flip her pencil on the eraser side. Instead, she just looked up at me, nodded, and wrote some more.

"Tell me," she began, as if there was anyone else in the room I could possibly tell, "what does it feel like when you have anxiety?"

You'd think a doctor would know the symptoms.

"Um, I usually get butterflies in my stomach, and I guess my heart starts going faster. But only if I'm really stressed out," I mumbled, wrapping my hair tie around my thumb until it turned red.

"Is that how you felt when you heard about your parents separating?"

I paused. I didn't know how to answer that one, especially because it just came out of the blue. Mom always got mad when people she barely knew would ask her about the divorce, like they were trying to be her friend, when all they really were was nosy. And usually, those people had at least started with a comment about the weather. This lady was bold.

"Liz?"

I was taking too long. Normal kids didn't take that long to answer a yes or no question. I tried to imagine what Lucy would have said, but she probably would have cussed out the lady for being rude, and she probably would have something written on her clipboard too. My leg was starting to tap against the floor, and each time it did I swore her pencil got closer to that stupid notepad, held at a perfect angle out of my view.

"No," I said. Mom told me once that normal kids weren't 'worry warts.' Of course, then I started to worry if one day I would wake up looking like a toad.

"And you didn't feel anxious when your parents told you the divorce was being finalized?"

It felt like a trick question. The raise of her eyebrow, the poised pencil; she was waiting for me to slip up.

I held my ground. "No, I wasn't anxious."

There was silence after that. I wanted to look at the floor, but I looked at her eyes instead; they were bright blue and made me uncomfortable, but eye contact was something normal kids were supposed to be able to do.

"Interesting," the lady finally said, and I knew at that moment I had screwed it all up: might as well start packing my things for the looney bin. Apparently, the worst thing you could tell a Dr-who-makes-you-feel-better was that you're already feeling fine. I guess she felt like I was threatening her job.

"Well, Liz. For the times where you do feel anxious, I would like to teach you some tricks. Coping strategies, if you will. Would that be alright?"

I nodded. I wasn't stupid; I knew I didn't have a choice.

"We're going to do some breathing exercises. I want you to copy exactly what I do. Hopefully you'll find it relaxing."

Doubtful.

"Ok, we're going to breathe in for 1, 2, 3, 4." I followed her lead, grateful to not have to talk.

"Now hold for 1, 2, 3, 4, 5..." My chest rose but my lungs started to tingle, and then to burn. "6..." It seemed like she was taunting me now, like Lucy always did in our underwater contests, before I learned that you could die from doing that. Could I die right now? "...and 8." Thank God.

"Now slowly let out 1, 2, ..." It took everything in me not to exhale in one big sigh. I didn't like this feeling, the panicky-ness. The lady told me to picture a balloon slowly deflating inside of me, but all I could think of was drowning. On land.

"Now before you inhale again, I want you to hold for 1, 2..." This was the worst part yet. Staying completely and utterly empty, without a single oxygen atom in my lungs. When you think about it, we are only ever a couple minutes away from dying, from running out of oxygen. But every time we breathe, we set back that clock. Over and over—and over again. At least you never really had to think about it. Because it's an automatic system: breathing. In fact, if you stay underwater for too long, your body will still make you breathe. It won't let you give up that fast. It'd rather make you inhale water, make you drown. It's slower. And it's painful. But maybe, just maybe, the lifeguard won't be on his phone that day.

Chapter 9

WAVING AND WAITING

I looked like my American Girl doll, Kit, only after the neighbor's dog had gotten a mouthful of her straw hair. I must've cut the back pieces too short because now it looked like I had those two long bits of hair in the front like some exaggerated version of what Lucy had told me, judgingly, were called slut strands. I didn't know it was even possible to be a slut before seventh grade. Speaking of which, seventh grade started in a week, and this was supposed to be my first day of school hair. I winced just thinking about the picture Lucy's mom would take of me. I looked in the mirror, and somehow the hair looked even worse, jaggedy around the edges of my forehead like I was wearing an upside-down crown. My dad would probably rather see me bald. But I mean, I was bald when I was a baby, wasn't I?

I looked over at my soon-to-be stepsister in the other room, her own short hair pulled back in a little pigtail. Her hair was so thick it looked like the hair tie only needed to have been wrapped around it once. I remembered how Mom would do my hair; she'd put it up so tight, so it'd never dare fall out. Except that then I'd get a headache and one time I even cut off the hair tie with scissors.

Balancing on the bathroom stool to get the better lighting, I grabbed the two bits, held them together, and cut them at the same time. The dark hair fell to the ground like leaves carried by the wind; you could try and do the tree a favor and reach out to catch them but you'd never be able to. They didn't belong to the tree anymore.

I hoped I wouldn't get in trouble for getting hair all over their house. It looked like they'd cleaned up just for me. I sort of felt weird about that.

I stared into the mirror again. The issue was that no one ever tells you that your hair pieces aren't going to be the same length because they're growing from different spots on your head. So now what I was working with was pretty much a micro-bob around my ears with a receding hairline effect right where my forehead started. I hoped it would come off as endearing. But maybe this is just what it would take to start undoing everything. Maybe it could make him stay. Or at least make him leave this house that I didn't fit into. I stared at the pair of scissors as I placed them back in their drawer, with the rest of my dad's fiancée's DIY craft supplies. She probably wouldn't need to make so many things herself once she married my dad.

I walked down to his office which was pretty decorated for someone who supposedly just moved in, stepping down one by one, as if it was my first time using stairs. To be fair, the stairs were the slippery wooden kind, without any carpet on which my dad had always complained about getting filled with crumbs and my mom had called homey. When I made it to the living room, which wrapped around into my dad's office, I tiptoed over to the wall so I could stand against the wall. His office had glass doors, so he would be sure to spot me. I carefully crept through the living room, keeping my back glued against the wall. I definitely didn't want Lisa to see me first. I sucked in a deep, shaky breath. With one more step I'd be right in front of his door, I could just imagine the endearment in his eyes.

I closed my eyes and made the final step. I waited, eyes closed, for him to say something, maybe he didn't recognize me. I waited some more, each minute building my desire for him to just open the door and put me on his shoulders and take me for an airplane ride. My eyes were getting watery, so I blinked them open for a second. My dad was staring at his computer to his left. I was right in front of him.

I practiced my smile in the reflection of the mirror, he typed something on his keyboard. I stood on my tiptoes to see if I could make myself more visible, but quickly went back on my heels, not wanting to appear as if I'd grown even more. So, I waited, flat-footed with a smile glued to my face while my dad worked. And worked. And worked. I was standing right in front of the clear door; all he had to do was look up. I wasn't going in there. I shouldn't have to go in there. Please just look at me. Please.

The keyboard kept clicking and clacking away and at some point, my legs must have started to tire because now they felt on the verge of collapse. So, I did. Well, technically I just sat down, still facing the door, but I did so rather loudly. Still, he didn't notice. And so, I sat there smiling at him like Anna waiting at Elsa's door. He didn't see me until he tried to open it, and it hit my knee.

"Liz, what are you doing there?"

I stared at him, and he stared back at my back blocking his exit. Just look at me.

Finally, he saw. "What the heck is that, kiddo—I mean, Liz?" he asked, correcting himself. I moved from the door so he could come out into the living room light.

"You can still call me Kiddo, um," I hesitated awkwardly, "if you want." I hated that word, but I hated seeing his stuff in this strange house more.

"No, no, no. You're a big girl now, and I've accepted it."

I looked down at the ground. This wasn't going the way I hoped it would.

"Turn around, let me see the back."

He didn't say anything at first and I thought maybe he'd left already. And then I heard him burst into laughter.

"Liz, oh my lord honey, did you not know mirrors existed or something? It looks like you took a chainsaw to that hair."

I couldn't help but laugh with him. He took a picture of the back so I could see it and he wasn't wrong; it looked more like some pile of mixed animal fur clumps than actual human hair. We laughed about it for a solid five minutes.

That means he still loved me, right?

Chapter 10

⌒

UNDER PRESSURE

The ocean is a body of pressure. That's how Dr. Chung had explained it to our seventh-grade science class. The cold, dense water sinks, while the surface water, heated by the sun, stays on top. The deeper the water gets, the more pressure it is under, pushing it down to the core of the earth. The ocean is so deep that it's divided into five layers. The sunlight, twilight, midnight, and hadal zones. There was one that came after the midnight zone, but I could never pronounce the name right. The water doesn't want to be under all that pressure; it wants to upwell and deliver nutrients to the surface. But it wasn't easy.

Dr. Chung did an experiment with the class, asking me to be the volunteer. I had to lay on the floor, with a piece of cardboard covering my body while the class placed cups of water on it. At first it felt silly. I was more concerned about giggling too much and knocking the cups over than anything else. But after the sixth red Solo cup, I started to feel the pressure. The weight on my chest felt like the heavy smock they make you wear during x-rays. Only this one kept getting heavier. Dr. Chung had turned the lights off at that point. He'd said we had reached the midnight zone. Even the sun was not strong enough to venture that deep. Dr. Chung had told me in the beginning to tell him when it got uncomfortable, but I never imagined the sick feeling in my stomach that would come. My heart began to race faster and faster as the Solo cups were replaced with buckets. I tried to tell them to stop, but the weight on my chest had grown so heavy that my diaphragm only had centimeters to breathe.

My voice caught in my compressed lungs. I remembered thinking I was going to die. In the dark. Where no one could see me or hear my silent screams. And that's when I couldn't take it anymore. Using my free arms and legs, I kicked and wailed my hands and strained my neck until my veins popped out. I looked like I was having a seizure. The big bucket tipped over and my pants were immediately soaked. The class was laughing and pointing at me, but I could finally breathe. I raced to the bathroom to grab some paper towels.

Chapter 11

GROWING TIRED

Of course it had to come the day before Lucy's slumber party. Brian said to use it as a motivator, but I had pretty much given up on getting my dad to stay. The haircut and the hugs hadn't been enough. I think the worst part was he couldn't even give me piggy back rides anymore, which he said used to be his favorite thing to do with me when I was little. I asked him for one the other day and he had tried, but he couldn't even stand up once I was clinging to his shoulders. He said it was a back problem, that he was getting older, but it was clear I was too. And heavier.

It was only a drop of blood in my underwear now, but Brian said it would get heavier, and heavier. Eventually I'd have to start using tampons which are basically little cotton rockets you shoot off into your vajayjay. No thank you. I guess I couldn't complain though, I was the last girl in eighth grade to get it.

"This is it, I'm never gonna be my Daddy's little girl again. There's nothing I can do to make him stay." Besides, he was going to have a new little girl soon, Lisa was pregnant.

I sobbed into my hands after I washed them six times after using the bathroom. Maybe this is what people meant about periods making you emotional. I had plenty of emotions as it is.

"Well, you're not completely hopeless."

"Um, I think I am. I mean after this comes actual bras and the birds and bees talk and soon, I'm just a 30-something year old still watching Gilmore Girls."

"Well, you know there are ways to look younger, Liz."

Brian and I were sitting on the edge of my bed, feet nearly reaching the floor now.

"There are?"

"Don't you remember what the teacher said in health class? She said sometimes girls who don't get enough to eat stop getting their period and stop developing. There are certain nutrients our bodies need in order to develop and go through puberty, which obviously is gonna make your dad want to leave the room, if not this country."

"Okay, so what should I stop eating?" I sort of already knew the answer.

"As much as you can," Brian confirmed.

I wasn't opposed to the idea of losing weight. In fact, I'd thought about it before, when I was looking in the mirror. Middle school made a lot of things clearer to me. Starting with the fact that I was not, in fact, pretty. I first came to that realization when I didn't find my name on the list of 30 girls the boys in my grade most wanted to kiss. I didn't find it on the girls you'd-rather-lose-your-Fortnite-streak-than-kiss list either. In a way that made it worse. I was just so plain. Pale, unremarkable, brown hair and brown eyes with teeth that weren't yellow but couldn't be called pearly either. And then there were girls like Aubrey, who walk down the hall and suddenly everyone forgets their own name, girls included. Their hair looks like a wig, but you know if you tried to rip it off her, you'd just be called a jealous psycho. And I was. I mean, who decided some people were just meant to be drop-dead gorgeous creatures of beauty while others have to live with being "not ugly" their whole life? And there's just nothing you can do about it. You're stuck. If I had buck teeth and a face full of zits, I would have something to work with, pimple patches to buy and a retainer to wear maybe, but no. I couldn't even tell you what was wrong with my face, it just wasn't right. I was forever stuck between not-pretty but not-ugly. I guess the only thing I could control was how not-fat I could be. It's ironic that making yourself smaller can actually make you stand out more.

Chapter 12

GETTING HEAVIER

"Guys, look at the clock," I turned toward Lucy's nightstand. "It's exactly midnight."

"Oooh, look at that, is the devil gonna come out now?" I joked, grabbing Dalia's shoulders and giving them a squeeze.

"Hey, don't joke about that," Lucy said.

I had forgotten her weird thing about superstitious stuff like that, in that she didn't ever want to talk about it. I knew she believed in hell and the devil and other crazy-religious things, and I knew she thought I was going to hell 'cause I didn't, but again, that was a topic we didn't discuss. I think maybe she thought if she pretended like she didn't know her best friend was a raging heathen, God wouldn't punish her for it as much.

"It's midnight guys, that calls for just one thing—" I turned toward Dalia, coming from her it could only mean one thing.

"Snacks!" she and Lucy shouted together. I cleared my throat.

"Shhh! Your parents are going to hear us," I warned. "Maybe we just wait." It was too late; they were both already creeping down the stairs like a bunch of Betty Crocker bandits and that icing Lucy's mom kept in the upper cupboard was Dalia's Kryptonite.

I followed behind them like the newbie on the job.

"Get the spoons!" I heard Lucy yell as Dalia made a clatter opening the cutlery drawer. My stomach sank a little. They must have already secured the dope.

We crept back carefully up the stairs, with Dalia's two hands wrapped around that container of chocolate frosting like she was worried it would just disappear back into her starved imagination if she let go. I looked at her tiny hands covering Betty's smiling face, I wished my wrists could look like hers.

"Ok, Dalia can go first because she was the first to find it," Lucy said, giggling at Dalia's drooling expression.

"Don't mind if I do." She ripped the pink lid off and dug her spoon into that dark brown, creamy goodness. The spoon was more frosting than metal when she pulled it out. Lucy and I watched as she brought it to her mouth. I was genuinely amazed she was able to eat all of it in one bite, it was sort of the sticky consistency of peanut butter, and of course none of them had remembered to bring up water. It did take a while of her just sitting there, eyes closed, smiling big, moving her lips around trying to savor every last drop of that sugary meth.

Lucy went next. She opted for a slightly smaller spoonful, probably because she could probably eat the frosting whenever she wanted so it wasn't that big of a deal for her. We never told Dalia that though, she had to be jealous enough that the thing was even allowed inside her own house. Besides, the whole sticky fingers act made it all the more special.

"Okay, you're up Liz."

I cleared my throat. It felt like we were doing some frat pledge and now I had to down the goldfish in the vodka shot.

I carefully took the spoon from Dalia; all their eyes were on me. I peeled back the plastic lid, but the nutrition label was still staring at me. 140 calories for 2 tablespoons. I looked at the spoon in my hand, it looked a lot bigger than a tablespoon, except that it was shallower and oval, so it was hard to gauge. Maybe I could call it 1.5, which would be 105. Still so much, all for a dollop on the spoon. I carefully lowered the spoon into the container, careful to coat only a thin layer. I brought it out: it was too much. I fake giggled and pretended to go back in for more and they laughed too, but actually I was wiping off the chocolate on the sides. The second I brought the spoon to my mouth, Dalia grabbed the frosting and dug in for seconds. I placed the spoon upside down on the carpet so they couldn't see that there was the same amount of frosting on it as when it went inside my mouth.

"Lucy, you have to tell us the tea!"

I looked over at her, I assumed it was already something I knew. Everyone knows that every trio has a secret, much closer duo.

"It's embarrassing." Lucy looked to the ground, and I could see her cheeks turning red beneath the lingering pits of brown frosting.

"Um, if I had my first kiss I'd be telling the whole world!" Dalia exclaimed, raising her hands into the air so dramatically that one of her palms almost slapped my face on the way. It may as well have though.

"I don't like Josh, let's make that clear. But he definitely likes me."

My heart sank, I kind of liked being the only person who appreciated Lucy's silly, unique confident persona. I didn't realize guys like Josh could see past popularity.

"We were just walking back from school one day, and he stopped to tie his shoe and then when he stood up, I was right next to him, and he just stared at me."

"Creepy," I said, even though I could think of nothing better than holding a guy's attention for longer than it took for him to turn and whisper something to his friend.

"And did he say anything?" Dalia asked, her excitement matching her blood sugar.

Lucy looked down at the floor again bashfully. "Yeah."

"Oh c'mon, tell us what you said," I told her.

"I said," she paused to take another scoop of the frosting, "are you going to kiss me or what?"

Dalia's mouth dropped open, and I grimaced at her brown tongue. At least that must've been part of the reason I was feeling nauseous.

We talked the rest of the night about boys and how Lucy would have to walk a different way home now, but I just couldn't stop thinking about how close it all seemed now. I always knew the day would come when Lucy realized she had too much self-esteem to be hanging around a loser like me. Not telling me something like this felt like the first step.

Dalia fell back asleep still holding the frosting so in order not to wake her I had to carefully slip it out of her hand and quickly replace it with a pencil case from her things. I figured her mom had packed the sleepover bag.

As Lucy and I stealthily walked down to the kitchen to put the stuff away, I looked at her in our special communication way and I hoped my eyes were asking why she didn't tell me about Josh. Or at least I tried to make that eye contact with her, but it was hard because she was looking at something else. It wasn't until we got to the dishwasher that I realized it was my spoon. She put it in the machine with the others without washing it off. We didn't say anything as we went back up the stairs. Not even with our eyes.

Chapter 13

LOSING STEAM

"It's good to see you again, Liz," she said to me, her hazel eyes lightening to green in the sun reflecting off the window. "How about we jump right into it, okay?"

I nodded with a sarcastic smile plastered across my face. After all these sessions, she still tried to make me feel like I had a choice.

"On a scale of 1 to 10, how overwhelmed were you this week?"

Overwhelmed. Even the word sounds like too much, too many sounds crammed into one overwhelming word.

I sighed. I wasn't particularly a fan of reminding myself of all the tests I hadn't aced this week and words I'd said all wrong. "8," I said.

"And how has your mood been?"

"Eh, fine. My dad just had his first kid."

"Liz, c'mon, you're still his first child."

I wasn't trying to be all pick-me, I honestly forgot. "Right, well I meant the first kid with his new family."

"Well, that's wonderful news. You're gonna have a little sibling now!"

I paused, again, I hadn't put the pieces together on that one.

"Yeah, I guess. I saw some photos, she's really cute."

She actually wasn't. Her eyes were too big for her head and her little legs and arms looked stiff and crinkly. Not to brag, but I had been a pretty damn cute baby. I guess looks weren't all my dad cared about though.

"How sweet. But Liz, I don't expect you to be over-the-moon about his news. I mean it's gotta feel…"

I could tell she wanted me to fill in the sentence, so she could pat herself on her stupid suited back and say, "yep, I know things about people." I wasn't about to let her have that.

"Feel like what?" I asked, trying not to smirk at her squeamishness.

"Well, um, I would think it might feel a bit like you're being replaced?"

I pictured my father, bending down to hold the hand of his new little girl. I imagined him tying her shoes and brushing her hair. I tried to recall how old I was when he gave me my first American Girl doll. Her hand was almost as small as mine was. But I stopped holding it once he bought me my first cellphone. Divorce gift.

"No," I said, and I watched as the lady's face made the oh-shit-was-I-being-a-bitch? kind of face. She was. Because replacements are meant to last. I'd give my dad three years. Even that was being generous. The man still couldn't watch a movie all the way through.

CONVULSIONS

Chapter 14

❧

SINKING

Present Day

I heard the faint ring of the doorbell followed by my father's loud footsteps shuffling across the floors overhead and I listened to the courteous, cautious exchanges familiar to all former couples who want to remain civil. I heard laughter at one point, but it was strained and trailed off for longer than it truly lasted. It had been two years since he last walked in this house, but he probably felt just as comfortable as I did in it. Without waiting for either of them to summon me, I made my way upstairs. And they say I never take initiative.

"Lizzy!" my dad exclaimed in an unnecessarily cheerful voice. "Oh, it's so great to see you, kiddo!"

He was wearing his classic LuLu joggers and Patagonia vest and smelled like the outdoors. His dark brown hair had thinned out more since the last time I'd seen him, his hairline made the shape of a "U" but the font size was growing larger every year. His Rolex looked a little out of place on his wrist, but he'd never cover it up. Mom says you can always spot new money.

"Yeah. I'm glad you're visiting." My formality countering my

81

dad's bubbling expression. But being my dad, he couldn't stay serious for long.

"You look so grown up!" He placed a horizontal hand at the level of my head and measured it up against some imaginary wall.

"I am." He seemed to forget I'd officially become a legal adult since the last time he'd seen me. I didn't remind him, but I hoped it would come up later and make him feel like a dick.

He laughed because he wouldn't be my dad if he didn't. "You crack me up, Lizzy!" he joked unconvincingly. "I've missed you so much." His arms wrapped around my shoulders, and his sudden closeness made me tense, as he pulled me in for a tighter embrace. Mom must have sent him one of those "actions speak louder than words" memes she's always sharing and leave it to him to totally misinterpret it.

"So, how has everything been around here? Have you two been getting along?"

I watched Mom's eyes fall to the ground and suddenly she didn't need all that blush she had on. The guy wouldn't even visit for two whole years and somehow, he made her feel like the shittier parent the second he walked through the door. It's easy to get along with someone if you know you won't have to deal with them in the morning. I bet he couldn't even handle the days I woke up on the right side of the bed. Not like I even got out of it at all these days.

Mom and I glanced at each other.

"It's nice having all this extra quality time together," she offered, unconvincingly, "especially when she actually comes out of that basement cave of hers." Mom let out a chuckle with her last line, but the hurt in her eyes was hard to miss as she glanced between me and her ex-husband. That and the sparkling eye shadow I just now realized she was wearing. I wished I could tell her she'd feel better when he didn't come back if she hadn't tried at all. It sure worked for me.

Sensing the tension in the room, my dad reached into his leather bag still slung around his shoulder and pulled out a bottle of red wine, flashing a smile as Mom and I exchanged glances. She only drinks white wine, she'd only ever drunk white.

He misinterpreted our wide eyes. "Oh, come on! You thought I'd show up empty-handed? What kind of guy do you think I am?"

But I knew exactly who I thought my dad was, and of course, I knew he would come with a gift. He was the king of gifts, but he never stayed long enough to watch you open one.

Dinner was awkward as usual. Mom overdid things in the kitchen which resulted in burnt lasagna and soggy green beans, while my dad repeated the same jokes he'd told last time he was here and rambled about his spunky stepdaughter, his adorable toddler, and Arizona: topics no one else wanted to hear about.

I reached for another helping, trying to excuse my own silence throughout the entire conversation.

"So, Liz, I see you've been enjoying Mom's cooking!"

My last spoonful hovered outside my mouth. He didn't realize it yet, but he'd just stepped into the lion's den.

Mom's face turned crimson. "And what's that supposed to mean, John?"

"Uh, I didn't mean anything," he stammered, "Liz seems to like it."

He should have just given up and apologized. There was no reasoning with Mom when you'd said something "someone else would find offensive." If he had just straight up called Mom fat it would've caused less of an argument.

"Well, at my house, we encourage having seconds!" Mom shot back.

"Marg, that's not what I meant! Liz, you know I don't care how much you eat," my dad replied.

"Then why say anything?" Mom escalated, glaring across the table at her prey. I took that as my cue to excuse myself.

"Way to go, Marg. You know, when you keep treating her like a victim like that, she'll act like one," my dad said as I left the room. That was probably the first serious thing I'd heard him say all night. I could picture Mom sitting at that table now, steam coming out both her ears as she tried to think of a comeback. All her makeup was probably melted off by now; she wasn't the best at comebacks.

I was only halfway down the stairs when I heard them whispering, in their old people hushed tone that was really just breathy talking.

"I found a new therapist, she has an appointment Monday," Mom said.

"Another one? Is this like the 4th, 5th 'expert' we've paid who hasn't been able to change a damn thing?" My dad spoke for me.

"John, do I seriously have to remind you how much you've spent on your stepdaughter's medical bills?"

I could practically see him rolling his eyes. They had a different definition of "medical."

Honestly, I did too. All this "treatment" was just money down the drain. The water in my lungs wasn't something you could evaporate out by moving to a warmer climate or by blowing out with an inhaler. I think it's a part of me now.

It's all pretty ironic though. I genuinely think Mom's told me there's "nothing wrong" with me just about as many times as I've heard her say "if it ain't broke, don't fix it." I've never broken a single bone. You tell me why I'm always seeing "the doctor."

"Let's talk about this another time," I heard my dad say.

"Oh right, so the next time you stop by in, what two years? Ok, I'll keep my calendar free." Mom shot back.

"We can talk over the phone, just let me have some time to talk with my daughter while we're together," my dad said to my own dismay.

"And what are you going to say to her, huh?" I could see where I got the bitchiness from.

"I'm going to tell her that she's got this, and I'm gonna remind her of how much more fun it was when she wasn't freaking out about every little thing."

"See, I knew it. Of course, you'd try to say something like that to her. That's very triggering for kids to hear, I mean like you would even know."

I loved that she seemed to know what would trigger me. As if I was just an identical copy of any of the case study mentally ill kids she'd read about. I was triggered though, not by the words, but the tone. And me being the cause of that angry tone. I mean when they were together it felt like a custody battle over my mind. What I should and shouldn't be exposed to. I felt like I was back on the staircase in middle school, overhearing them argue about which one of their families predisposed me to an eating disorder.

I retreated to the dark basement, crawled under the covers, and listened to James Taylor like I'd also done in middle school. Sometimes when I play music, I pretend my life's a movie and everyone is just sitting in the theater snacking on their popcorn while I'm tortured on screen. I imagined this depressing picture of me, accompanied by the tormenting crescendo of "Fire and Rain," during the character's rock-bottom part of the movie. I guess I just wanted the audience to feel bad for me.

Sleep was already starting to gnaw at me when my dad's thin figure came into view, and I closed my eyes in a last-minute effort to avoid the awaiting conversation. Whether my dad thought I was sleeping or not, he didn't seem to mind, and took a seat next to me, his hand rubbing circles on my back.

"I'm glad I got to see you today, kiddo." I knew he wanted a response, but I felt too weak to deal with his impending sympathies.

"No offense, but this room looks like a pig sty, Lizzy!" his hand lifted from my back. I realized he hadn't been in the basement since I'd moved down here. I could only imagine what he thought I'd done with the place. The combination of unwashed clothes, dirty dishes and food scraps created a sharp odor that almost overpowered the basement's natural musty smell. Almost.

"So, erm, I was talking with your mother, and it seems like

you're not doing one hunno percent right now? Is that right, kiddo?" I rolled my eyes beneath the covers.

"I miss my old Lizzy. The one who would jump into my arms when I opened the door. Lizzy who wanted to wear a tutu to school and not care what anyone said." It was as if my dad was talking about another girl, like he did with his new daughter, and I was tired of listening. "I know she's still in there, all that bubbliness. I just wish you would let her out more. I feel like I've lost my daughter, my favorite little girl..."

I felt my cheeks heat up; I hated the way he acted like I wasn't lying right next to him, and how he expected me to mold myself back into an innocent 6-year-old again so that he didn't feel like he lost me. Even if that meant I was losing myself. If I had learned anything from all my years in therapy, it was that people only became "concerned" about me when it starts to negatively affect their lives. Both of my parents had clapped me on the back when I sewed them and my grandparents' masks during flu season. It didn't matter that I stayed up all night making them, worried my family would die if I took a break to sleep. I was pretty sure I had even made it on my mother's Facebook page that night. In fact, I'm sure I did, because I remember my grandma commenting "what a blessed child."

But my dad's words seeped in, and again I wondered how I had become this mole of a person rotting in my bed. It didn't feel so long ago when I was a spunky six-year-old splashing around in the pool. Where was that care-free kid now? And where was Lucy, my "best friend" who hadn't spoken to me in months?

If this wasn't rock bottom, I didn't want to dig any deeper to find out what was. I could've complained as much as I wanted in that high tower locked up with 20 ft long locks of golden hair and my mother and Brian manipulating me, but it turns out that sometimes he really did know best. The world was no place for an anxious girl like me. At least rock bottom in a tower is still a couple hundred feet above everyone else. I mean, Brian wasn't all bad. He would be horrified if he could see me now or maybe he'd be vindicated. Because I had basically become his worst nightmare, the thing he always warned me I would become without him: nothing.

"Lizzy, you're gonna get out of this. Whatever kind of slump this is, you're gonna get out of this. I want you to know I believe in you, to the moon and back, kiddo." That had been our phrase, "to the moon and back," except I had stopped saying it once he had left and didn't come back.

It was curious that my dad never brought up Franklin. I'm sure he was proud of himself for "fixing" all my problems by calling in a favor to a friend at a shitty college. Margaret must have gotten word to him that I was not in the mood to discuss my future.

"Please just let me hear you say it, Lizzy. Just give me something. Just a glimpse of my Lizzy Bear. I'm... I'm really at a loss here." I could feel the trembling of his words in my own throat, and I wanted him to leave, so I gave him a thumbs up. I felt his two hands wrap around my own and squeeze, saying, "Everything is going to be okay, it's all gonna be just fine," but I wasn't exactly sure which one of us he was reassuring.

I cleared my throat as soon as he left.

Chapter 15

PLUG YOUR NOSE

Three Years Ago

I stared in the mirror. I liked the way my hair was tucked behind my ears so you couldn't see how fried the front pieces were, yet you could still see that it was long enough to touch my elbows, which was how I liked it. Mom had finally let me get highlights this summer and I loved my new blond look. Well, maybe blondish is a better description. I liked the way I'd built my mascara up so my lashes covered the ugly wrinkles on my eyelids. I liked looking at that girl in the mirror, because I could already picture her in a blue robe, ready to throw her cap into the sky with the rest of her worries. I couldn't wait to go to college, I was sure once I was there, I wouldn't even remember what anxiety felt like. Sometimes when I thought about crushing beer pong records (I'd never played but it was one of those things I knew I was destined for) and tailgating football games (and then leaving before the game started) like one does in college, I would kind of forget school was still a thing. I mean can you imagine that? Me, forgetting school exists? I suppose I could only really see that happening if Brian and I went to different schools.

I sighed. I wasn't in college yet when all my worries would

evaporate. Instead, I was at the beginning of a very, very long journey: high school.

The good thing about high school, at least for my town, was that only one middle school fed into it so each grade was the same size as it was in middle school and I didn't have to worry about meeting new people. The bad thing was it meant all those turds from Maple Brook Middle were now pipelined into this shithole. That and the boys had gotten smellier somehow. I took note of that right as Slim Jim from my old advisory walked right in front of me and Lucy. He completely photo-bombed the first day-of-high-school blackboard her mom was making us pose with again.

I looked around for Lucy when I finally got to my locker, but we'd been separated the second we walked through the main doors. I looked at the paper the admin lady had given me. It was my schedule. I liked the way the H's next to the courses for honors were in bold. I had a feeling Lucy would complain to me about not being in any classes together.

But before any of our real classes started, we had a freshmen assembly. The second I walked into that auditorium though, I cursed the fact that the "universe" randomly chose a short skirt for me to wear. It seemed to punish me a lot, which is sort of hard to not take personally. The seats were made of that scratchy fabric that was poison ivy to bare legs. They were an anxious kid's worst nightmare. Every time I squirmed, my legs scraped against the little spurs of wool, and it felt like fire ants were crawling up my skirt. I'd be lucky if my butt cheeks didn't look like two hot tamales by the end of the assembly.

"Okay, everyone take your seats," the Dean said into the microphone. He was one of those really unfortunate looking guys, with the early onset balding head and a perpetually sweaty forehead. If I wanted to, I could probably see my reflection in both. I guess he must have said something important though because soon the whole room started to play musical chairs. Kids were scrambling and pushing each other to get over to where their friends were. A few of them had ditched the aisle all together and were just stepping over rows of seats: the boys had the legs for it now. Suddenly I felt like I'd missed the memo. My head swiveled around in a frantic fashion, scanning the sea of heads for Lucy's light brown ponytail. It would've been a lot easier if she was still wearing those JoJo bows to school. The lights went out before I even got through searching the third section. I had no other choice, I just had to sit down where I was in the back rows, where the zombie kids roamed.

"Now I want to start off today's presentation with a reminder that you are no longer in middle school."

I genuinely don't think any of us were confused about that.

"Grades aren't just something you get a sticker for having an A in. The stakes are higher for you guys now," the sweaty Dean told us.

A rock began to form in my stomach.

"You need to be putting in 100% effort, 110% for those of you who want to see your name up on that wall over there."

I looked at where he had nodded his head to. "Cum Laude" was written in cursive on the top of the plaque. One of the boys with legs that had doubled in size over the summer pointed at it and started laughing at the name.

"Cum Lord," he called it. I couldn't believe we were sitting in the same row.

"Now I know some of you guys think that because you're teenagers now," the Dean continued, "rules don't apply to you, and you can do whatever the heck you want. But what happens when you decide you want to make the big bucks and work on Wall Street, but you spent your entire year of Econ playing Super Mario or whatever it is you guys do."

I got the message the first time he went about saying it. But he just kept going. He dragged on and on about how high school mattered and teachers expected more from us and that rock in my stomach was starting to fall faster and faster, like someone standing on a bridge had just dropped it into the water.

By the time the tides had turned to drugs, drinking and parties (turns out you just had to say no) there were audible snores coming from the back rows of the room. Some of those kids could use the sleep though. I remembered how Dylan had come to school with bloodshot eyes. So then again, maybe he needed to hear all the D.A.R.E. stuff.

The front few rows were like a sea of glasses, tapping feet and nodding heads. It literally gave off a buzz, their nervous energy. One of the girls had an actual pencil tucked behind her ear, like in the movies. It must have been just for presentation though, because the girl had her laptop out and was pounding that keyboard so aggressively, I thought one of those keys might just pop off and hit the dean in the face. I hadn't even thought to take notes.

"I want to tell you all about a little thing called the 'butterfly effect,'" the dean started.

"It's essentially the idea that every little thing you do has an impact on your future. You think it's not gonna matter if you skip class? Think again. A flap of a butterfly's wings here can lead to a tornado all the way over in Japan." For a second I thought it was Brian on stage.

It didn't take long for the water to start filling my throat after that. I made my way to the girls' room across from the auditorium. Walking into the first stall, I took a seat and stared up at the dimly lit ceiling above. I could feel my knees beginning to tremble. Then in an instant I felt myself being transported back to my elementary school days. I remembered hiding in those stalls, perched on top of the toilet seat while my heart tried to escape my chest. Some days I would run in there because we had to write a story and I couldn't think of an idea, or sometimes I was afraid of the new food options in the cafeteria. But no matter what changed around me, the bathroom was always the same. The bathroom I was in now looked the same.

I took deep breaths as I focused on slowing down my heart and calming the quenching feeling of anxiety that was eating away at my stomach. I brought my knees up to my chest and squeezed them until there was no space for my heart to try and run to and my lungs could barely heave. I kept my eyes trained on the tiled floor as my mind tried to place itself anywhere else.

Suddenly I heard noises in the hallway; the assembly must be over. I froze as I saw a pair of black heels strutting across the floor towards my stall. The feet continued past me and a wave of relief washed over me; if the teacher actually tried to open my stall I probably would have had a heart attack on the toilet. Just like Elvis. As quietly as I could manage, I unlocked the door and darted across the room, not even bothering to check the girl in the mirror; I had a pretty good idea of what she would look like right now.

As I emerged from the bathroom, I was shocked to see everyone had already cleared out of the hallway. An entire ocean, completely empty. Except for Brian.

"Took you long enough!" he exclaimed.

"Oh, sorry."

"You wanna tell me why you were hiding in there?"

"I wasn't!" I shot back defensively, hoping he wouldn't detect the slight crack in my voice.

"Hiding, isolating, taking a break away from other people in a confined space; call it whatever you want," Brian mocked me with a smile I couldn't help but cheekily return.

"Come on, let's get to class, it's the first day and you've got to make a good impression on all the new teachers!" Brian said as he steered me down the empty hallway.

I'm not sure if there is any one way to show you love some-one. I'm not even sure I knew how I knew this relationship had become something more. I didn't think about him much in middle school, he was just kind of there. But now I found myself wishing he were around more, just there as a source of calm. The right guy isn't always the one that makes your heart race, sometimes it's the one that slows it down.

∽

I told Lucy we could give her a ride home the first day. She had wanted to hang out, reminding me that even high school teachers wouldn't give homework on the first day, she'd checked. But Brian didn't care about the rules, and he wanted to come over and study; these days I found myself spending more time with Brian than Lucy. Lucy was right, I didn't need to, but today I'd learned that this whole high school thing was actually way more life determining than I'd taken it for. I guess it always just seemed so far away I didn't see it sneaking up on me. College was practically around the corner. No more packaging it up in a box and shoving it under my bed.

Lucy was already waiting inside my car by the time I made my way down those big steps. I could see Mom swiveled around in her chair hammering Lucy with questions which would've been torturing me if I'd gotten there first. I took my time walking around to the front seat.

"Hey Liz, how was your day? I was just asking Lucy all about it, did you know she has this cute boy in her math class, oh what did you say his name is?"

"Ashton," Lucy said from the back seat. She was smiling at me in the rearview mirror.

I turned to Mom. "Did you seriously ask Lucy if there were any cute guys in her classes? God, you're so nosy."

"No, I just told her, Liz," Lucy chimed in, "and plus I think she'd think he's quite handsome too."

Mom started blushing and told Lucy she'd always liked blondes in junior high. I rolled my eyes. I didn't know how she did it, but Lucy was the best at talking to grown-ups. She knew all the ways to make them feel young again but also respected, and how to be witty and charming so that she was not just another "nice girl" you were introducing to the parents but a real "keeper." I tried telling her once that my mom already loved her and she could stop trying to be so friendly with her now, but she'd just told me she liked talking to my mom and that it was called having manners.

By the time we dropped Lucy off, Mom had heard enough about her day. And she must've figured mine had been just as fun, so we drove in peace. When we got home, Brian was already waiting on my doorstep. This wasn't unusual; we'd been "study buddies" all summer and had gotten into a routine of hanging out every day. He made sure I never forgot to do my summer reading again after the Wonder incident in sixth grade. In fact, we read all the books on the list, not just the ones we were supposed to select, just in case.

I grabbed my backpack from the car and let him in and we both raced to my room. I went to my wobbly desk and sat down in the pink Ikea chair which is just a perpendicular piece of wood with random holes in it to somehow make the thing even more uncomfortable. I would've sat in my white fluffy chair that felt like a cloud on your butt, but Brian said I'd be more motivated to finish my work if my body wasn't comfortable. He had all sorts of weird rules and tips, but I found it best to follow along rather than question him.

"That grade meeting was kind of an eye opener," he commented.

"I was just thinking that."

"We wouldn't want to be making any habits now that could negatively affect future success, you know?"

I did.

"Yeah," I agreed, "people always say Junior year grades are the most important, and choosing hard classes and whatnot, but you can't even get into some of those APs if you haven't been excelling in the honors track as a lower classman."

"The best day to start preparing for anything is always today."

I nodded but I don't think he made up half the quotes he told me in that prophet-like voice of his.

"I just don't even know how to prepare. It'd be one thing if I had homework to do and stuff, but they've given me like no material so far."

"Yeah but let the lazy kids who aren't shooting for the Ivies use that excuse. C'mon, can we at least start making a plan for how we're going to get work done?"

"Sounds good." Anything he said always sounded good. "Now, where's that planner of yours?"

I pulled the pink pad out of my backpack, admiring the glitter lettering, and placed it on my desk next to my LED makeup mirror.

"My dad bought me this," I accidentally said out loud. I thought it was the best gift ever at the time, until I scheduled all the days he was supposed to visit us. I shouldn't have used that sparkly gel pen it came with. The ink was permanent.

"That's the best your dad could do?" Brian declared sarcastically, nodding his head back and forth; or at least I figured he was, I wasn't looking at him. "Shit. I'm sorry, I forgot you had daddy issues," Brian apologized, peering his head down to try to meet my eyes in the mirror.

"Well, you can't really have an 'issue' with someone you never see," I admitted, though I regretted the cringey line as soon as it came out.

"And how does that make you feel?" he asked.

"Hey, don't get all therapist on me," I joked, "I swear next thing you'll be telling me is 'it's not your fault.'" Not like that was remotely close to how he'd framed it 3 years ago.

"First of all, therapists scare me more than you do. And secondly, I mean, I don't know: It could be your fault," Brian quipped. I hadn't thought it was funny when he'd implied it the day they told me, and I definitely didn't find it funny now. If it was even meant to be a joke.

"Very funny, but I'm pretty sure my dad getting cozy with his assistant for three months behind my mom's back may have played a larger part in it than me."

"Well..." Brian began, "maybe he didn't feel like he was getting enough attention at home, didn't feel loved, didn't feel like his kid appreciated the ways he provided for her. I mean, you're in that position and some younger, attractive lady is throwing herself at you, values you, yeah, I think we'd all take that."

I stared at him with wide eyes. He was still that little kid with absolutely no manners.

"Jeez, who hurt you?" I shot back sarcastically, trying my best not to seem phased by his last remark.

"I don't know, but it sounds like you clearly hurt your father."

Ouch.

"Yeah, well, it's all in the past now. He's got his new perfect, happy family." I answered, embracing the pick-me-ness at this point.

"Well, I bet he can't be that happy, without you."

"Well, I guess he isn't the happiest man alive. Every family has their problems."

"Oh, I'm sure they have problems. But I'll bet you he'll run away from them in a decade too."

"I'm not so sure." It's not like he didn't know what he was signing up for when he married a woman with a chronically ill kid.

"Well damn, Liz. I feel like you must've done something

then," he paused, reflecting on something invisible to me. I could never tell when this guy was just joking with me. "I don't know, we all can have a lot to handle sometimes. You should call him, thank him for everything he's done for you." I didn't know what to say.

"Well, maybe I will."

"You should, you never know when it's the last time to say things, and then it would actually be your fault."

"Yeah, I guess it would be."

Chapter 16

SUBMERGED

I had my free third period, so as soon as second period ended, I ran to claim the best study spot in the library. It wasn't a rule or anything, but there was a tradition at the high school that all the nerds kind of had their own designated nook, where they'd plop down all their stuff and then that was it: it was theirs for the year. A lot of them would even decorate it, just like you would at a work desk. Kind of like a dog marking its territory. I scanned the library and looked around at the few kids who had chosen to spend their free in it. And then my eyes fell on the perfect desk: it was tucked back in the corner right next to the water fountain no one used. It was in the old "tech pod" section of the library. A couple years ago, when they'd just introduced computers as part of rebranding the library as a "Media Center," the school was too dumb to figure out screen monitoring and Andy King and his crew had spent a whole semester having "study sessions" during lunch period. I was the only one with access to the internet now. That was a pretty big honor for a freshman.

I took a seat at the desk. Apart from the large Mac computer in the middle of it, there was a stapler, several pens and pencils, and a notepad in the drawer. It seemed to already have everything I was going to need, but as I scanned the other desks in nerd hostage, I noticed how bare mine looked in comparison. The desk on my left looked like it belonged to a new freshman, with a whole assortment of small potted plants, an inspirational quote and a small mirror in the corner. It also had one of those things I never knew the name of—one of those metal structures with a number of silver balls on a string that was always moving once someone pulled back one of the balls. I could watch that movement forever. I liked knowing it would never stop on its own.

Turning my focus toward the back of the library, a bright orange pile of Post-it notes caught my eye. Scanning the rest of the desk, I noticed a set of rainbow pens set in a perfectly straight row, neatly stacked color-coded binders, and picture frames that all seemed evenly spaced. I'd always wished I could be organized like that, but I never felt that inclined to make things look "perfect." I usually focused more on being "perfect" myself.

Scanning around again, I realized that all the other desks seemed to be set up in a similar manner to the sticky note one. Their papers were stacked perfectly if they had any, their pens all faced the same way in their containers, and even the Librarian's desk with a hundred pictures had some order amidst the chaos. Looking back at my own desk, I decided it was time to do some of my own decorating.

I reached for my backpack. I pulled the little stand-up mirror from the front pocket and placed it on my desk. But as I emptied the rest of it out onto the desk, turning it upside down to get all the stuff out, I quickly regretted not looking at what was packed inside first. Two packs of pencils spilled across the desk, breath mints which I'd practically inhaled this morning came tumbling out next, followed by a mountain of crumbs from a variety of sources I had no interest in identifying. As quickly as the mess had escaped my bag, I tried my best to scoop it all back in, leaving a littering of crumbs and eraser dust and dirt all over the floor and chair. I was mortified as I looked around the library to see if anyone had seen the utter chaos that had just engulfed my desk and was almost satisfied that everyone was staring right at their textbooks. That's when I caught Brian's eyes which seemed fixed on mine. Watching Brian's eyes reminded me of the way Mom's looked at me, searching; but where Mom's eyes were trying to ignore the darkness, Brian's eyes seemed to be fixed on it, analyzing it even.

Suddenly uncomfortable, I left my stuff on the desk and headed to the bathroom. As soon as I entered, I felt like I'd resurfaced, like the water pressure just wasn't as strong in this one little patch. I wanted to stay in front of that mirror, looking at that girl: because for the first time in a while she was actually smiling. Mirrors are cool because, being the self-obsessed kid I've always been, I was curious to see how other people saw me. Mirrors couldn't lie to me: they wrote out the story in plain words. My mind wasn't always a reliable narrator.

A pattering of footsteps outside the door, however, caused me to jump, and I quickly made my way into one of the stalls. Those were a different part of the ocean. The bathroom was where groups of cliquey girls went to gossip and reapply makeup, or where the stoners went to get high, or maybe it was even a hookup spot: I wouldn't know. The stalls though, they were different. The stalls were where losers ate lunch alone, where nerdy boys hid from their bullies, or girls who didn't think they were skinny enough made themselves throw up. The bathroom was like a cool coral reef, where you could be safe from the sharks; the stalls were like the sea anemones inside of them: where you hid from other fish. As I sat on that cold toilet seat, with the door safely latched in front of me so I could physically see it was locked, my conversation with Brian the other day replayed in my mind. All the dad stuff was a joke, but a tiny part inside of me told me it still held some truth.

I sat in that stall, in that little cluster of protective tentacles for what felt like only a minute, but I knew it must have been longer than that because I started to hear people going to lunch.

I should've given it another minute. I opened that stall door, and it was like this girl had manifested out of thin air. Her hair seemed to be in a constant state of hurry because the back of her dark ends stuck out to the right as if she'd turned her head when she was blow drying and never did the other side. It gave the effect she was always on the move. Apart from the crazy hair, the girl was gorgeous. Not vanilla type pretty but pretty in the rainbow sprinkles way, heck I wouldn't be surprised if she put gummy bears in her ice cream. If she were a fish, she'd 100% be the rainbow one from that children's book we used to read in school, the one with all the metallic scales you could actually feel on the pages.

I guess I'd been staring at her for a little too long because I suddenly realized she was looking at me too. No one looked at me just to look at me.

"Hey," I said, because if you break the silence first you can usually get away with breaking eye contact too.

"Hey, what's up?" Clearly, she was not one for cop-outs because she was still staring at me: hard. But again, maybe she was just flexing her not-poop-brown colored eyes. God, what I'd give to see an ocean every time I looked in the mirror.

"Nothing much. Nope." Nope? What was it about cool people that made me even more awkward?

The girl must've been used to this kind of reaction to her chillness because she just smiled at me and said, "Oh, that's annoying. I hope you still find something fun."

Hold up, was she going straight to pity mode? Last time I checked, you're supposed to say "nothing" or "not much" or something conversation-ending along those lines when people asked you "what's up?"

"Wait a second!" I guess she'd been holding off on her colored eye powers because with her eyebrows up to her forehead those things were opened real big and on full blast too.

"You're Lucy's friend, right?" she suddenly asked me.

At first, I thought maybe there was another Lucy I didn't know about. Lucy and I weren't losers, but I wouldn't expect either of us to know a cool girl like this.

"I met her in Drama Club," she explained.

Now this made more sense. Although this girl seemed too cool to be a theater kid.

But I could tell she was probably like those other girls in high school, the kind where because they're popular it's cool to get really into the spirit games and actually participate. God forbid I wore school colors on Homecoming, I'd be branded the school try-hard. The football captain wore an inflatable blue and yellow dinosaur costume. But nope, it totally made sense.

As we walked out of the bathroom she dug into her bag and pulled out some lip gloss.

"You want?"

I almost didn't look at her because I assumed another friend of hers was standing behind me.

"Suit yourself, but I've got Mr. Connor next, and I'll be needing this." She winked at me like she was some female lead in an indie movie and walked away with her hips swaying side to side like they couldn't decide which way they wanted to go.

"If I didn't know better, I'd say you have a crush on her."

I rolled my eyes. Of course, Brian was there. My cheeks were probably just red from embarrassment.

"You're so insecure," I told him. "You have nothing to worry about, I'm not gay."

"Right, and denial is a river in Egypt. I always thought you were secretly in love with some of your friends."

I just shook my head at him and kept walking down the hall, trying to ignore the queasiness in my stomach. If you could be drowning and not know it, could you also be gay and not know it?

When I finally made my way back to my desk in the library, I decided it was time to lock in. History was next period, and we'd probably have a pop quiz on the summer material. I looked at the 50-page study guide Brian and I had designed. I knew the work would be easy but the sheer magnitude of it made my knees wobble as I rushed to sit down.

I could feel myself becoming more and more overwhelmed as I worried about the space left in my folder to fit all the papers, the probability that I might lose one or spill something on it; my mind was thinking of everything. Before I realized what was happening, I felt the upper half of my right foot make contact with the floor below me and my leg started to bounce. I wondered if I bounced fast enough, maybe my heart would slow down to balance everything out. It didn't. My breathing started to quicken, and I felt my pulse throbbing through my wrists, until I felt a familiar shadow form around me.

"You okay? You look stressed," Brian questioned in a concerned voice. It felt like we were twelve again.

"Oh, yeah, I'm fine. I'm just a little disorganized right now." My eyes traveled with embarrassment to the crumbs that still stuck like glitter to the fabric of my pants.

"I can see that." If I wasn't mortified before, I certainly was now, and I kept my eyes on the floor as I felt Brian's penetrating the back of my head.

"Let me help," he said.

"Thanks," I said, shocking myself that I was actually accepting such an offer from someone like Brian, even though he didn't really seem like he was offering it when he said it either. Brian was going to help me; it was a fact.

"Okay," he said, clapping his hands as he made his way over to my side of the desk, "let's plan this out." He was one of those quiet clappers, those ones that clasp their hands instead of slapping them together.

"What do you mean, like make a plan?"

"Yeah, like an action plan for fixing this," Brian said as his pointer finger drew circles around my desk space. "Everything goes smoothly if we know what we want to do and have some idea of how we get it done."

"I guess," I mumbled skeptically. He seemed to be brushing over the actual energy it took to do something. You could meal prep and map your route as much as you wanted, but a marathon is still going to be a fucking marathon.

I was never really the kind of girl to carry around an organizer or even a notebook in my purse, so I wasn't all too convinced by Brian's proposals. However, by the confidence in his voice I could tell he'd done this a million times, and clearly it must've worked or else his desk wouldn't look like it belonged to Mr. Clean over there.

"So where are we going to start?"

Brian looked up at me as he planted his spread-out fingertips on the desk. Noticing my messy backpack, Brian emptied its contents once again so that both of us could see what they were working with.

"Umm..." I was still unsure about what Brian meant by this; I was just trying to organize my desk; it didn't seem to be a big deal; but I got the sense that everything with Brian was going to be a big deal. But hey, who was I to judge? He wasn't the one with croissant crumbs sprinkled across his keyboard.

"Ok, I'll tell you where we're starting—left to right."

"What do you mean left to right? Like reading a book?"

"Exactly." Brian moved over to the left side of the desk while I gave him a questioning look. "When you read a book, it's calming right?"

"Yeah, I guess," I responded.

"Wouldn't it be a heck of a lot less relaxing if you started at a different page each time? I mean, you would probably miss a few chapters and never even know." Brian's eyes lit up as he talked about this.

"Ok, let's start with your phone. We'll put it on the top left corner of the desk," he started, grabbing my phone and placing it neatly on the corner of the desk, ensuring that the top edge of the phone and left side of the phone were exactly parallel to the corresponding top and left edges of the desk.

"Now let's move over these scattered pens," Brian continued as he looked at my collection of unsharpened pencils and orphaned pen caps that lay to the right of the phone.

"Oh, I think these should go in my pen pouch," I suggested, grabbing my old cosmetic bag I'd converted to a pencil case before forgetting about it at the bottom of my backpack months ago. "Oh, and I bet I could also put my notecards in this little tote," I added excitedly, pointing to another repurposed cosmetic bag I'd forgotten about. I was getting the hang of this, and it felt good.

"We can deal with those later," Brian responded hastily.

"But why not just put them away now?"

"They're not next in the order," Brian said with a tone of finality that I didn't feel like questioning.

After I finished putting away the pens, and then the files in their correct folders, and then the crumbs in the trash, everything was starting to look neater, and my heart had quit the race it had seemed so intent on winning earlier. I was just about to sit down and enjoy the fresh working space when Brian gave me a quizzical look.

"Perfect!" Brian responded after I gave him a thumbs up. I looked around myself again, and Brian was right, everything really did look perfect.

"Do you feel better now?" Brian asked me timidly, as if I might tell him I didn't.

"Yeah, I feel so relaxed now. Your strategy works!" I told him, as I thought about how helpful it was to separate out each part of the table, so it wasn't so overwhelming.

"Told you." Brian said with a smile as he retreated to his own desk. "Everything always works out."

"Thanks for doing this."

"Thanks for letting me. It's like I always say: if your space is messy, your headspace won't be clean either."

"I swear I should hire you to organize my room for me," I joked.

"I'll take you up on that," Brian said with a smirk as I walked into English class.

~

I had a substitute for my third class, so he ended up just giving us the work and letting us leave. Naturally, I went to the library. I guess some other kids had the same idea, because it was more crowded than normal. The whole place seemed to take a breath and hold it, as if they were scared to let it out as they would blow me over. Or at least make me stumble, I wasn't exactly the most petite lady in the room.

I felt their eyes follow the folds along my back that the little top tried its best to stretch itself around as I made my way to my small desk, arms folded across my chest. I put all my work, which was a stack of papers in a yellow folder in the middle, and whatever peace through cleanliness I had preserved the day before, had now been dirtied.

I pulled out my notecards with comments and reminders and they sprawled across the desk and water must've spilled somewhere in my backpack, because some of the papers were damp. I tried my best to smush all the papers together into one pile, flipping and folding and flattening to make fifty tasks look like one.

I tried dealing with the first paper on top, a list of math formulas we'd need to memorize by the end of the week. The first few I'd already learned. I quickly made some flashcards for the rest.

After I recited the trig identities twenty times, I could feel the toll of monotony starting to affect my movements, as I groggily reached for the next paper on my homework stack. What made the work even more boring, was that the work was categorized by classes. This meant the top ones were all asymptote and limit nonsense, the middle was History bullshit, and I didn't even know what to look at what Mr. Davidson had assigned. Bio was at the bottom.

The period droned on and finally by lunch I'd made it through the first third of the stack and I decided to eat in the student lounge. I grabbed the leftover Sloppy Joe Mom had packed and opened the large glass doors that led into a small room with a wooden table and nearly the entire Robotics team eating. I sat down at the end of the table.

Surreptitiously glancing around me, I observed the other kids talking and laughing with each other; but every time I tried to chime in, my voice was unheard, drowned out by the roaring of the ocean.

Brian suddenly appeared by my side and nudged his head in the direction of the empty chairs towards the back of the room, which were disconnected from the larger group.

"Over there, Liz!" he said a little too excitedly, but no one even looked up from their food when he raised his voice. Brian and I both felt kind of invisible in this school sometimes.

Relieved to have a destination, I smiled and made my way to the back, awkwardly asking people to scoot in their chairs as I tried to squeeze myself along the sides of the room. I felt butter-flies starting to flutter in my stomach as I wondered what Brian was up to. He was always up to something.

"Soooo, how's it going?" Brian inquired.

"It's good, you know, boring but good."

"Yeah, I know what you mean. My day's been like that too, doing the same thing over and over."

"Literally, I feel like every hour turns into Groundhog Day."

"Yeah, well we've only got 3 more hours."

"I just feel like it's been two days and how am I supposed to stay motivated?"

"Well, it definitely gets boring sometimes, but you get used to that boredom. It's like a safety net, like nothing can go bad cause we're literally doing the same exact thing we did the day before."

I'd never thought about routines in that way, but I did relate to that feeling of comfort in consistency, with the bathroom stall, with my bed.

"But still, don't you get sick of it once in a while," I responded. That was one thing that sucked about our school, they don't even bother to switch the schedule up, it's the same order of classes every day. No 8-day rotating schedule bullshit around here.

"I mean sure, anyone who says they love school 100 percent of the time is 100 percent lying to you, but I guess I've found ways to spice things up," Brian said in a whimsical tone, "I just like to be spontaneous now and then, you know, like kind of randomness."

"Yeah, I know what the word means," I said in mock annoyance, "I just don't understand how you can be so spontaneous in a red brick high school walking through the halls like they're conveyor belts." I said it sarcastically, but my point was valid, and I really did want to know.

"I'll show you some tricks, after lunch," Brian replied, and as I looked down at my own meal, I realized I'd forgotten to eat the entire time. That was a first.

"Sounds like a plan," I said as I began to shovel the food into my mouth, trying my best to smother the butterflies with the cold sloppy joe meat.

"You know I love plans," Brian said. It was no use, the butter-flies were invincible at this point, and I threw out the rest of my lunch.

Walking back to my desk, I again retrieved the stack of home-work. We still had 30 minutes left in the lunch period, so I had time to get some more work done. I looked at the first assignment, it was still History. I'd already written three DBQs, and whatever this SAQ shit was, I wasn't in the mood for it.

Brian watched me as I stared at the paper like it had just called me lazy.

"Sick of school already?" Brian teased playfully.

"I've been doing this for two hours," I complained, rolling my eyes to emphasize my exhaustion.

"And what is that?"

"Just going down this stack of homework."

"Not very spontaneous I see."

I laughed, even though Brian seemed to be making a general statement instead of a sarcastic comment.

"I'm not so sure it's possible to be very spontaneous."

"Sure, it is."

"And how exactly would that work?" I replied, hoping my voice didn't give away the real desperation I had in finding entertainment.

"What's your favorite number?" Brian suddenly asked, quickly turning his gaze in my direction.

"Ummm, I don't think I really have one?" I stammered; those kinds of decisions were usually too much pressure for me.

"There isn't any number that makes you feel happy, or content, or you'd just prefer some amount to be?" Brian said with a hint of judgment, making me feel stupid for not giving him a number.

I tried to think about what he was saying, tried to remember what number made things "feel right" like Brian had explained, but the only thing that came to mind was singularity. I liked there to only be one thing to work with, one stack of papers, one choice.

"I guess 'one'?" I said tentatively, as if Brian could really tell me which number was supposed to be my favorite. To be fair, in middle school he used to tell me my favorite food was kale. He used to make me practice saying it in the mirror until it felt a little less gross on my tongue and a bit more believable. We had moved past that now, though. Right?

"Okay then, perfect," Brian continued, "go down the stack and work on every other assignment."

"But won't that be just as boring, I mean I'll still be doing history all in a row." I wasn't sure how this was all supposed to make my work more enjoyable.

"Hmmmm," was Brian's only response as his eyebrows furrowed together, and his eyes seemed to dart between prospective ideas known only to him. "I guess, just this one time, you could do roll a die. There's a Yahtzee in the game closet." Apparently, we were not past telling me what to think. I wondered how long it would take for me to just start thinking the right things on my own.

"I mean who cares if it's more fun, right?" I said with a chuckle as I went over and grabbed a die from the closet in the back of the library. I rolled the die and tried to ignore the slight change in Brian's demeanor. It landed on six. English the sixth paper down. He was right though; I already was more excited to start English: at least it would be a change of pace. The fact that it wasn't just the next paper in line, made everything seem a bit more...spontaneous?

"Well, tell me if you like it," Brian finally remarked as I started to read the passage assigned: "The Invisible Man." I smiled; I loved that horror movie.

"Yeah, I'm sure I will. I'm surprised you like it, aren't you such a rule follower?" I responded teasingly.

"I wouldn't say it's breaking the rules, just choosing which one to follow," Brian whispered. "Who knows, maybe I'll convince you into doing the same thing for your course list next semester."

Brian disappeared right about the time I figured out this story was not in fact the same stalker thriller I had been thinking of. I sometimes get overwhelmed reading; one of my old therapists told me to put my hand over the rest of the page so I could only see the line I was reading. That helped stop me from mentally aligning up the letters and words, but my mind still wandered.

I wrote down my "observations" or whatever and put the sheet back in my folder, this time being careful to gently place it back on its holder rather than slam it down as I usually did with the frustrating assignments. Following Brian's advice, I counted down six numbers from the top of the stack and pulled a sheet out. Before flipping it over, I imagined all the different classes it could be, and the fact that it truly could be any one of them made me smile, in fact I almost wanted some crazy fish-themed bio project: it was unexpected. Spontaneous.

Chapter 17

S.O.S.

"Does he sound like he misses you?"

"What?" I asked. We'd been studying for my math test a minute ago.

"When you're on the phone with your dad or you visit his house, does it seem like he misses having you around?"

He must have seen me hesitating too long over the word problem with the name "John" in it. He could spot my triggers a mile away, like some supermom scaling the house for pointy corners and opened Tide Pod containers.

"I haven't called him in a while," I said, playing with the bits of eraser littered across my paper. "It's not like he calls me ever. So, I guess that's the answer to your question: he doesn't miss me."

The real answer was that he couldn't possibly be missing me if he was ready to board a plane and move to Arizona with his new family when school got out for the summer, which was only a month away. His step-daughter had asthma, she had an inhaler and the whole works. He and Lisa thought the polluted Seattle environment was too much stress on her body, seeing the way her skin would get all clammy and hearing her wheezes all up the three flights of stairs. Still, that's 1500 miles they were moving. But hey, a parent will do anything to stop seeing their kid suffer.

God, forbid she had to go a few seconds without air in her lungs. Try having water in there instead.

"That's one option, but maybe," Brian paused, sensing the worried look on my face, "you haven't talked to your father in so long you forgot what he sounds like. Maybe if you called right now, you'd hear that strained, longing tone in his voice."

"He never calls me," I repeated, shocked by the defensiveness Brian's innocent words were bringing out in me.

"I wonder why..." Brian replied, alluding to his remarks about our relationship earlier: how I had hurt him.

I didn't say anything to Brian but that was just because deep down I knew what he was saying was probably right; my dad had been visiting less and less often, but I couldn't ignore the fact that he also had a new family now, which is why I always found excuses not to visit him on the weekends I was supposed to. I considered defending myself to Brian, but somehow, I knew it wouldn't change his mind, and I'd probably end up feeling worse about myself.

"You know what, you're right, I should call him," I said resolutely. "That's what a good daughter would do."

Suddenly, with a wave of guilt, I remembered I didn't even have contact information for my dad saved in my phone. Scrolling through my numbers, I pressed on every random one, telling myself I'd recognize a conversation with my own dad over one with an Uber driver. It's crazy to think how quickly someone can go from being your home screen to a deleted text thread.

I had other contacts saved, like Mom's for example, but they still seemed like a string of numbers to me, a formula for a person who really only existed out of practicality. Almost everyone in the world had "Mom" in some language on their phone, you don't need to have anything to have a mom but apparently you have to be something if you want to keep a dad.

I placed my finger at the bottom of the screen, but instead of calling that last number I flicked it upward, letting the nameless numbers scroll freely down my screen. When the number beneath my finger finally stopped so I could read the clip of a text next to the number, my hand immediately rose to my mouth, as the word 'KIDDO' stared back at me. I had found my dad with just one swipe; Brian had been right: one was my favorite number.

I considered pressing on the conversation, opening up a world where my dad stayed only a text away from home, where family only meant two other faces to him. But a part of me didn't want to open that book back up, sometimes it felt better just to rip out the pages.

And I probably would've just deleted that number right there and cleaned my hands of the man, but Brian was right there. So instead, I pressed on the number, and then on the call button. I knew the phone was ringing, but it was hard to distinguish from the ringing in my own ears, the kind you get when you swim down too deep.

"Liz?" my father's voice sent ripples along the ocean's surface: I considered hanging up right at that moment.

"Kiddo..." I winced as I imagined that name calling out to another young girl, "I'm glad you called," he continued, "it's been a while."

I'd be lying if I said at that moment I didn't want to shout back the same thing to him. I wanted to tell my dad that maybe the only reason I never called him was because I was waiting on him to call first. Maybe I would have forgiven him already if he had only apologized to me first. I mean, the parent was supposed to do that. But Brian's denunciatory voice echoed in the back of my mind, and the butterflies turned to moths in my stomach, and I reconsidered. Maybe he would have been there for me more, if I hadn't pushed him away first. Maybe he wouldn't be moving 1500 miles away.

It's weird how I still couldn't remember it. But there was this one night, when I was in 6th grade. I only know it happened because Mom told me about it, and my therapist—the one with the sweater vest and Lipton tea who only lasted three months— played the videos for me that I guess Mom had taken. I was pretty sure there was some rule in court about not showing videos that were taken without consent.

I'd gotten my first B on a math test. Brian reminded me about it the whole car ride home, telling me how I should have listened to him the night before when I went to sleep instead of reciting my times tables. I remember screaming at him to shut up with tears in my eyes and Mom looking at me with her eyebrow all up like I was the crazy one.

I ran right into my room when I got home and slammed the door so loud I thought the hinges were going to fly off. I could still hear Brian on the other side though. I started screaming so loud I think I probably burst his eardrum because he finally left. Unfortunately, Mom replaced him.

Sitting against that door I could imagine her scrambling for her parenting textbook or going through her "anxiety coach" flashcards. This was her moment to shine, and I could tell she didn't want to screw it up.

"Ok Sweetie, I understand you are experiencing strong emotions right now."

"I am here to listen and validate."

I remember it sounding like she was trying to negotiate with a terrorist. I wasn't going to put down the gun that easily though. Brian was probably still in the house; his words were still in my mind. I stared down at the crumpled-up test.

"Please let me in, I want to do some breath work with you, it will help."

I screamed again. I guess she realized her stupid textbooks weren't going to be of any real help in the field. She started to improvise.

"You know, Liz, when I was your age, I got more Bs than As, and I think I turned out pretty well."

There was a reason my mom quit the improv club. She also just quit a lot of things. I cried some more.

"Hey, okay, just let me in and let me try something. Please Liz."

I felt like we were in the movie Frozen and then I opened the door because I suddenly imagined her dying on an icy ship like Anna's mom.

"Oh, ok, good." She was beside herself. "Liz, I want you to look at me," she said. "We're going to focus on our breathing."

I took a deep breath in with her just so she would shut up. I took a few more. But that didn't get rid of the B on the paper.

"Just focus...on your...breath."

Suddenly something I'd read about respiratory rate came back into my head. How sometimes when you're drowning you can actually hyperventilate and that knocks you out first. It was something like over 20 breaths a minute.

I stared at the watch on my wrist and started counting. "1...2....3" the distance between them started to shorten. "4, 5,"

"Now one big bre..." Mom started. She lost my count.

I started saying the numbers out loud and I buried my head in my knees so the only thing in my vision was my wrist against the carpet.

At some point my dad joined us, all huddled on that nasty rug. I do remember that.

They told me I was just counting; I remember my breaths coming and going so quickly that my brain had a hard time keeping up with the records.

I don't remember much after I reached around 300. It had only been ten minutes.

Apparently, I just stayed there, curled up with my head buried murmuring numbers to myself. My dad tried to put his arm around me, and I just started rocking back and forth, my body heaving up and down.

Mom told me he started crying, that he was screaming in my ear and I just kept rocking back and forth like there was some other world I'd entered, and they didn't know how to get me back. I think my therapist had called it catatonic.

It's hard to imagine my dad like that, reaching out to me and being shut down. It sort of breaks my heart, just the picture of it all.

It's like trying to talk to your grandmother with dementia and she doesn't know who you are and eventually they tell you to stop scaring her. It was sort of like that.

Mom told me she stayed all night with me on that rug. She said that my dad wanted to, but it just hurt him too much to see his daughter like that.

I've only ever watched the recording once, in that stale, dark, therapist's room where mom had handed over her phone on the witness stand. I'd just spent the whole session convincing the lady I was fine too. My dad drove me home before the video finished. Mom said he was in denial. He told her she didn't understand as much as she thought she did.

"Lizzy? Are you still there?"

"Yeah..."

"Well, Mom told me the college tours have been going well. I, uh, heard you've been studying hard and doing really well in school," John added, rather tentatively as he couldn't read my silent words.

"Yeah, it's been pretty good. I'm really liking it, I'm a lot happier now," I stressed, reminding myself more so than him.

"That's wonderful to hear, I want you to know I'm very proud of you," he said genuinely, which made me cringe. If he had wanted to share his pride so badly, why hadn't he called me on his own accord? His words made me feel like a little kid again, as if all my self-worth stemmed from the roots of paternal pride, but again I reminded myself that the little girl all those years ago had let her father down first.

"Mmm" was all I could muster.

"I'm serious, I'm proud of you kiddo." I rolled my eyes.

"Save that nickname for your daughter who's actually six years old, please," I replied sarcastically, although I regretted my comment instantly. The topic of his other family would get him on a whole other tangent.

"Ha! It's funny you say that 'cause I actually have never called her that even though I'm sure she wouldn't try to rip my head off like you if I did."

My dad's response caught me off guard. I had assumed he was the same corny dad he was to all his kids. As much as I hated it when he called me that, I was glad I was the only one that got to hate it.

"So... how is everything going over there?" I asked out of politeness. I didn't really care about the answer.

"It's fine, yeah. The baby's teething, we're getting ready to move, and I'm not sure I'll be winning stepdad of the year, but it's all good."

My eyes widened, I'd forgotten his "new family" was just as new to him as it was to me.

"Oh, well I'm sure they all love you: everyone always does."

"Yeah, well everyone apart from your mother."

I laughed, although to be fair, I thought, Mom wasn't the one who cheated.

"Hey, listen kidd... Liz," he quickly corrected himself, "I'm so glad you called. It's nice to hear your voice every now and then, especially since you usually never pick up."

"What do you mean, you never call me!" I exclaimed, annoyed I had let my defensiveness out through my tone.

"Um, what do you mean?" he shot back, matching my defenses. "I've called your number a million times, and you never pick up. I literally just called you last week to remind you Grampa's birthday was May 5 but your voicemail box isn't even activated."

Scrolling through my phone, I saw the same number appear again and again on my calls in red and I could have sworn I felt Brian's minty breath brushing against my neck as my cheeks lit up.

"Oh, um, I guess I just thought it was a random number." I finally answered, knowing it would hurt my dad that I hadn't saved his contact.

"I see...well nonetheless thank you for calling, it sounds like you're doing really well over there."

"Yeah, it's nice talking to you."

"Ok, well I got some stuff to take care of now, so I guess this is goodbye, kiddo."

I knew that whatever he had to do was likely a family matter and he didn't want to ruin our talk by mentioning their business, which to be fair, I was glad to not have heard about. I imagined him.

"Ok, love you, Dad."

There was a small pause after that, I hadn't said those three words, or at least said them together since I was in middle school, and I knew what he wanted to say in return.

"To the moon and back, Kiddo." He hung up. I was glad he did, I wouldn't have been able to say it back. We both knew that.

Chapter 18

CLEARING OUT THE LUNGS

Brian was waiting for me when I got home from back-to-school shopping with Mom. Sophomore year was here and none of my clothes from freshman year seemed to fit anymore. Mom pretended to ignore that fact and just said every high schooler deserves a fresh wardrobe each year when she convinced me to go to the mall with her.

"Hey, I thought I'd follow through on my offer to help organize your room."

"Um, that was like eight months ago, but ok. I should have known you wouldn't forget."

"I never forget anything," he said in an unsettling voice that I wasn't sure was a promise or a threat.

Walking into my room with Brian, I saw it with fresh eyes and wished I'd at least picked the pillows up off the floor. I wondered what he thought of my pink and gold aesthetic. Between the hot pink comforter of my twin bed, baby pink curtains, furry pink beanbag chair and gold chrome floor lamp, desk lamp and mirror, it looked like a sixth grader's room, which was how old I was when I decorated it. Divorce guilt gift from Mom who only took part in therapy if it was of the retail variety.

I glanced again at my messy bed; I couldn't imagine Brian

120

leaving a bed unmade in his life. It's crazy how we could coexist. This put-together figure of organization and a literal pig sty. There are times when I feel like we're the same person. And there are times like these where I question whether we even know each other.

"Oh, wow Liz." He began, peering around the room.

I stared at the floor. Only small patches of the light pink carpet were visible under all the clothes strewn across the room.

"How bad is it?" I asked as I picked up a pillow from the floor and jumped onto my bed with the pillow over my face. He hadn't even seen the closet yet.

"Well, I'm not gonna lie, it's a big job. But I can be your motivation, you know, help you stay on task."

I wasn't stupid. Brian's "emotional support" was more like getting reminded of all your mistakes at the same time. I couldn't even look in the mirror after my 8th grade gymnastics competition, not even to check if the gold medal clashed with my leotard. But how could I complain that Brian wasn't one of those lovey-dovey "you're doing great" kind of cheerleading partners? No one's ever gotten a trophy for being lied to.

"Okay, why don't you start here." Brian said, moving over to stand at the left-most corner of the room. "The same principle applies as with your desk: start with the top left corner and move on from there."

I lifted my head up from under the pillow, feeling like somehow even my brain had gained weight. I crawled out of bed slowly. Bending over, I lifted a gum wrapper from the floor, groaning as I carried it over to the gold chrome trash can that seemed disproportionately empty compared to the chaotic mess of the room.

"A jog would be faster."

I rolled my eyes, but my legs had already started moving. My body had that response to Brian. That was the thing about him, he wouldn't ever force you to do anything. But you hear enough observational statements undermining your slacking performance and you feel like you owe it to yourself. It'd been the same case with tricking me into confessing to my teacher that I'd somehow looked at Katie Song's test before I handed mine in. I sounded delusional when it turned out she was taking a completely different class.

I looked back at the spot on my stained rug where I had just gotten the wrapper from, and miraculously another one seemed to have taken its place. I started to doubt whether I had even thrown the other one away at all, or if I had just imagined myself doing it, and had groaned at the effort of even that.

"Didn't I just pick that up?"

"I don't know, did you?"

I again made my way to the gum wrapper, picked it up, and brought it to the awaiting trashcan across the room. When I peered into the bin however, I quickly spotted the previous wrapper, and while I was glad I hadn't been hallucinating, it was pretty obvious I needed to get my shit cleaned up.

When I turned around to face the room with my newfound encouragement however, I felt my stomach sink to the floor. My heart began to pick up pace, as the sheer magnitude of the task dawned on me. I tried to picture just how long it would actually take. Imagining the time things would take always made things worse for me, as if the time in the day I spent doing other things was really that valuable.

"Don't let yourself go, Liz. Picture who you'll become by what you're choosing not to do."

In my mind, another movie began to play, and I saw exactly how I spent that time away.

"Imagine a girl who spends more time slumping back into her crusty bed than she spends leaving it. The girl just adds more and more bowls to her tower when she just as easily could have brought them back to the kitchen a staircase away. Who does that?! Who would want to be around her? Look, now she's finding one dirtied sock after another and unwashed underwear in her covers, and—"

"Turn it off!" I didn't like watching scary movies by myself.

"But it's still playing, the girl's still refusing to clean her..."

"I get it. Okay, I'm the pathetic girl in the movie. I get it. Just let me fix this."

I don't think I've ever felt more self-conscious, as if someone was peering into my memories, judging me from the walls of a room that wasn't full of dirty clothes and gum wrappers, with air that could move on its own without being forced by a fan.

I pictured how his room would look, how beautiful it would be, how full it probably was, though not in the same way my room was full. My room was so disorganized that it physically hurt your head. I knew I wanted a clean room, and with that a clear head. I didn't want to drown anymore; I just needed some swimming lessons. I mentally cursed myself for being so cheesy. I blamed it on all of Mom's stupid podcasts seeping into my brain while I had to ride passenger patient.

Brian had helped me earlier, his strategy: "like reading a book" he had said. I stared out at my cluttered room and watched as the floor turned into pages and each object into a floating, out-of-place word, calling for my attentiveness.

Starting in the furthest left corner of the room, with the threatening movie still playing in Brian's eyes, my own fell upon a large tower of cereal bowls, some with milk still dripping down their sides. The tower was disgusting, and most of me was mortified, but at the same time, a silly little part inside was amazed at just how many bowls made up that tower and how they had managed to stay balanced for so long.

I carefully made my way over to it, which took some time given the room was large and my steppable floor space horrifically small. I started with the bowl at the very top, with the most recent smelling cereal milk. Thankfully the tower was straight.

"I would have made you see exactly which bowls were furthest to the left. You're lucky." Brian said as he watched my every move.

He was always saying those sorts of things. Like just because it could be worse automatically meant you were being treated well, no matter what all your friends said about him. Sometimes I didn't think I deserved all this "good luck."

I scanned the room and landed on my desk chair. The chair looked clean enough itself, but hanging off its back was a smelly, stained cardigan, whose skinny sleeves wouldn't make it halfway up my arms. Brian probably put it there to taunt me. I considered dealing with it later, but I quickly saved myself from that self-fulfilling prophecy and kept to the system. That and Brian was sure to jump on any mistake I hoped he might overlook.

I smiled proudly to myself as I threw the sweater into the laundry basket. Liz: 1; Brian: 0. Except technically my shot actually missed the bin and I had to go pick the sweater back up. Nonetheless, I was starting to get a hang of this thing Brian called "position-based organizing." The job became less like a dangerous, unpredictable ocean, and more like a regulated, lifeguarded pool.

Lucy was always telling me not to listen to him, said he was always barking orders at me, she said he treated me like a dog. But do dogs get their own personal lifeguard? Maybe my friends were the bitches after all. No pun intended.

When I walked back into my room from the laundry room, I confronted a bit of a problem, and suddenly the lanes of the pool seemed a bit too blurry for my liking. Averting my eyes to the right of the chair, I faced my nightstand, which was surprisingly clean except for a dirty napkin and an old water glass which was not to the left or right of the napkin, but directly behind it. Shit.

My anxiety began to build, and even though I knew it all didn't really matter in the grand scheme of things, it was hard to ignore the lifeguards' blaring whistles, reminding me I was breaking the rules. Reminding me I really ought to have read my summer reading in 6th grade. Positioning my head level to the table, I squinted as hard as I could to determine if one of the objects was just slightly more to the left: but neither was, they were exactly in line with each other. That's the problem with these Brian rules, they're extremely rigid.

"Too much slack and you might as well let go of the reins 'cuz they're not doing anything." Leave it up to Brian to come up with a quote for it.

He had never told me what to do when this happened though and part of me wanted to ask him. But what if I wouldn't like the answer? "It's better to beg for forgiveness than to ask for permission." Even worse to ask for instructions and then ditch them because you're too lazy. I didn't really know why I cared so much either way, but it felt good to feel like something mattered again: even if it was just a stupid cleaning technique or the boy who would always break my heart.

I figured I was just going to have to improvise something or maybe move one of the objects slightly out of line, though that felt like cheating. Part of me was tempted to do the "Eenie meenie miny moe" song that had rescued me from things of this nature when I was younger. But Brian had informed me the rhyme had long since been canceled. Something about the song being used to pick between slaves to buy. I never thought about racists having anxiety too. Now that I was older, Brian said I had to use more complex ways to let the universe decide. There were a lot of things I didn't like about getting older.

Glancing around my room, I searched for any inanimate object I could get an answer from. Brian, of course, offered no help. I spotted a couple of coins on my countertop, but I was awful at flipping them. My Alexa probably had some feature to pick a random outcome, but I was a little creeped out over the idea of a machine having control over me. I was at a total loss.

I was practically ready to just spin in a circle with my eyes closed until my hand landed on either the napkin or the glass, when a scattering of cards spilling from an overturned Monopoly box caught my eye. I had absolutely no clue how the game got into my room, as despite being one of my favorites, I hadn't played the game since middle school. Resting on top of one of the Chance cards was a dice—or a die technically. Facing directly up at me, two dots rested on the top of the die. As I looked at the table again, my eyes went to the napkin first and then to the glass second.

Coming over to the table, I picked up the glass, carried it to the sink, washed it out, and brought it up to the top of the stairs where the kitchen was. I then returned to the table and threw away the napkin.

Brian stopped blowing his whistle. I hadn't realized when he'd started.

I continued moving to the right across the room. I folded my clothes one by one, laid them in my dresser, and flattened down the pizza cartons that littered my floor. Annoyingly, as I got closer and closer to completing the task, Brian seemed to get pettier and pettier about every little thing. He even made me put new batteries in my toothbrush when I finally made it all the way over to the bathroom on the right side of my bedroom an hour later, even though I had just replaced them last week.

By the time Mom called me for dinner, I had cleaned out my entire room, and everything in it was assigned a place. My brush was always on my nightstand, my mirror was placed on my desk, and my photo books and spare sheets were under the bed. I tentatively walked around the room.

Brian was right, rules were like a roadmap for your life, telling you where to go, lining you up for success. For the first time in a very long time, I didn't feel like I was walking through water: the air was as light as I was. *So again, not quite perfect.*

∽

"Hey Liz," Mom began as she entered my room, "I wanted to..." She was cut off when she saw the room. I really hadn't done much, just folded a few blankets and thrown the trash away.

"Um, I don't remember telling the cleaning lady to come today?" Mom began, testing the waters of what she believed her daughter capable of. "Did you do this by yourself?" she asked, in a tone that seemed to be preparing for disappointment, as if I would bring some stranger into the house to clean for me.

Although honestly, I didn't really feel like I could take credit for it. It's kind of all because of Brian.

"Um yeah. Someone at school gave me some tips, I probably wouldn't have done it otherwise, and I mean there are still a lot of like crumbs, and my bed isn't made or anything bu—"

"I don't even know what to say." Mom's eyes danced around the room, each patch of cleanliness flashing an incredulous look across her face.

"Perfect, don't say anything."

Chapter 19

BUBBLE ALL THE WAY UP

"Oh my gosh, he's here."

I turned my head to see the guy Lucy was staring at. I'd seen him before; tall, slim but toned, blue eyes, dirty blonde with a big smile. His tray was stacked high with two sandwiches, a cheeseburger, a bag of Lay's and a protein shake. Damn.

"I think I'm in love, Liz."

I nearly spit up my smoothie. Lucy and I were close, like born-and-raised together type of close, but there were certain things we just didn't talk about with each other. It was more of a guy friendship in that way, trying to make the worst smelling fart and then collect it in a jar, pranking our teachers, ranting about girls that lived for the two seconds Kyle Moore would look in their direction. I was never sure if it was the whole Christian thing or not, but for whatever reason, Lucy was adamant on not talking about crushes.

"I'm not kidding around Liz, I really, really like him."

Of course she did, who wouldn't. Those eyes alone seemed to lift me out of my seat and drop me in the deep blue ocean. But a hallway crush isn't love. I would never dare admit it to Lucy, but I lived for that walk between classes. The school offered some prime real estate, with the gold star going to the intersection between Dr. Turner's lab and Mr. Mill's history class.

"Yeah, he's hot. Ooh, check out his friend! The one chugging that carton of milk."

I wasn't kidding. The dude had a full gallon of milk next to him. They had to be athletes.

"They're on the soccer team."

"Oh yeah, is one of them wearing a backpack?"

All the athletes wore their team backpack, the ones they were given when they first got put on varsity. They wore those things like those two straps were the only thing pulling them out of the normal kid pond, and they'd rather tear their ACL than be caught dead mingling with the rest of us sorry lot. Seriously, the way those guys shuffled their feet in sync, so many one-eared AirPods you never knew who was listening with who, all traveling in one big pack, you would think we went to two completely different schools.

"Probably, I can't see from here. God, to date an athlete."

"How do you know they're soccer; did you follow him to the field or something?" I didn't mean for it to sound judgy, there was no shame in the stalking game.

"Um, no? He told me. I mean, I already knew the answer since freshman year Liz, when I first started crushing on him."

I didn't say anything, but I was pretty sure I would have remembered if she had told me anything remotely guy related. "So, you really went up and asked him what team he was on?"

"Obviously not, he came up to me at the end of our class, and we just started talking."

I nodded, wondering which class Lucy had with a jock.

When I finally made my way out of the library after school, I saw Mom's annoyed face through the dirty windshield of her car. The little scar between her eyebrows would always crinkle at the bridge of her nose when she was upset. I'd forgotten she was picking me up.

Today, she was also wearing makeup (definitely a bad sign) because I couldn't see her usual chestnut freckles, which were splattered across her face as if Jackson Pollock had just used her as his new canvas. She always told me it was sun damage, but my grandma had had the same look. That was where the comparisons ended though.

My mom, unlike my lipstick-loving "Gama," didn't wear makeup because she wanted to prove a point. She told me that not wearing makeup showed people that she was secure enough with the way she looked, and didn't have the time nor patience to spend an hour in front of a vanity each morning. "Guys don't like girls that hide themselves beneath a layer of foundation" she loved to say. Ironically, now that I think about it, she seemed to start wearing it more after my dad's wedding to a makeup artist.

"What took you so long? I've almost finished the crossword already!" Mom yelled, shaking the New York Times in my face. I glanced down at my watch; it was nearly six.

"Yeah, sorry about that, I just had to finish up some work."

"Well, it's great you're liking your studies, but you have got to call me ahead of time, Liz."

"Ok, sorry, can we just go now?"

I looked at Mom. Her eyes were amber in the sunlight coming in from the windows. When she rolled them, it sort of looked like the sun rising and falling.

We sped out of the parking lot in silence. Well, almost in silence. I had pretty much mastered the art of drowning out whatever new podcast Mom would play at me when she was driving. Honestly, if I hadn't, I probably would have been forced to jump out of the car by now.

Today's episode was on "Becky's 12 Reasons why You're

Scared of Losing Control." I guess "Dr Happiness'" 10 reasons weren't enough for her yesterday. I don't understand how she could honestly enjoy them. Part of me didn't believe she did, the way she'd only play them when I was in the car, constantly glancing over at me from the corner of her sunlit eye. As if listening to other random people who took a psych class once in college drone on and on about human nature could magically cure me. A podcast won't stop the water in your lungs from killing you. Everyone knew that. Secretly, I think my mom knew that. But what can I say, we all make up our own realities sometimes. The real world was a scary place.

We finally reached the driveway. It turns out, just as I could've told you without a $2.99 subscription and a mic, that "humans like having control because uncertainty is scary." And as for the other 11 reasons, just flip the words around and check out a thesaurus. "Humans often fabricate a sense of control to avoid feeling hopeless" was the final one. This time I was the one side eying my mom.

Honestly though, I didn't mind if the stupid podcasts made her feel like she was being that kind of Fix-It-Felix mom she always wanted to be. It beat her doing shit, like sending me off to some wilderness program like Dylan's mom, that's for sure. She was gripping the steering wheel so hard now her fingers turned white. That's when I noticed the nail polish. I couldn't even remember the last time I'd seen her clip them.

I made a mental note not to bring up the phone call with Dad the other week.

The second we got home, I emptied all my stuff on the floor and climbed into bed, without bothering to tidy up my room like Brian had reminded me to do immediately. I just lay there, fading into the mattress, while sleep offered its lazy hand to me. My eyelids started to become heavy, and my body felt depleted. In this position, almost identical to how I started my day, it started to feel like I'd never left the bed at all, that the day held no meaning other than being a vessel to the next one.

Chapter 20

OUT OF VIEW

We'd never been home alone before, but there was no way in hell I was flying to Arizona in July to be in 108-degree heat, so my dad had agreed to visit me while Mom was with her parents.

Of course, then he called last minute to say his stepdaughter was in the ER and he'd make a rain check. When Brian heard I'd be alone all weekend he insisted on staying with me.

"But are you sure the doors are locked? I wouldn't want anyone breaking in and hurting you," Brian continued.

I was thrown off by his sudden interest in my safety, and while I was initially flattered by his protectiveness, I couldn't help but feel like his tone was more condescending than concerned.

"Um, yeah." I answered in an attempt to wrap up the discussion. He always had a way of dragging on the most boring conversations. Honestly, what does this say about me, what kind of girl could talk to him?

"You don't sound certain. Did you check the lock?" he persisted.

"Um, yeah, I think I checked last night."

"Well, thinking you closed it and knowing you did are two different things."

"Oh my god, why does it even matter?"

"Um, maybe because some creepy dude could be peeping on you all night and you'd never know it. Who knows, maybe there's a serial stalker on the loose..."

I rolled my eyes, but I knew he was right, to some degree.

"Fine, would you feel better if I went over and checked it right now?"

"I would, and I think you would too," Brian replied.

Begrudgingly, I walked back downstairs and checked both the front and back doors. Both were locked.

"I told you so," I sneered as I made my way back to my bedroom.

"But aren't you glad you checked? I mean, it could have been a much more dangerous situation."

"Yeah, yeah, whatever you say," I joked.

"I just want to look out for you Liz, that's all."

The butterflies were back in my stomach and the waves were crashing in my ears, but for the first time in a very long time, the wings didn't fly up my throat. I felt like I was swimming rather than drowning. I felt like the luckiest girl in the world, the kind of girl who had someone protecting her, keeping her safe. There was the feeling of comfort and there was the danger of that comfort's fragility.

~

"Earth to Liz," Brian cooed in my ear causing my heart to beat so rapidly I swore there were hummingbirds rather than butterflies flapping their wings inside of me.

"Huh?" I asked groggily.

"Well, I was just wondering what you do in the morning. I mean, it's already almost nine."

The wings stopped flapping, and my gut began to sink as the

rest of me felt stranded on land, inhaling dirt as if it were air, seaweed intertwined in my hair.

"Well, it's the weekend," I replied, "and I don't have any homework due Monday, so I should be allowed to lie around all morning until I meet my friends at the mall later."

"No." Brian said sternly.

"What do you mean 'no'?" I asked.

"I mean I'm not letting you stay in bed and watch your weekend go by with your eyes closed. Liz, I'm making you a morning routine," he announced, "a schedule, if you will."

"Like the one you so kindly gifted me in 6th grade?" I asked.

"You mean the after-school routine that consisted of doing homework, then a shower, then a Facetime with Lucy?"

"Yes, that lowkey saved me from flunking out of middle school. God I was one unorganized kid."

"Yeah, well you still are, which is why you need a new routine. That old stuff was just the basics, I was an amateur back then too. But no, Junior year is gonna be busy as hell, you're gonna need a routine, not a distracting friend."

It was true, sometimes Lucy could convince me to skimp out on my extra credit assignments so I could have a sleepover with her. I could tell why Brian never approved of Lucy.

"Ok," he instructed, "you're gonna want to take notes."

I unlocked my phone, opened the Notes app and typed "Daily Routine" on top of a new note.

"So, school starts at 7:45. The car ride shouldn't be more than fifteen minutes with traffic." Brian began; his eyebrows knitted together in concern as he peered over my phone.

"Ok, so I'll get up at 6:45. Easy-peasy."

"No, you'll get up at 5:30."

"6:30."

"6:00 and that's my final offer." Brian announced. There was a sense of confidence in his voice that made his words sound final, and even though he wouldn't be there every morning to pull off my covers, I knew I'd probably still get up when the alarm went off.

"Fine."

"Now, if you get up at 6, then by 6:01 you can be in the bathroom."

"Oh, don't tell me we're planning out every minute of my morning."

"You think we need it down to the second?"

"No!!! I just think this whole time regiment thing is going to stress me out."

"So, waking up five minutes before school and doing whatever you remember to do before you're out the door doesn't worry you the tiniest bit?"

"Well..."

"My concern for you is this: with vagueness and cloudy directions, come one of either two things: laziness or guilt. Neither of which I would ever wish upon anyone, especially you."

I knew all about guilt. Brian made sure about that.

"I just don't really think I'm gonna stick to the schedule like let's be realistic here."

"Okay, well your reality is never going to be anything other than what it is now if you're not willing to do anything that doesn't fit your current lifestyle." Brian exclaimed, a little too loudly into my ear.

"Okay, okay. But how about we just map out every ten minutes at least for now I think that would be easier."

"Fine."

"Ok."

"So, by 6:10 can I safely assume you will have had enough time to travel across your bedroom floor into your bathroom?"

"Correct." I answered, rolling my eyes.

"And in those ten minutes I believe you can effectively use the toilet and wash your hands."

"But what if I don't have to pee?"

"Well, by sitting there and forcing you to go in the morning you will be doing yourself a favor later on in the day so you can save time at school and be more productive."

"But I love my bathroom breaks!" I exclaimed, thinking of my comforting sea anemone.

"Well, you'll just have to think of another excuse for time theft."

"Time theft, give me a break," I replied, rolling my eyes again.

"That's exactly what a time thief would say." Brian countered back, clearly way too proud of his pun.

"Okay, so first..." Brian paused, "you're gonna want to write this down."

I pulled out my phone and created a new Notes page, "Tooth-brushing Technique."

"Start with the front of your teeth: top and bottom, you'll be doing them twice, as they're what people will see most often."

"Makes sense."

"Then, to make it easier to remember, you will start with your gums—on the top, then down to the front of your top row of teeth."

"But I just will have brushed those," I remarked, looking up from my notes.

"I said you'll be brushing them twice, didn't I?"

I nodded, though it still didn't make complete sense to brush the same spot without practically any break in between.

"Anyway, after you brush the front ones, you will brush the bottoms: of the top row. Think of trailing the brush down through your mouth. And to finish the top, you'll curl beneath the back of your front teeth."

"Let me guess, we do the same thing on the bottom row now?"

"Essentially, except in the opposite order."

"Okay, so I do that, now what? Am I done yet?"

"Not quite."

"I swear to god, there's no way I'm brushing the fronts for a third time."

"No, but I like your idea of symmetry it's just lacking a little, um, diversity."

"We're still talking about teeth brushing here, right?"

"Yes. And one of your last steps will be to brush the bottom part of your top and bottoms, as while the beginning was for appearance, the end will be for health."

"Interesting."

"Not really, you're just brushing your teeth," Brian replied, shooting me a smug smile. "And lastly…"

"I thought that was the 'lastly.'"

"Almost. The last step you're gonna want to do is quickly trace your brush in a zigzag from the back of your top right corner to the back of your bottom right and then snake back. And finally, you'll scrape your tongue, and for some extra symmetry, you'll also do the roof of your mouth."

"Great, makes total sense."

"I think so. And you've got that all recorded right?"

"Right down to the 'snaking' of the toothbrush around my mouth."

"Great. I've never mentioned it before, but your breath is pretty nasty."

I dropped my mouth in shock and was preparing for a nasty comeback when I paused for a moment and actually got a chance to smell some of the air I just let out. And in that moment, although I could think of nothing that would be more humiliating, I couldn't help but recoil from the revolting smell myself.

"Fine, perhaps it will improve my breath, but it's not gonna help my anxiety. I mean all I'll be thinking about is if I started brushing in the right spot or if I brushed for the right amount of time."

"In the beginning maybe, but it'll get easier. You won't even have to think, it'll just be muscle memory."

"Yeah, but in the beginning—"

"In the beginning you'll spend all your brain power focusing on and worrying about the brushing technique so that you won't have any room left to stress about the other stuff. All that anxiety, structure contains it."

I hesitated, I tried to imagine a morning when I wasn't thinking about my schoolwork, or my dad, or what kind of desserts were gonna be in the cafeteria that day.

"Fine."

"So, you promise you'll try it? I swear you won't be able to stop once you start."

"Yeah, I'll test it out."

After we covered the teeth, we discussed how to brush my hair, how and when to apply my makeup, and then jewelry.

"I don't feel like doing any of this," I admitted.

"Don't say those sorts of things Liz. You'll feel guilty soon enough."

He remembered. Of course he did. When didn't he have the perfect tactic to cut me down and sew me back together with his rules? Of course I would feel guilty. I always do. Sometimes I feel like I was some sort of mass serial killer in my past life because that's the only thing that would make sense for the amount of penetrating, darkening, guilt that I feel. It's nauseating in the way your stomach plummets when you've just gotten in trouble or been caught talking bad about someone behind you. It's frustratingly painful like a brain freeze you're powerless against until it just fades away. Only you can't ever get rid of it because you don't know where it's coming from. It was bigger than Brian, I knew that.

Brian's routine may have been a bit over the top, but there was something reassuring about having a path to follow. Sometimes I wondered how my life could have gone, if I hadn't been so worried by uncertainty. It felt stupid, living my life like I was playing "line up," the game I'd invented when I was in kindergarten at my grandma's house.

She had an attic full of toys she'd been hoarding since the '80s but I was the only one with good enough knees to make it up those steep narrow steps. There were all sorts of vintage relics up there, from Cabbage Patch dolls and action figures to Matchbox race cars, and Playmobil sets; the room was loaded. The only modern toy was a giant Barbie Dreamhouse with like seven different rooms, all bigger than my head.

So naturally, I decided to make it a tourist attraction for my toys, and, like any organized establishment, they would have to wait in line for it. There were probably over 100 toy figures I would stand one after the other starting at the door of the house to the literal door of the attic on the opposite side of the room, winding through tea party sets and Twister mats along the way. It was my masterpiece, but it didn't just end there.

When I was a kid, there obviously needed to be some fun involved. So, every day of winter break I'd move each toy up one spot in line while moving the ones inside the house to the next room over. Over and over and over again, I inched the figures forward, satisfied by visible progress they continued to make on their journey.

To this day I don't know why I did it, but I guess maybe I liked the order and predictability of it. Looking back on it I can understand why Mom got me tested for autism that year (I didn't have it). It might sound like a boring game, and I hated waiting in line myself, but there was something about watching Superman and my clan of spikey-headed trolls moving slowly along their pre-ordained path that was sort of comforting. They knew they'd reach the Barbie dreamhouse eventually. I guess that's why I always threw tantrums when we had to go back to Seattle before they'd all gotten their turn. I didn't like disappointing them. Imagine waiting in line your whole life and never getting anywhere.

I glanced at my watch. I was running out of time myself.

⌇

I couldn't believe it was somehow 2:15—had I really spent that much time working on new routines with Brian? I was surprised I hadn't gotten any texts from Lucy or Dalia since I was supposed to meet them at the mall about two hours ago. I suppose they could probably guess where I was, or rather, who I was with.

Honestly, I was kind of surprised I still managed to make the invite list today, judging from all the times I'd flaked on sleepovers to finish up the homework. And then there was the time I missed Dalia's birthday party because I had a crazy, time-consuming history project to do. I never knew if Dalia was more hurt that I hadn't remembered we had class together, or that the project took only took her ten minutes to complete.

I couldn't exactly explain to her that Brian thought it best I make a timeline for every year within the timeline of the period Ms. Walter assigned us. It took up to four pages and 14 hours. In general, I tried to avoid having classes with my friends. Going completely overboard on an assignment like that and then telling them about their timeline with two dates is exactly what the teacher's looking for is just as bad as telling them their C is "practically better than my A."

Remembering Brian's warning the night before, I suddenly had the urge to recheck the lock; after all, it wouldn't be that dramatic of me to have falsely convinced myself of having felt it lock earlier. Walking back to the door and grabbing the handle, I felt the same resistance that meant the door was, indeed, locked, and for a moment, I felt comforted.

"You should jiggle it. Just to make sure it's actually locked." Brian's voice came from over my shoulder.

"That's stupid."

"But you're gonna do it."

I sighed. Defeatedly, I moved my hand back to the door handle, and jiggled it, first softly then again more forcefully. It was locked.

"It's locked," I told him, but he said nothing back. Any answer would have been more settling than his silence.

"Routine completed," he finally said.

"Routine completed." I sighed in relief.

⌇

Having Brian over while my mom was away made me feel safe, but I also knew that meant he'd be checking up on the routine he'd made for me. It didn't surprise me, however, when at the exact second the clock reached 6:00am, Brian was up.

"Why are you still in bed?!" he yelled, practically pushing me out of my bed.

I'd been expecting a yawn, or an arm stretch, maybe even a nice "Good Morning" but no, I was working with a drill sergeant.

I went to the bathroom and then to the sink. Before the water even had time to warm up, I saw Brian's reflection in the mirror.

"Oh my god, you scared the shit out of me!" I exclaimed, turning away from the mirror.

"Hey, watch where you put those nasty potty hands of yours!" Brian yelled, sounding even more terrified than I'd been.

"Whatever. Can you just show me the 'proper' way to wash my hands?"

"Fine, but you should have always been doing it this way. I didn't come here to teach you. Only to supervise."

My eyes fell to the floor. It was clear he only came to make sure his machine was still running smoothly.

"It's ten seconds for the initial rinse. God. I hate people who think it's okay to just go right in with the soap, I mean the sheer feeling of dry hands scraping a soap bar it gives me the chills!"

"Do me a favor and shoot me if I ever care this much about handwashing!"

"Well, you'll die either way. Most of the world's deadliest diseases spread by germs carried on the hands."

I rolled my eyes, already dreading the rest of the day.

When it was finally time to get dressed, I practically sprinted to my dresser. Instead of having to dump out all the clothes on the floor and make random piles to blindly pick from, I had strategically divided my clothes collection into the dresser, whose drawers would now act as the piles. I'd been following another routine Brian had taught me that would prevent the misfortune of the same clothes being selected at the top of the drawer: every time I put clean laundry away, I dumped out each drawer and put both the new and old clothes back in randomly. It took a lot longer to put my clean laundry away this way, but it was worth it to know everything would be random. In order to know when to wash my clothes, Brian instructed me to do laundry every five days, on days ending in a 5 or a 0.

"Are you forgetting anything, sleepyhead?" Brian said in a mock tender voice that sent shivers down my spine.

"Huh?" I already felt like I had been getting ready for hours, and I hadn't a clue what Brian was hinting at until...

I'd forgotten I needed to put jewelry on before my makeup.

"Took you long enough." Brian sneered, turning to observe me.

"Yeah, well I forgot. Sorry."

"You forgot, you were lazy, whatever you want to call it." Brian said, a little too passive aggressively for my liking.

"I wasn't being lazy Brian, I literally just forgot."

"Mhm," Brian nodded. Another one of Margaret's coveted remarks.

"Brian, I'm telling the truth here. I'm not lazy!" I shouted, surprised by my own reaction towards the accusation.

"Fine, you really want to prove it to me?"

"FINE!" I yelled back, even though I still felt kind of stupid for caring so much.

"Start over." Brian stared at me; eyes fixed on my own.

"Excuse me?"

"I said 'start over.'"

"Yeah, I heard what you said. I just don't understand." I countered back.

"My apologies. Allow me to be as clear as I possibly can: if you want to show me that you aren't lazy, then I implore you to start from the beginning, the whole routine. Do it again. You clearly need practice anyway," Brian said it in a tone that I'd never heard him use before but knew better than to mess with.

Normally, if anyone talked to me in that commanding, patronizing voice of his, I would probably have just stopped listening, put my head underwater so all I could hear was the morphed, distorted sounds of words that turn to melodies in the ocean. And if it were anyone else, I would've done just that. But it was Brian, and the only way it seemed possible to drown his voice out was to drown myself. And so, instead of asking him to kindly get the fuck out of my home, I instead asked him for a glass of water.

"Why do you need water right now?" Brian asked, anticipating my disobedience.

"Well, if I'm going to pee on the toilet again, I'm gonna need some fuel."

After Brian left, over two hours later, I checked the door, jiggled the handle twice. The door was still locked. I went back to my room, exhausted, and fell asleep.

Chapter 21

I WONDER IF ANYONE KNOWS

Somehow summer had come and gone before I ever got a chance to sit down and enjoy it. It's like school ended in June, Brian and I opened my APUSH textbook, and fast-forward 71 days and we're here now, Junior year.

As I entered the school, I immediately felt self-conscious, which was new for me—at least at school. I kind of ruled the academic world here. I couldn't put my finger on it, but something about Junior year had a different vibe to it.

My first class was AP Biology. I spotted my name tag where it always was, in the very last row. That's what you get for having a track record of paying too much attention in class. Brian was next to me.

The teacher, Mr. Smith, was a tall brunette with eyes that were spaced just slightly too close to either side of his nose. If you wanted to make eye contact, you were also committing to counting his nose hairs. He wasn't the most exciting to look at, and his belly drooped over his belt and jiggled up and down as he crossed the room, but I appreciated the clean and orderly look about him.

"Class, welcome to your first day of AP Bio. I know you're

expecting one of those boring teachers who starts the year going over the textbook and syllabus, but I'm not that kind of guy."

Clearly. I noticed a circular tattoo design poking out from one of his sleeves. I really hoped it wasn't a Mickey Mouse logo like I thought it was. God help me.

Mr. Smith continued, "I want you guys to get to know me better. And I believe there's no better way to do that than to introduce you all to my favorite little Cymothoid friend of mine."

The whole class looked at each other. Truthfully, I didn't even know what a Cymothoid was, but I just nodded and smiled. As much as it pained me to encourage this unqualified buffoon, this was Junior year, and teacher recommendations mattered.

Suddenly, a giant picture of a fish appeared on the projector screen, with its mouth wide open like the dentist had just told it to say "ahh." I pretended to laugh. "Fake it till you make it," my dad always said. But he also always knew what he was doing, at work at least. Sometimes I wondered what thoughts went through his head whenever he would tell me, "See you soon!" after one of his bi-annual spontaneous visits.

"Anyone know what this is?" Mr. Smith started weaving through the desks now, leaning from side to side, trying to find anyone who secretly shared his fish fetish. The signature off-white layer of stickiness coating my desk felt like slimy gills against my white knuckled hands.

When he finally passed my row, I let out a large breath of air I hadn't realized I'd been holding.

Suddenly, Mary came through the door with her dark hair frizzed out an inch from her head, and her makeup had clearly been slept in. I would know, I didn't even own makeup remover.

"Sorry, late night," Mary said as she flew into the room in a whirlwind of messy papers and clacking boots, a smug smirk set on her face as she made her way to the front of the class where her name tag was placed. I knew Brian was judging her. He'd made a comment earlier of how just about everyone got into Bio this year.

"Seems like that's every night for you, Mary," one of the boys said with a laugh.

"It's a fish!" Another boy in front shouted.

Mr. Smith put his hand on his face in mock disappointment. He zoomed in the projector so we could all see the fish's nasty mouth better.

"I want you all to look very closely at the fish's tongue. Do you see anything there?"

I leaned forward on my desk, squinting my eyes. It looked like part of the fish at first, this slimy blob, but when my eyes focused, I saw it. I mean I actually saw its eyes. It was a whole other animal living on that poor fish's tongue. It looked like a little sand crab with grubbing claws and a curve at the bottom of its face that made it look like it had a Glasgow smile.

"It's called a Cymothoa exigua."

"Ewww," the class regurgitated.

"It feeds on the tongue of its host."

Mr. Smith was smiling at us just like that creepy little bug and suddenly I felt like swallowing my tongue too.

"I caught this fish myself. It was my first big catch of the day; I was about 12 years old. My dad and I pulled this little guy out of the water and what do you know, he brought a little friend with him."

It didn't look like a friend to me.

"He sure was tasty though."

I wanted to gag but I cleared my throat instead.

⌀

Still feeling nauseous after class, I headed straight for my bathroom sanctuary. I hadn't been in there long before Ms. Rainbow Fish herself walked in.

"Hey, Liz, right?" I couldn't believe she remembered my name.

"Yeah, and you're Mary, right?" Duh.

"You were in my Bio class just now, right? Isn't Mr. Smith gross?"

"Yeah, but not as gross as that thing on the fish's tongue."

"Eeew. I almost barfed," she paused like she was reconsidering it, and then proceeded to ask, "Oh, do you have tickets to the play?"

I had no idea what play she was talking about.

"Umm, no," I mumbled.

"You totally need to come!"

"Oh, you know what, that's okay. I don't know, I might have something tonight."

"Oh, don't worry. I'd be shitting my pants if we were performing tonight."

I know that's just an expression, shitting your pants, but I still believe only those who have actually done it reserve the right to use it. Mary looked like she'd never even wet the bed before.

"We go live in a month. But they told me to start giving tickets out early because it's gonna be really fun."

She was holding out the crumpled ticket to me now, like it was the last of her shiny scales she was giving away to the last ugly fish in the pond.

I accepted it slowly; fully aware I hadn't heard the bathroom sink run in about an hour so we were both spreading a million germs to each other right now. But hey, half the ocean is basically just fish pee anyway.

"So, what's the play?" I asked to distract myself.

It took her a minute to think of the name.

"Legally Blonde, yep. Apparently, there's a movie. I play Elle."

"You're joking, right? You must've seen Legally Blonde." I

mean she'd have to actually be blonde if she thought I'd believe she was too cool to have seen such an iconic movie. And that was the other thing, she wasn't even blonde!

"So, are you going to wear a wig or something?" I asked.

"You know, I'm not sure yet, I actually never auditioned for this, but this kid in my theater class I accidentally signed up for told me to join the cast, he just gave me the role and everything."

"So, no audition?"

"No audition."

"So, it can't be like the big official school play then?"

"What? Yeah no, I don't think so. It's just a dozen kids from this guy's drama club. It's gonna be so fun though, you have to come!"

I smiled.

"So, you'll be there? It would mean so much for the cast. Me, Derek, Lucy..."

"Wait, Lucy's in the play?"

"Yeah, she's Brooke Taylor."

I couldn't believe this. I didn't know if I should go call her right now and yell at her for not telling me or start rolling on the ground with laughter. I looked up at Mary, but she didn't seem to see my amusement.

"I guess I'll be there," I said, finally.

"Great, it means a lot!"

I'm sure it did.

Ms. Rainbow Fish slipped out of the bathroom, leaving me in her wake. I stared in the mirror in wonder. I mean what kind of person can get out of a stall, meet a stranger, and reach into their pocket to give them a ticket to their play that they just learned they were starring in? I still couldn't get over the fact she wasn't even blonde. I could have been the spitting image of Reese Witherspoon, and I wouldn't even make it to callbacks.

I came home and the whole house smelled like spices. Mom didn't cook much, but crockpot chili was one of her specialties. She handed me a bowl full of her "famous" chili, but she didn't let go when I grabbed it, like she was trying to keep me hostage in the kitchen; I normally grabbed my dinners and ran to my room to eat over homework.

"Sooooo...how was it?" Mom began with excitement that faded throughout the sentence as she tried to interpret my expressionless face.

"It was fine," I went with, hoping a neutral approach would lead to the least amount of pestering.

"Oh please, Liz, this wasn't the first day of middle school, tell me how it went!"

"It went okay, I don't know."

"Liz, I won't push it, but I hope you know how proud I am of you."

I nodded as I began to move towards the stairs, leaving my mom to eat alone in the kitchen. I could almost hear what Brian would say to me if he were here, "You're gonna make that poor woman who had to push your fat ass out of her, eat all by herself?" Unfortunately, you couldn't just talk back to someone who wasn't there.

"Hey Mom," I began, shocking myself. "Maybe I'll eat down here with you tonight. I wouldn't want to spill any of this on my homework."

Mom's face seemed to take a pause before she quickly recovered to accept the offer before I had a chance to retrieve it.

"Thanks for the chili," I mumbled, playing with the brown mush in my bowl.

"Of course, I'm just so glad you want to eat with me," Mom

responded, trying to read my face while I kept my eyes on my meal. "You are okay though, right?"

"Yeah... sorry I just didn't want to eat alone for once."

"No, no, that's not what I meant, I just didn't know if you wanted to talk about something," Mom started, sensing the defensive walls starting to build.

"Mom, I'm 16, I don't need to confess all my feelings to you," I said sarcastically, even though picturing that scene felt oddly comforting.

"Right, I know that. I'm just here if you want to talk, that's all, I guess."

I rolled my eyes. I wondered what kind of relationship she thought we had.

At this point, I realized that Mom had long since dwindled her bowl down to a few bits of meat that her fork seemed to break apart with each bird-like bite, and it was clear she was trying to prolong our conversation, or at least time together.

"I mean school wasn't terrible," I started, feeling a little guilty seeing her face light up just by looking in her direction.

"Oh yeah?" Mom asked, trying her best to mask the hope in her voice.

"Yeah, I got to meet my advisor. He was nice, and fat," I elaborated, remembering the older man with the jiggly belly.

"Oh, that's good, I was worried he'd be some grumpy guy. I always got stuck with the worst teachers."

"Yeah, everyone seemed nice. I mean it was only my first day, so I don't know, maybe it actually sucks."

"Well, that's terrific to hear," Mom replied.

"Yup," I said, pushing my chair out and standing up from the table.

"I guess I can take these and start working on the dishes, unless..." Mom paused, "unless you want to help me?" She finished with an overly eager raise of the eyebrow.

"Don't push it," I returned as we exchanged knowing smiles and Mom gathered our bowls.

I tentatively climbed into the driver's seat. I hadn't driven since the day I got my license, almost four months ago, but I insisted on finally driving myself to school. As I settled in, I looked back at Mom, standing in the doorway biting her nails—her long jeans rolled up a couple of inches at the ankle, her tan Ugg boots slowly getting darker as water dripped from the gutter above. I'd hoped she would be excited for me; I didn't want to see her worried face. I already faced one in the rearview mirror.

Nevertheless, I made my best effort to back out onto the road without hitting any of the cars parked along the street. Once I successfully made it out of the driveway—most likely leaving the garage door open—I remembered to pause at the stop sign, my fingers digging into the sweat-soaked steering wheel. My GPS burst out in a jumble of rights, lefts, and 200-foot turns, and I tried my hardest to keep my eyes on the path it illustrated. There were so many options, so many ways to go and paths to take—it felt terrifying. With one wrong move, I could cross the double yellow line into oncoming traffic; even worse than my fear of doing so was the temptation.

Chapter 22

SWALLOWING WATER

There were donuts at the cafeteria to celebrate mid-terms being over, and after spending my entire morning begging for the car, I hadn't gotten a chance to eat breakfast. They were from Dunkin': my favorite. My stomach growled, scaring off the butterflies.

I grabbed a strawberry one; it had pink frosting and rainbow sprinkles on top. Before I could drool over it anymore, I quickly stuffed it into my face until all that was left was a glob of pink hanging from the tip of my nose which I tried my best to lick off with my tongue. No matter how cute I felt in the morning, at that moment I knew I looked like a clown; and no one was better at laughing at that clown than Lucy.

"I think you got a little..." she motioned with her finger to her nose.

"Uh, yeah, I'm aware."

"Do you want a napkin?" Lucy asked with a smirk frosted across her face, gesturing to the pile on the table.

"No, I'm good."

"Mmm, that frosting does look good." She teased, reaching out her finger to my nose jokingly.

I turned away from her so I could get the frosting off myself.

That's when I noticed Brian had appeared. I didn't want to hear his thoughts on my eating a donut.

"No way you did that with your tongue." Lucy chuckled with disbelieving eyes.

I opened my mouth cheekily revealing the pink icing.

"Fake." Lucy rolled her eyes.

"So anyway, how has your day been going?" she asked, after I had managed to polish off every last crumb of my pink prize, as if I were hiding the evidence from Brian.

Just then Mary and a group of her friends from the play joined Lucy's side.

"Hey guys, some of us are going out to dinner tonight if you want to join?" she asked.

I held my breath. Aside from Lucy and Brian, if you even want to count him, nobody invited me to anything; unless, of course, their mom made them invite the whole grade to their birthday party.

Lucy smiled that big toothy grin of hers and I heard Brian snicker. I'd almost forgotten he was there. I guess he was invited too. I tossed my head to the side to tell him to leave us alone. He didn't.

"Yeah, that sounds great!" I said.

The second those words came out though, judging by the vibe Brian was giving off, I knew I had said them all wrong. Seventeen-year-olds weren't supposed to get so excited about going out to dinner; they weren't supposed to be surprised every time a class-mate asked to grab food. Teenagers worried about curfews, or getting into college; teenagers didn't worry about saying the right things or saying them the right way.

"Um... yeah I mean we're probably just gonna go down to that cheap Italian place." Mary said.

I could tell this was the sort of thing they did all the time.

"Oh, the one with unlimited breadsticks!" I had done it again.

"Um, I'm pretty sure you're talking about Olive Garden?"

"Yes, I love that place." I said, realizing halfway through that my response had not been the right one.

"Oh, well it's not that; it's called 'Il Pasto,' on Alaskan Way," she corrected me.

Lucy came to my rescue, "I can pick you up if you want?"

"Ok, so then I don't have to drive," I nearly shouted. I hadn't realized until that moment how much driving really stressed me out.

"I'll scoop you up at 7:30. Is that good for you?"

"That's awesome!" I blurted out.

"That's awesome!" Brian mocked me in a snarky tone.

I wanted to die over the words that just left my mouth; I wanted to tie a boulder to my back and jump in the ocean. I didn't care about Lucy, but what about Mary, and what if someone else in the hallway heard? What new embarrassing things would I say at dinner, in front of Lucy's new friend group I was somehow supposed to be adopted into? And then there was the whole Brian issue, he'd never let me go without him.

～

The second I got home, after one of my tensest drives which left my fingers momentarily stuck gripping the air, I raced upstairs to my room. Thankfully I had already cleaned it.

Climbing into the shower I heard Mom call down, "LIZ! You're home so early, did everything go okay at school today?"

The sound of the shower water pouring down around me drowned out any of my desires to respond, and within minutes I had forgotten my timeframe that had previously been crunching over my head, as the ocean always seemed to do. I liked the way the water droplets poured out from the faucet and rolled down my body, never getting stuck, not even in my head which had a tendency to suck things in and refuse to spit them out.

"Liz? Why are you taking a shower already? Is this some new routine?" Mom called again.

I turned the knob, and the waves dissolved against my skin.

"I'm going out, Mom," I couldn't hide my annoyance; she was always so dismissive of Brian and his routine. I think she was threatened by him because I listened to him more than to her.

"Oh, you are..." my mother started, and I could imagine how hard it was for her to stifle her million questions. "Well, have fun."

I doubted I would: especially if I never made it out of the house. Lucy was coming soon, and I'd barely started my routine.

⁓

I quickly picked out my clothes: reaching blindly into my shirt drawer, I grabbed a white t-shirt, and I was relieved when I pulled out a pair of jeans from my pants drawer. I didn't need Brian hovering over me to know how to do it anymore, it was all routine.

Unfortunately, because I hadn't bothered to open the pack of socks Mom had just bought me at Costco, when I pulled out one Puma sock, all eight pairs came out of the drawer with it. This meant I'd have to wear them all. Brian had made it very clear that there was no cheating the universe.

To my relief, the next and last two picks got me a nice fresh pair of underwear and a white bra, which went perfectly with the white t-shirt—something I used to always forget to consider.

After I got dressed and did my makeup and jewelry routines, I was pleased with what I saw in the mirror. Sometimes the universe is generous. Except to my feet. They were sweating with eight socks on each foot; I couldn't fit them into any of my shoes, so I had to wear my mom's ugly Birkenstocks that were two sizes bigger than my shoes.

I looked at my watch. I'd done all my routines in record time. I heard a honk outside the window on cue.

⌁

As I climbed into Lucy's car she smiled and said, "I forgot you had your license, I guess you could have just driven yourself."

"I've had it for four months, you're the one who just got your license."

"Yeah, but I've been driving my dad's pickup since I was 14."

I laughed, but not because she was joking. I never told her about the thoughts I'd had when I was driving, that I may have killed someone, or that I was one impulse away from it. Even if I didn't believe in it, I didn't want her thinking I was going to Hell.

"Yeah, well I didn't exactly want to show up alone, so thanks for taking me."

"Tonight will be fun, there's nothing to worry about."

I looked at myself in the visor mirror. "Should I be worried?" I asked, tapping my foot against the carpet of the car.

"No, I'll introduce you to some of my new friends." I saw her size up my outfit, with a look of relief. She clearly didn't see my socks.

"I hope so, I wouldn't want to emb—"

"Ooh, I really hope Ashton will be there."

I wanted her to let me finish my sentence, to apologize for hurting her rep, even if they were just a bunch of theatre kids. Instead, I said, "Yeah, me too." I didn't even know there was an Ashton at our school. I mean, is that even a real name?

"And their food is really good. I'm craving their spaghetti and meatballs." Lucy said dreamily, wrapping her finger around her hair like it was a fork.

"They are the best kind of balls."

"Like you would know," Lucy laughed.

"Hey!"

"Who knows, maybe there will be a cute guy there for you tonight." She was never subtle about trying to get me into a new relationship.

I rolled my eyes, but my feet kept tapping on the ground, faster and faster. I wasn't excited to talk to other people; if it were up to me, I'd stay with Brian the whole time. I'd stay with him forever.

"Ok, GPS says we're here." I said, nodding my head toward a white brick restaurant with a red, green and white banner sprawled across the doorway. The smell of freshly made pasta wafted through the car windows, and as soon as Lucy parked— rather poorly, might I add—I jumped out of the car. My sudden wave of hunger was so great it was like I was being pulled to the door, and was ready to dive right in, as I waited for my swim buddy.

Just then, Brian showed up and pulled me to his side before I could go inside with Lucy.

"Liz, are you sure you want to go? It looks crowded tonight."

His questioning tone created a doubt that seemed to sink me down to the seafloor, plummeting like an anchor. The restaurant did look busy, at least busier than my usual dinner company. I looked for a sign that Brian wanted to get away as fast as I did, but the flicker of excitement as he tapped his feet to the music told me the opposite. Maybe he was just trying to test my confidence. I looked over my shoulder for Lucy: she'd already found her crowd.

"Yeah..." I answered him tentatively. Besides, I told myself, swimming up too fast can leave you paralyzed.

"Hey," Brian said quietly as he nudged my shoulder, "everything is going to be fine." It was hard to read Brian sometimes; he was so full of contradictions and mixed messages.

Walking through the restaurant, I quickly realized there were not nearly as many people as I'd thought, and the large crowd I'd noted on my way in was merely the group surrounding the bar in the front of the room. Looking over at the tables, I noted that most of them were empty, except for a few couples and a family with a bunch of grumpy kids. I wonder if they had also been expecting breadsticks. My stomach growled.

Brian and I sat down at the end of the table, Lucy was already seated at the opposite end but there was no more room over there.

"Wow, these menus are huge." I muttered as I unfolded the three-page list of different salads, pastas, "antipasti" and pizza. I loved to eat (much to Brian's disappointment), I just didn't love choosing what to eat, ever since I was a little girl in that Rapunzel dress. And tonight, there was a lot more than chocolate and vanilla to pick from.

"Yeah, I've been here so many times and I still haven't tried more than a fourth of the menu." Mary said.

"That's better than I could ever do. Once I order something I like, I rarely try anything else!" I giggled nervously, but I knew that probably made me sound boring.

"Huh, interesting." Brian muttered under his breath. "I'm sure there's a lot of pressure when you'll be ordering the same thing every time you come back here." I was glad he was whispering but it was still loud in my ear.

"I'll probably end up getting something I know I'll like, a pasta dish to be safe." I said.

But I didn't need to hear Brian's reaction to feel the way my body reacted to him. My feet were back tapping on the floor in seconds. Or maybe it was my feet's way of trying to keep circulation moving under eight pairs of socks.

"That's low-key a good idea," one of the girls said to me from across the table.

I would've said my cheeks were red from blushing if Brian didn't completely embarrass me.

"Wrong," he practically shouted. Thank God the music was

so loud that the rest of the table didn't seem to hear it. While the group was busy talking about some boy one of them liked at the other table, I whispered to Brian, "What's that supposed to mean?" I couldn't believe he was the one who'd be judging me tonight.

"Nothing."

"Right," I muttered under my breath.

"What do you think about him, Liz?" Lucy said, reeling me back into the conversation. She must have noticed I was drifting.

"Oh, yeah. He's hot." I said with a giggle. I just hoped he wasn't one of their boyfriends. Before I could get a look at the guy in question though, Brian decided he actually did have something to say.

"I do think that you're missing out. I mean how are you going to know if there isn't something else on the menu you might like even better than pasta?"

"Not now, Brian. I need to be social." I turned my attention back to the group, but they had moved on and were now talking about the play. I knew there was no hope of trying to contribute anything besides a head nod now.

And I knew what Brian was saying was right, and it wasn't the first time I'd thought about it. In a way, it was just like picking out my clothes: how could I know which choice was the best? Tasting good was the least of my worries; nutritional content and calories made the decision that much more stressful. Maybe that's why I liked math so much: there was always an optimal solution.

I knew I was missing out, but I'd rather just order the first thing that looks good than mull over the menu for an hour reading every ingredient. I mean, that's what my dad would always do, and he'd always end up regretting whatever he got anyway and complaining about it the rest of the meal. Sometimes my mom just got tired of it and ordered for him. It's funny how he couldn't pick an entree but seemed to have picked a perfect new family with no regrets.

"Has everyone decided what they're getting?" Mary asked,

sitting up in her chair so she could see everyone. Now I was the only one not head nodding.

"Liz." Brian whispered in my ear. I pretended to ignore him and didn't say anything back.

"Let's try something out, see if you like it," he continued. "You know how you chose your outfit this evening?" I remained quiet, which was his invitation to continue. "Well, I think we should do that again, with dinner."

I wasn't exactly sure what he meant, but I was intrigued.

"Now, in order not to always get stuck with appetizers as they're always listed first," he explained, "we won't use the favorite number technique, we'll just pick randomly."

I was confused at first, not sure how this would work. Did he expect me to bring a blindfold so I could both spin around and pin the tail on the tagliatelle?

"Bruh, where's our waiter?" I heard someone say.

Again, seeming to read my thoughts, Brian continued with his instructions, "It doesn't have to be complicated, I say you just close your eyes, and place your finger down somewhere on the menu, wherever you feel called to and that's what you order."

This sounded reasonable. Brian appeared pleased with himself, while I tried to take a mental note of where the pasta section was located.

"Ok, now close your eyes and put your finger down wherever it feels right."

How do I know when it feels right? I wondered skeptically to myself, still hesitant about the whole plan.

"You'll know, trust me." Brian was seriously in my head tonight.

I rolled my eyes and then checked to make sure all the other girls were too busy talking to notice me. Only Lucy was looking in my direction. I couldn't tell if she was mad at me or glad I wasn't talking because I'd probably just say something to embarrass her anyway. Her eyes were still on me when I closed my own.

Following Brian's instructions, I stuck out my pointer finger, flipped the menu over a couple of times, and circled my finger around the surface of it. I'd expected to feel stressed out by the idea of not knowing where I should place my finger, but Brian was right, I just knew. It felt like a magnet, from the universe or something, and when I felt my finger placed down on the laminated sheet—sticky too, like my desk—it felt right. Whatever feeling I'd been chasing my whole life, this was it.

Opening my eyes, I looked down at my meal: "Lampredotto." The ingredients were in Italian, but looking at the header above, it seemed to be some sort of small sandwich.

"I hope you didn't peek," Brian warned.

"Um... I one hundred percent did not cheat." I whispered, grateful that the rest of the table seemed to be distracted with their menus and weren't paying attention to my indecision.

"Good because you probably wouldn't even be able to enjoy your meal if you did, knowing it wasn't actually the meal you were supposed to eat." I didn't exactly understand how a person was supposed to eat a certain meal.

"Hi, are you ready to order?" A woman with pencil thin eyebrows, and undyed roots asked, pulling a notepad from her side and a pen from her pocket.

"We've been ready, yeah," Mary said with a sarcastic smile. I couldn't imagine Lucy approving of those kinds of manners.

"What drinks can I get you started with tonight?" The lady asked, unfazed by the rudeness.

"Tell her you're good with the water," Brian said, elbowing me. This annoyed me because even if Brian wasn't a drinker, he shouldn't force me to do the same. I wasn't stupid, Mary chose this place because they didn't card. The waitress was now looking at me expectantly, along with the rest of the table.

"Water's fine."

"Have you decided on your food?" The waitress asked politely, looking at me for the answer.

"Yeah, I'll have the lasagna." Mary interrupted. The waitress wrote it down. I didn't know if I was more taken aback by

Mary's lack of manners, or her decisiveness. And man, I loved lasagna.

"Yes, may I please get the Lampredotto? Thank you." The woman's eyebrows rose to the top of her head, looking like twigs, trying not to break from the arch.

"Oh, the Lampredotto, great choice."

I smiled, but I couldn't help noticing the woman's words, she had said "great choice," she could have said a meal, or order, or sandwich. Brian seemed relaxed though, which meant the universe was as well.

After the woman walked back to the kitchen, Brian turned his attention back to me.

"Well, this is going to be exciting!" he said mischievously.

I looked at him skeptically, imploring him to explain what was so exciting.

"Well, did you read the ingredients in your sandwich?" I didn't say anything; he knew the ingredients were in Italian.

"So, that's a no then?"

I felt a drop of panic and wondered if I should Google it. What was it called again? My fingers threatened to quiver while I searched for the menu left on the table.

"No, don't do that!" Brian said forcefully, causing me to freeze my hand in mid-air, "it's so much more fun to be surprised. I mean that's the beauty of randomness."

That should be a quote, I thought as I placed my napkin on my lap as if it were a towel, transitioning me back to dry land.

"Yeah, well on the idea of being random, how is your dad these days? Have you guys talked recently?"

Wow, Brian really liked to bring up sore subjects. I smiled, trying to delay the conversation, while I simultaneously tried to remember the last time I'd spoken to my father. I hadn't talked to him in a few months, but the last time we did, when his daughter picked up, it was nice.

"I'm glad you're starting to make an effort," Brian said, a little condescendingly. I nodded, I had thought of it more as mutual effort, but thinking back to the missed calls, it seemed Brian was right, as usual.

The waitress with the splinter eyebrows came over and dropped a plate down in front of me then bustled her way back to the kitchen. I blinked, and then I blinked again. I shut my eyes, really hard this time so I could feel the darkness and then opened them. Brian was laughing, but I felt like I was going to vomit.

On the plate in front of me, practically spilling onto the placemat was a giant, overstuffed sandwich. Only instead of any normal deli meat, there were heaps of what appeared to be shriveled up, soggy gray strips of leather. To make it even worse, rather than having any regular condiments, the sandwich was oozing with green slime, like the trail left behind by the snails in my mother's garden, only chunkier.

I didn't know what was worse; looking down at the monster of a meal in front of me or looking back at everyone at the table who I'd practically tuned out this whole time and now suddenly became all too aware of. They weren't gawking at the sandwich though; all their eyes were on me. I felt like I was back in the school cafeteria, in those tight plastic chairs that squeezed my hips and made loud creaks when I squirmed around.

From the corner of my eye, I could make out two people from my English class. I watched as their gaze traveled up and down my body, lingering on the sides of my shirt where my belly protruded from. At the end of the table I saw Mary and another girl exchanging looks. I recognized the girl from school, her eyebrows scrunched together, and her eyes squinted; it was the kind of face that popular girls made when some loser guy dared to ask them out. "As if" had always been Aubrey's go-to. Mary said something to the girl next to her I couldn't make out. Whatever she said though, it made them laugh, like real laughing: it pushed the other girl's eyebrows right back into place. That's when Mary winked at me.

I was never very good at telling whether someone was laughing at me or with me, but at that moment, across the table with a cow's guts under my nose and my eight pairs of socks, I sort of felt like laughing too.

"Ew," Mary said as she took a bite of her lasagna, "this isn't beef, it's lamb, what the hell?"

I caved and googled "Lampre Dotto" and almost hurled.

"You knew, didn't you! You knew I'd end up with a gross meal." I hissed quietly at Brian before clearing my throat.

"Well, too bad you can't enjoy the tasty cow stomach in front of you." Brian responded smoothly.

My stomach growled before I could answer, "You know what, I think I will."

I knew Brian didn't believe me, which turned my bluff into a statement I was now determined not to let down. Carefully, I did my best to dig my fingers under the soggy bread and lift the sandwich. Bringing it closer to my mouth, the meat did not nearly smell as bad as it had when it was first served, and my green sauce looked more and more like salsa rather than slime.

Slowly, I took my first bite as Brian watched in horror. My mouth shriveled up at first as the meat's rag-like texture flopped around my tongue. But, to my great surprise and utmost relief, the spicy, warm taste of the green salsa and fresh bread paired well with the slow cooked meat. And as soon as I managed to swallow the first bite, I kind of found myself craving a second one.

"Well? Do you need to run to the bathroom so you can puke your brains out?" Brian asked.

"You know, I actually think I like it."

"You're kidding."

"I'm not."

"Are you sure you're not just saying that to make a point?" Brian said, curious to find my true opinions of the daunting meal.

"You just can't believe I like the sandwich you tricked me into ordering."

"Well, I'm not surprised you did."

"And why's that?"

"One word—" I raised an eyebrow as he continued, "Fate."

～♪

Standing in my bathroom back at home, wiping off my makeup and airing out my sweaty, swollen feet, I was tempted to go to bed without brushing my teeth as the taste of the dinner was still lingering on my tongue and I had a feeling I'd be fantasizing about it all night. How random it all was, I thought, the odds that my finger landed on something I ended up loving. And the lasagna I thought I wanted ended up having lamb in it! Perhaps it was only mind over matter, and perhaps it wouldn't have tasted nearly as good if I had picked the sandwich out myself, but that didn't matter to me. I didn't need a golden halo; I had Brian. Last time I checked, having a prince was the sole requirement for being a princess.

～♪

I had just sat down to breakfast when I heard the knocking. I didn't have to check the window to know who it was, I could tell by the incessant nature of the knocking it was Brian: as if his fingers were thudding on my brain. It's easier just to open the door and let him in than to listen to that sound all day.

"What are you doing here, Brian?"

"Just thought I'd join you for breakfast. What, is that not ok for me to want to spend time with you?"

"No, of course not... I mean, yes, it's ok. I'm just having toast."

We both looked down at the toast on my plate; the butter was cold and lumpy on the toast.

"Smear it, c'mon it's gotta be balanced out," Brian urged as he took his seat beside me.

Quickly taking a knife, I tried to fix it. It sounded stupid but it made me feel better. Brian knew it would. I brought the knife to the crust of the toast and began to edge it toward all sides of it, fixing it. I took about five minutes making sure that every particle of burnt bread, every grain of toast, and every seed of the crust aligned, it was finally going to be perfect.

I stood up and put my head to the piece of toast—according to Brian, "anyone even with an A- in Geometry would know that this is the only way to accurately observe the angle at which one is leveled to." I started in the middle, careful to keep my eye out for any stray smears of butter or burnt edges but found none, or at least not in the first check; so it was on to the left-hand side. That was all clear too. Next it was the right side, which took a bit more time but eventually I reached the point where Brian was almost certain I had "fixed" it.

"Clear," he approved. He could sound like a drill sergeant sometimes.

Finally, it was time for the return to the middle, the one that determined it all. I got back down in the position, tilted my head for the best accuracy, and began to observe as if I was a soldier on the front line except that I was searching for toast and butter slabs rather than bullets, but equally important.

It was almost done, I just had one last row of toast particles to go when Brian and I spotted it—the pesky, no good, destructive toast crumb that was going to cost me another 'tardy' at school.

"Well, you're not gonna leave it like that, are you?"

I went back at it, smoothing with the knife as fast as I could across the rough surface of the now cooled dark chestnut brown toast. I checked it once: spotted a crumb and a melted piece of butter that was slightly higher than the rest. Twice: this time I had accidentally cut into the toast and caused there to be an indent.

"Liz, you gotta fix it! You're not gonna be able to focus at school!" Brian screamed. It was true, I was already behind schedule. I forced myself to look back at the bread, eyeing it with the cost of my morning, my day, and above all, Brian's satisfaction.

"You've got one more row of bread to go."

I scanned it once, twice, three times before it was "cleared." Finally, after letting out a sigh of immense relief, we both looked at the toast—it was perfect. On that note, I lifted the small triangle to my mouth and Brian relaxed. Buttered toast never tasted so good.

Chapter 23

THRASHING AROUND AGAIN

"Hey, how are you girl?! We haven't talked in so long!" Lucy's raspy voice shouted through the phone.

"Jeez, chill out, it hasn't been that long!" I replied, slumping down on the couch, Brian by my side as usual.

"Yeah, only a million years!" Lucy's voice blasted in my ear.

"Well, what have you been up to?" I asked, feeling guilty about being so out of the loop with my best friend.

"Well, the other day, I was feeling crappy about being a couch potato literally my entire life, so I just spontaneously decided to go on a run, and it was awful, but I got lost and ended up running five miles! FIVE miles!"

"Good for you!" I responded, never really knowing what to say when people told me about their fitness accomplishments.

"I know, and here I was thinking I couldn't run for more than five minutes!"

Suddenly I felt Brian stir, and he whispered in my ear, "Are you going on runs?" in that judgy tone he often has.

I muted the phone, while Lucy was telling me something about her "runner's high," I had a side conversation with Brian, "Um... no why would I ever do that? I mean unless of course I'm being chased by a tiger, but we live in Seattle..."

"Ok, you can quit the sarcasm. You're avoiding my question." Brian was in one of his intense moods, I could feel it. No joking around when he gets like this.

"What's that's supposed to..."

"Anyway, so after I got back from my practical marathon Liz? Are you still there?" Lucy's voice again burst through the speaker, reminding us we weren't alone.

I unmuted the phone. "Yes, I'm still here. You're right, that sounds like a very productive morning!" I said, trying my best to sound supportive, while Brian was glaring.

"Ok, yeah. Liz, I'm telling you, when I got home from that run, I totally thought I was just gonna get inside and faint," Lucy's voice droned on, "but no! I filled up a big glass of water, added ice and a lemon and stretched on the back deck while..."

"That's impressive. I didn't know you even had friends who worked out," Brian mumbled.

"Yeah, well this is new for..."

"...and while I was doing my yoga and meditation, you know I really felt like I was just letting everything go, and if I could only have had one of those heart tracking watches, you know..." she went on. I knew she'd quit this kick of hers before she even had time to forget she wanted a watch in the first place.

Clearly Brian had other assumptions. He didn't even have to say anything for me to know how he felt, I could feel it in my body, in the waves that rose and fell in my stomach: the moths that flew further up my throat with every breath I took.

"Okay, well I think I'm gonna have to go now. I gotta finish my homework." I interrupted, sounding eager to end the conversation.

"Okay... Well, I'll talk to you later."

Now it was just me and Brian.

"What is up with you today?" I asked angrily, "Hello?!"

"Stop that, you know I can hear you, trust me, I can always hear you," Brian snarked.

"Fine, then talk to me. Why don't you tell me why you're acting so grumpy!"

"Oh. I wouldn't call that grumpy, more just…"

"Just what?!" I asked, not sure I really wanted to hear what he had to say.

"I don't want to be accused of sounding like your mother again."

"Just say it!"

"Fine, I guess that phone call made me feel a bit more disappointed than usual."

"Than usual?"

His tone made me angry, even though I didn't know exactly what he was referring to. There was a plethora of things I had done in life that "disappointed" my mother, probably more than those that pleased her.

"I just think, now more than anything, there is more we could be doing with our lives," Brian responded in an accusatory tone.

"Ok well you don't have to say it like that; we both know who you're talking about when you say 'we.'"

"Fine, then, at your request of frankness, I don't even know what you're working on even when you're physically working." Brian finished.

"Well, what do I do?" was the only comeback I could think of, but thankfully, Brian was usually a fan of anything action-oriented, as long as I actually did it.

"Well, with your AP course load and applications, you have a lot of different things to work on and I feel like things could slip through the cracks without you even realizing it.

I didn't know what to say to him, I didn't even know if there was anything to say to him. His words were true, they spoke right through me and left my throat dry, unable to produce a sound that felt worthy of all the wavelengths of sound he had wasted on me.

"You know I'm always trying to stay on top of everything,

you're always on top of me to do that. How could I forget something?"

"Well, it's not exactly about trying though, it's about commitment, not moving on to the next thing until the first one is finished. You have to be harder on yourself Liz, I mean I can be there to support you, but in the end the only motivation you're really gonna listen to will be in your own words."

I felt what he was saying or at least the last part. When I was younger, just hanging out watching TV instead of doing the dishes, I would hear my mother complain about how lazy I was, telling me I wasn't doing enough around the house, but it all kind of washed over me, like one big wave. The kind of wave you could hear but never feel, because you were already wet. Walking around the world my feet rarely felt the ground; I was normally swimming. The only place that eluded this was my own head. You die if your brain takes a bath.

"Do you understand what I'm saying?"

"Yeah."

"So, what do you want to do now?"

"Work."

"I love it."

"Love is a distraction," I responded coldly, repeating one of his favorite phrases.

Chapter 24

FIGHTING FOR AIR

"After the war I went back to New York. A-after the war I went back to New York." My phone lit up the walls of my room like a boombox as the familiar Hamilton tune woke me from a deep sleep. I forced myself to roll over and turn it off. Every morning, he called me, without fail. I know I should probably feel grateful that I have a guy that is that obsessed with me, but at the same time a part of me is thinking like, something has to be wrong with this dude. It's me we are talking about here.

"Good morning, Liz." His perky voice mocked my hoarse one.

"Morning."

"What are you up to?"

"As of two seconds ago - sleeping, Brian."

"Oh, well, we're going to have to work on that."

I hated when he talked to me like he was the boss. I could never tell if he was awkwardly failing at cute banter or actually implying he was gonna show up at 4 am at my door with a blow horn to whip the laziness out of me.

"Do you have plans today?"

"Um, yeah actually, it's Saturday... so I was planning on sleeping in...." he didn't seem to catch my sarcasm, "Then I was going to do some homework then pick up some flowers for Lucy before heading over to the play."

"You're going to the play? And you didn't invite me?" If there was anything I hated most in the world, it was Brian's stupid baby voice.

"I didn't think you'd want to come. It's just a bunch of theater kids singing and dancing."

"No, no you're absolutely right, I don't want to come." I waited for the "but..." that was sure to follow.

"I don't want you going either. Have you even started writing your college essays yet?"

"Jesus Brian, junior year isn't even over yet and you're already talking about college applications?!"

"You want to go to college, don't you?"

I threw my phone across the room and dove back under the covers. I got a solid 3 seconds of peace until Lin Manuel Miranda's pitchy voice was screaming in my ear again. I would have to get out of bed and walk across the floor to turn it off. I tried to just ignore it instead. I heard once that anything can turn into white noise if you hear it for long enough. Which is questionable because I also heard the FBI used the Peppa Pig theme song on loop for psychological torture. The phone paused for a minute and then the music came back on. And that's how it went, over and over-and-over again. It didn't matter how tired my body was, the noise was penetrating my brain. They use 'sound torture' because it causes so much unbearable stress on the body's systems without even coming in contact with it: so in other words, completely humane. Only I wasn't hearing Peppa Pig snorts or Hamilton's voice cracks, I was just hearing: You want to go to college, don't you? Over, and over-and-over again. You hear it so much your body interprets it as a threat. A very, very real chance of you going to community college if you don't write these essays this instant. So that's what I did.

It wasn't just the essays though, because Brian could tell you right now that Princeton, Harvard and Yale would also be looking for a 1600 on the SAT and 5s on my 5 APs to pair with a perfect transcript like the holy fucking trinity for the holy fucking trinity. I didn't even know why I wanted to go to any of these snobby schools, apart from Brian insisting that I not settle for less, but like I said before, you hear something told to you for long enough and you lose the ability to forget it. Prisoners come out of those sound rooms still hearing frickin' Peppa oinking her fat ass off in the back of their heads. Good luck getting any information out of those guys apart from "What does the pig say?"

Right now, I was at a 1580. It was a perfect split: 790 Math, 790 Reading & Writing. It was practically a perfect score. But according to Brian, close to perfect and perfect were a million miles apart. 1600 says, "that's all you've got? Please, I could do this in my sleep," and technically they couldn't call your bluff. You walk in with a 1580 on the other hand and they'll slap that smirk right off your face, because that's the best you could do ... not "literally the best anyone could do." Big difference.

I hadn't been under my covers long before Brian showed up.

"Well, well, well, look what the cat dragged in," I sneered sarcastically, gesturing for him to come inside. Brian had no issues showing up at my house whether he was welcome or not. No room for boundaries with that one.

"Good morning to you too. Now what are you still doing in bed? You've gotta get started on those Common App questions and your personal statement."

"It's a little early for that isn't it? I'm pretty sure the essay questions won't even come out until August."

"Liz, I don't have to explain myself, that's your job."

I should have known he'd pull some shit like this. But I didn't feel like fighting.

"Yeah, fine whatever, but you're gonna need to help, I've never written a college essay before. Where do I even start? I don't know what the questions are," I said, cursing to myself as I opened a new document.

"I'm not telling you. Do your own research. They really don't vary that much year to year."

"Ugh. Fine! I don't know why you have to make this so hard for me, I mean it'd be so much easier to wait until I knew what the questions were before I tried to answer them," I complained, pulling up last year's list of prompts.

"Liz, I don't care about what's easier; besides, I'm sure your daddy could get you a job wherever you want after college."

"THEN WHY AM I WRITING THIS?!"

"Because you have to get used to putting in the effort for something that actually isn't useful in itself."

"I'm so confused right now."

"Okay let me try to explain this. Um, say you're in the final week of school, and your grades are already set, but your bitchface English teacher decides to assign the class a six-page essay on censorship presented through magical realism. Do you write it? Does it meet the requirements? Do you turn it in?"

"Hmm, well I know what I would want to do. I mean no thought necessary. Six pages of 'fuck you,' and yeah of course I would turn that in."

"But in reality..." Brian prompted.

"In reality..." I paused, tapping my finger against my chin and pretending to think hard as my eyes looked up above, "yeah I suppose I would write the essay."

"Great, well that's exactly what I want you to do, and no half-assing it either."

My eyes widened and I knew I'd been hoodwinked, "Woah, woah, woah. Stop right there. Since when am I writing a random essay? A minute ago, this was all hypothetical. We agreed on a college essay, remember?"

"Yes...but I changed my mind" Brian replied, with a tone of finality that seemed useless to argue.

"Fine."

"Great, well let's get started!" He pointed to a stack of paper underneath the table, and I winced.

"Hey, you're not gonna make me hand write this essay, are you?"

"Well, no, I guess not since I've seen your handwriting. I mean seriously Liz, write your name in crayon, throw some macaroni on it and it's a fridge masterpiece!"

"So, you just knew I would agree to this stupid essay idea of yours?"

"Let's say it was a strongly felt prediction."

"Mhm."

"That's right. And speaking of 'write' it's time for you to do that!" Brian said with a finishing smirk.

"What's it about again, some realism and censorship shit?"

"Right."

At some point my brain just stopped recognizing there was even an option where I didn't follow Brian's orders. It was like he was the puppeteer, and he'd finally pulled all my strings. In a way it made the tasks easier, almost mechanical. Getting yourself to do a thing you don't want to do is half of what makes the hard thing hard.

∿

I stared blankly at the pen and paper in front of me. I couldn't remember the last time I wrote without the help of a computer. I so despised all the cramping and discomfort the pencil brought. Thinking back to middle school, I tried to recall the stupid food acronym I'd been taught, the one that gave a format of where certain things went in a paragraph. R.I.C.E? No. B.E.E.F? No, that was basketball.

I squeezed my eyes shut, racking my brain for the word. I knew that it really didn't matter, and that I really didn't need to remember the pattern, since I was pretty sure like every dorky

English teacher had their own one. A paragraph was a paragraph, and some silly four-letter word wasn't gonna write it for me. And yet I knew if I could remember it, I would just feel a whole lot better. I liked having my hand held, I just hated being touched.

And then, suddenly, it came to me: who knew milk's favorite cookie was going to be helping me write this essay? It wasn't difficult to remember what the letters stood for and honestly it wouldn't have really bothered me if I couldn't think of all of them, because as long as I could come up with a word that started with an "O", followed by an "R" and so on, it didn't matter what their meaning was. Rules made the stress go away, it was like a map to follow, as Brian would always say. Nonetheless, Ms. Jenny, my third-grade teacher, had gone over-and-over this acronym so many times it would have been impossible to wipe it from my memory; that and the fact that it was pretty damn obvious. Opening, Reason, Evidence, Opinion.

I began writing, "Censorship is the stealer of stories while Fantasy saves them from the depths of reality. To begin with, magical realism is often used to highlight the flaws in censoring a society, by attempting to cover up their stories. But even though words can be written, and books can be burned, a story that isn't real can adapt into a million different tales that neither the producer nor the sensor has control of."

Taking a break and staring down at my work, I smiled. I'd always liked writing, even when it wasn't one of those "write whatever shit pops into your head" kind of assignments. In fact, I tended to get into a bit of trouble with those, back in my elementary and middle school days. Like when the teacher would tell the class to write "little moment" stories, trying to steer us away from the tried and true "and then and then" stories that were dear to any second grader's heart. All my friends would write about one of their birthday parties, or when they got a new dog, or some other happy, meaningless moment. Not me though. I would rack my brain for anything bad that had ever happened to me, because before I knew what love was, I thought sadness was the strongest emotion you could bring someone. And I wanted my writing to make my teacher feel something. I wanted adults to know that I was deep, not like the other kids in the shallow end of the literary pool.

"Liz??"

"Oh yeah sorry," I immediately responded, my eyes returning to the scene.

"Well?" he asked, "how far along are you?"

"Um, I'm nearly done," I bluffed.

"Really? You shouldn't be, I told you I wanted you to actually put effort into this," Brian challenged, his face becoming more stern.

"Well, yeah, I'm gonna go back and edit it after. To, you know..." I paused, almost fearing my next words, "make it perfect."

Brian smiled, affirming my fear that this really was going to have to be one of my better writing pieces. And what sucked about that, was that I was a damn good writer.

But the worst part was I knew that whatever I created, it would never be enough for Brian. And if it wasn't enough for him, it shouldn't be enough for me either.

"Okay, so I'm assuming you are satisfied with the essay due to the fact I haven't heard the paper moving around in the last fifteen minutes?" Brian finally asked, coming back into the room after disappearing for a while as I wrote furiously.

"Um, yeah," I responded, hoping my tentative answer wouldn't lead to further questioning.

"And it's perfect?"

"As perfect as it will ever be." I stated, looking down at the worn notepad that had marks and rips and arrows spilled all over it. The words seemed to jump out at me, screaming 'we could be better!' Sweat built on my forehead, I had just spent over an hour brainstorming, writing, rewriting and editing the essay before me, not to mention the fact that it was on paper and my hand was currently crumpled into the grip of my pencil, refusing to let go of the hold: though the pencil was no longer in my grasp and the paper was in Brian's hands now.

I had never questioned my writing before, I had never needed to, because any teacher that had ever graded my work had always given me an "A" whether I tried or not. But it was different with Brian, it was like he was reading it to judge me not the writing, and I knew the paper was good enough.

I swore I heard Brian whisper in my ear, making my eyes sting from trying to open them underwater. There was just something about him, the ability to transport me to another world, that excited and scared me at the same time. In all my years at school, I had never been this on edge after turning in an essay, even the SATs didn't have me shaking my knee so violently I genuinely thought it would be dislocated. It wasn't even the fear of him criticizing my writing that frightened me; to be honest with myself, the last piece of "constructive feedback" I had ever taken seriously was when my first-grade teacher introduced me to capital letters. I didn't really care if he thought my work was bad, I just knew the consequence was going to be worse.

"Liz?"

I knew what was coming.

"Liz, I'm talking to you." I continued to pretend not to hear him.

"I'm never gonna leave you alone until you listen to me." I slowly raised my head and mumbled, "What!"

"First off, you have to write this again." Brian's voice ordered me quietly, as if he had somehow used the exact frequency so that his words echoed in my brain, bouncing around my skull and creating a headache. Dread filled my body, tying my muscles in knots as they seemed to remember in vain the previous torture the former essay had provoked. There was no way out. And I wasn't stupid, I knew from the moment I could stand on my own I didn't have to do anything, that no one could ever force me to do things. Part of the reason I had done my chores so well at home was because I knew it was my own choice. Despite all the meaningless threats and ultimatums and time outs, I knew when my parents said the words "have to" it was all just a ton of bullshit. I was always in control.

"You know I'm just looking out for you, I'm here for you, Liz. I've always been here." Brian whispered in my ear, and in less than a second the pencil was back in my hand.

He was right, I thought, thinking back over the years. There I was, a little girl all curled up in a ball, shaking back and forth. And he was at my side. The night before middle school when I almost had a panic attack, he was there. The day I stood in line shaking and shivering on the cold December morning outside Washington High School for the pre-SAT, he was there. The day my dad left, he was there. But he was also there the days I spent beating myself up over my summer reading, wetting the too-close-to-perfect 1580 on the College Board's letter until the score was translucent with tears, and he was there when I wondered why my dad wasn't. I'd be lying if I said I liked him all the time, even back then. But some people are just hard to resist. You try so long to pull away that you lose all the elastic in the rope. All the tensions are gone. You sort of just let go.

～

I want to say I would have remembered, I really do. But my brain was just so fried after all those essay drafts that by the time I could catch a breath I had little to no stamina left to recall the little crumpled up paper in my pocket. It wasn't until I was searching for the one sugar free piece of gum I was allowed a day that I found that ticket instead. A lot of the words were faded but 7:30 was clear as day. So was my wristwatch: 9:21. Shit.

I raced out of my house without even telling Brian where I was headed, I was so late I couldn't risk him wanting to join me.

He always ruined shows for me, anyway, having to constantly whisper in my ear about the spit spraying us in the front row seats. Shame on me for wanting to do something fun for once.

I got there right in time for the applause and thankfully the lights were still off, so no one saw me creep in. There were more people there than I had thought there'd be, but not as many to guarantee Lucy wouldn't recognize a new face in the crowd once she stepped out for her bow. I took a deep breath waiting for her to come out. The audience was so far back from the stage and with all the bright lights shining on them, the actor would have to be actively searching for someone to realize they weren't there. That wasn't really Lucy's MO. She looked for no one, they came to her.

And just on cue, there she was in all her Party City blonde wig glory. Before her real bow she pretended to do a little bend-and-snap curtsy that got the whole crowd hollering and I kind of started laughing too. Mary gave her a hug in her own pink jumpsuit. I wonder if Miss Elle Woods had watched the movie for this role. I watched with even more surprise as the two of them began to do this little square dance skit. Lucy was kind of a mess of clacking heels, but Mary—she didn't miss a beat, I mean she was perfect. It wasn't even the makeup or anything, it was just her. I mean we all knew those pretty girls who used their looks to pass for not trying at anything besides Spirit Day of course and everyone would still clap for them just because hey, they're not hard on the eyes. I mean you had to wonder why there were more people in the audience for Miss Universe than any of the Nobel Peace prizes? But Mary wasn't one of those girls. She knew her stuff. I kind of felt bad I'd always assumed she'd just blow this thing off like she did with all the other things she'd signed up for.

It took a while to find Lucy and Mary amidst all the crew and friends of the crew congregating around the stage as soon as the curtains were drawn. A couple of them were crying. Mary was in the middle of everyone, naturally, and beaming. I'd never seen her this happy. It kind of gives you a warm feeling, watching someone just existing where they are so clearly meant to be.

Suddenly Lucy was pulling me into the circle.

"Liz! Omg yay!"

I almost forgot we were friends for a second and I felt like a fan girl, running up to hug her.

"You were so so so so good!"

"Thanks," she said, seeming to agree with the compliment.

"No like, Hamilton was good, but you..." suddenly Mary was by my side. "Both of you were like good, good. Honestly!"

Mary smiled and said thanks but something about the way she smiled made me think she knew better than to ask what my favorite part had been.

"Lucy, over here! We're taking cast photos!" Someone called from the other side of the lawn.

"Just a second, I'll be right over! Can you hold these?" she said as she shoved a bouquet of flowers into my hands, reminding me I had meant to buy her flowers too, "I have to throw up real quick."

"I'm sorry what? OMG is that cause of that crazy run you went on. Are you okay?" I asked, worried about the friend I'd never seen sick before.

"No, it's just all the nerves. I went on the run and did all that stuff just to distract myself from all this so I wouldn't throw up before the show. You think I'd willingly go on a run if someone wasn't chasing me?"

She was off running toward the bathroom before I could respond. I kind of wish Brian had been with me just to hear that part.

It did surprise me though, not the whole sudden life-improving health-kick thing which I knew had to be a phase, but the fact that Lucy was actually nervous for something. And not just anything, but this. I mean, in my opinion, she was the coolest person here by far and everyone would be happy just to get a chance to be around her confident energy. I mean that was the other thing, she was so fucking confident. I didn't think a person like that could worry the way a person like me worries, like your whole body is feeling it. But I suppose we could all drown. Hell, Whitney Houston did. I guess I always assumed Lucy just lived in this constant bubble of never questioning her decisions and always doing whatever the hell she wanted that I never really realized she could be drowning sometimes too. I wonder how she was able to get the water out of her lungs without any help.

Chapter 25

HELP IS COMING

For the remaining six weeks of Junior year, more hours than not, I found myself scratching down pages after pages of words that would ultimately end up being erased, or as scrubbed away as I could with the little nub of the pencil's eraser. I still hated all the work, and my hands always felt like they were about to give way at any moment and simply refuse to pick up another pencil whose mark would be written over.

The only thing that made these "assignments" slightly more tolerable for me was that Brian had started making the writing prompts more and more class related, to the point he even had me work on an actual homework task from my AP Lit class, which of course he made me go the extra mile on, but nonetheless it actually made sense.

"Okay, I like this one, good job," Brian remarked, staring down at my essay on Wuthering Heights.

I didn't respond. I dare not risk it. I was shocked to say the least. Never in all the months we had been together had he not found something critical to say about my work, especially if it was his first time seeing it. Maybe I just understood Catherine Earnshaw. Brian always told me that working hard would pay off one day, but that's what everyone said, and they usually meant it literally.

But at that moment, I wasn't thinking about money, or success, or even my grades at all. Because nothing felt better than hearing Brian's words.

It wasn't so much pride I felt towards the quality of my writing, because I had always known what I was capable of, but rather a sense of accomplishment in all the effort I put in. It was almost like a high, this feeling that Brian's approval gave me, and no matter how many bad moments plagued our relationship, when he would yell and criticize me and demand essay after essay, I knew in that moment that it all was worth it, I would always stay with him.

In a way, the lows made these moments even stronger, made the rose sweeter because the thorns were sharper. But I wasn't thinking about the sweet smell of flowers; all I could currently smell was the salty ocean: nothing could convince me to jump off the wave I was currently on top of.

꩜

All that extra writing for Brian seemed to be paying off. I might not have been getting much sleep, but I was getting great grades, and the moderator of the newspaper, Mr. Swanson, was taking note of the volume of articles I was submitting.

"Liz, I've been very impressed with your writing. Not just the quantity, but the quality," he said after our last Newspaper meeting. "I wanted to ask you if you'd be interested in the role of Editor-in-Chief next year. It's a lot of work, but something tells me you can handle it."

I blinked in surprise. Reaching my right arm under the desk, I pinched my leg, almost hoping it was a dream so it all would make more sense. Of course, the hard-working extra-miler Liz would want to take on more work. But it wasn't the new job that scared me, it was the sudden wave of imposter syndrome that had washed over me: a lazy girl hiding in the shell of an overachieving scholar.

"Of course, I'd be honored, thank you!" I heard myself saying. I was going to have to make sure Brian joined the newspaper staff.

As soon as I made my way out of Mr. Swanson's office, I made a beeline for the bathroom. It had been a while since I visited my anemone safe haven. The walls felt like sponges on my skin, their vinyl paper pressing tiny indents into my fingertips, as if I was touching coral. The splatters of soap decorated the countertop like bubbles on the water's surface. And just for a moment, the world felt small. In a way it was ironic, as scientists know more about space than the ocean.

I didn't want that title, as guilty as it made me feel to say it. It was like I was admitting that being successful wasn't worth all the effort. But then again, how could success really be measured?

"I heard you got a promotion," Brian exclaimed in a sing-songy voice when I came out of the bathroom. "You know how proud it makes me to see you get recognized for your achievements!"

"Ew, you sound like my mom," I jeered back. Though I meant to say, 'a mom.' I couldn't remember Margaret ever saying anything along those lines. I think she thought she wasn't putting pressure on me if she acted like she didn't care about my grades or other achievements, but in reality, withholding her praise made things worse. If I couldn't rely on her to apply pressure on me, I had to put it on myself. Passengers can die if a plane loses pressure.

When I got home, after closing the front door and locking it, making sure that it was really locked by jiggling the doorknob, I ran up to my room and sat on my bed.

Glancing around the bedroom, I tried to take it all in—the clear, organized desk, the spotless wood floors and rug—it almost seemed impossible. Not too long ago the entire room would have been covered in dirty clothes and used water bottles. It was like, in just a few short months my life had done a total 180, and now I was starting to feel the whiplash.

There would always be a part of me that missed that old life, the apathy that made things feel worth doing, probably because there wasn't really a consequence if I didn't. And it was this lingering desire to watch life from the couch, or maybe it was Brian's constant warnings that "laziness is a drug, one hit and you're lost again," but my attitude towards life had begun to change, or perhaps I simply just had one now.

Pride was not a feeling I had ever become accustomed to growing up, so it made sense when Mr. Swanson asked me to be Editor-in-Chief, I couldn't really describe how I felt. My emotions were nowhere near the times I'd mistaken pride for acting upon spite. This was a new kind of pride for me. It felt empowering, to feel validated by achievement solely from my own hands. Not only did I feel as if I had scaled a mountain, but it was a hill I had built myself.

Laziness may have been a drug, but success was intoxicating. Brian drove me crazy at times, but I had to admit I owed all my success to him. I was too afraid to find out who I'd be without him.

Chapter 26

WATER RESCUE!

When school got out at the end of junior year, we all finally had our licenses and Ruby Beach was calling our names. I couldn't tell you how excited I was for this trip. Actually, let me just tell you. I was really fucking stoked. Independence was addicting and Riley's rusty 1994 Ford Tempo (aka the "Tempo of Doom") was our gateway drug to the strong shit: 2 am bonfires and unlimited boozy seltzers.

Who cares that the beer in the overheated trunk would probably be skunked by the time we made it off the highway and the engine sounded just about ready to smoke a joint itself. APs were done. Tests were done. Pre-college programs were still two weeks away. And the best part about everything: no parents. I lied and told my friends I told my mom the same lie we'd all agreed on: that we were staying at Andy's grandparents' cabin in Tacoma. Secretly, I had practically come sprinting home to tell my mom the rebellious little scheme we had devised. Proud was an understatement; the woman was beaming.

It wasn't that she was like Abby's mom, who lived for her old partying days and who we also didn't tell for the sole purpose of not having to awkwardly decline the funky smelling edibles she would've tried to pawn onto us, but because my mom was always worried about me. She was always on me about getting out more and taking a break from studying because "you only live once" and "you have the rest of your life to work, enjoy your youth!" I figured this trip would distract her from my pathetic social life for at least a year. Who knows, maybe she'd even realize how lucky she was to have a kid who wasn't pregnant or flunking out of Gym class.

I could never complain about my mom encouraging my rule breaking though, because poor Dalia had it the worst. Her mom, Jena, was this tiny, Coraline-character-looking scrooge with a face like she was always sucking a lemon which I wouldn't be surprised if it were all she ate by the looks of her skeleton figure. Dalia had been taught from birth the necessity of continuing the family's long line of Princeton graduates. Instead of nursery books, I remember her playroom being filled with math work-books and every AP textbook that ever existed. Every single thing in there had come straight out of the Kumon library, I swear to God.

Poor Dalia didn't even have a choice in becoming so brilliant. I don't think people always think about that enough, that some people never asked to be smart. That not knowing things makes life more interesting. Because for people like Dalia, she really couldn't learn a new thing every day. There'd be nothing left to learn by the time she was out of diapers.

The funny thing was, Dalia would be making paper airplanes in Math Foundations 1 if she could. She even tried failing tests once, but the girl was so smart that by purposely choosing the wrong answer each time she actually impressed the teachers more. I feel bad for Dalia a lot. All she's known for is being smart and if it were up to her, she'd have donuts for brains: her words, not mine. That was the other thing, no sugar allowed in that house.

So, to say the least, Dalia and the rest of us were having the time of our lives without our parents around to make us feel like shit. I didn't want Brian coming and making me feel like shit either. He'd been so hard on me the week of AP tests and I needed a serious break from his judginess and bossiness. I was glad it was strictly a girls' weekend, no guys, no drama.

Our first night at the Airbnb was slightly less glamorous than we'd imagined. I guess we were still picturing the apartment from "Friends," not what five young people can actually afford. The place was more hostel-y than homey, which I thought was Airbnb's whole brand. The floors made our feet turn black and the "Queen Bed" turned out to be a toddler sized mattress with a fairy net and some lights taped to the sides. But it was a roof over our heads, and we didn't plan on spending most of the days inside anyway.

That first night we decided to do a little exploring, some scoping out of the market if you will. Let me just tell you, there were some fine selections. The first beach we hit was housing two separate parties at the same time, with a keg in the middle for communal use. On the far side of the sand, there was a group of what could only be a herd of hockey boys, with their backwards hats and shaggy mullets. Even barefoot in the sand they were still shuffling their feet. Impressive. I wondered if they had come down here from Canada, which would make them foreigners. Exotic meat.

On the side of the beach closer to us stood a fusion of different flavors. There were some cute girls, mostly blonde doing blonde things, and guys with their shirts off for no greater reason than why sweet girls bleach their hair. The two went hand in hand, among other things. Most of the kids looked our age, or possibly seniors on their last hurrah before college, but certainly none of them were old enough to be lawfully engaging in the activities that they were. And it certainly didn't take long for Dalia to go up and join them. She was always the boldest out of all of us. I made a point to tell the story of her beating a frat bro in a keg stand any time I heard someone calling her a nerd behind her back. They had actually tied, but Dalia appreciated the rep boost and sometimes a little exaggeration was needed to get people over the hump of their stupid stereotypes.

I was the last one to muster up the courage and carry my red Solo cup up to the keg. Brian didn't like me drinking, especially if he wasn't there, which was pretty much the only time I drank because he was a shitty drinking partner. He didn't drink, but he'd make you feel worse than the hangover ever would. The whole trek in the sand over to the keg felt like that scene in Nemo where they're all chanting "Don't touch the butt!" and I'm just swimming right toward it like the stupid moth that thinks "one light can't hurt." Well, it turns out a couple cups full of Coors Light can indeed hurt. It also made an hour feel like 2 seconds.

⌇

I spotted my friends a couple feet away, holding Dalia's hair back while she puked into the ocean. God, if Jena could see her now. I would've gone over to help, but I felt like shit. There was still some mashup of pop songs going on, with each one only playing for as long as our fucked-up Gen Z attention spans could handle, and the resulting noise pollution was only egging on my headache more.

I laid down in the sand, trying my best to block out the blaring music and whatever gross noises were coming from the bush behind me, surely some shirtless blonde duo, you pick the combo.

A few minutes later, the smell of Dalia's seaborn vomit had effectively cleared out this side of the beach, which left us five all laying on our backs in the sand. The smell was horrid, especially considering the girl had eaten nothing but McDonald's and Chipotle after escaping her house last night. The sand was even worse, in that it stuck to all the wet parts of us, which was pretty much every part due to unidentifiable substances. If there was anything I hated more than feeling hungover, it was feeling sticky.

But what made up for everything, was the stars. You could make the Big Dipper out of satellites in Seattle, but this sparkling sky was nothing any of us had seen before. I wished Lucy could have been with us, she loved stars as much as I did, except I'm almost certain she'd ruin the magic with some Bible reference. I hoped she was enjoying her church trip.

We didn't talk. Just lay there gazing at the stars and listening to Usher and the ocean. I'm not sure I'd ever felt as calm or as gross as I did that night.

The five of us were drunk on dreams by the time we stumbled back to our Airbnb, because for anyone wondering, all stars are shooting stars when you can't stand up straight. I guess that's probably why I didn't see Brian when he was standing right in front of me.

"You look pathetic, Liz." His words pierced my twinkling thoughts. There was something so sobering about his voice.

"Your summer course at Yale starts in twenty days and this is how you're preparing? Seriously, what are you gonna have to say for yourself when they ask you what you've been doing this summer?" His words didn't sound like words, they sounded like control, and there's nothing a drunk person hates more than being controlled.

"Did you even bring your AP Euro textbook?"

"Shut the fuck up you controlling asshole!" I slurred. My friends were too far gone at the moment to know Brian had made a guest appearance. I wish they could kick the crap out of him and kick him out. I mean this was just too much. Right?

"Are you hearing yourself? Please Liz, you slurred half the words in that sentence!" Did I?

"God, it feels like you're trying to be my mom sometimes. You're supposed to have my back."

"And you're supposed to be going to Duke in a year, Liz. Can't you see I'm looking out for you here?"

"I, I know you are, it's just..." I tried to put my frustration into words, but they all tasted funny in my mouth.

"I know you wish I was more laid-back Li; look I get it. But when you love someone, you can't help but want to do everything you possibly can for them, even if they say they don't want it."

I thought about my friends and their boyfriends. Tom, Dalia's secret boy toy in Robotics Club, programmed her phone to read positive affirmations about herself out loud in the morning. Abby's boyfriend came to every single one of her painful one-woman plays. That's what support looked like. It's putting in a positive review for a restaurant you've seen a mouse scurry across. It's calling that girl beautiful in her baggy T-shirt and retainer instead of writing her instructions on how to lose face fat.

Maybe I was never going to find a supportive boyfriend if I continued to let Brian treat me this way. All I ever wanted was for Brian to believe in me like how we all believed in those stupid flying stars in the sky. Like there was some other way dreams could come true without staying up all night writing college essays and hating yourself.

"Let's get you home."

"No, Brian you need to go home. I told you not to come."

"And sometimes I just have better judgment than you!"

"Then how am I ever going to learn to make these decisions on my own! You have to let me be free, can't you see that?"

"Wait, what? Are you seriously breaking up with me? After I came all the way here because I knew you'd be getting yourself in trouble!"

He reached that conclusion before I did. It's not like I hadn't thought about breaking up before or even started to try before chickening out. We went on a temporary break in seventh grade because he wouldn't let me try the new Oreo Cakesters that were all the rage at the time. But I came running back the second I popped a button in my favorite jean skirt. To this day I still wonder if it just hadn't been sewn on properly. If it had, would I still be submitting this Stanford application?

"Liz, c'mon you aren't thinking rationally."

Now that pissed me off. This whole conversation had practically reduced my blood alcohol level back to 0, and if anyone was known for acting nonsensical it was him. I needed to find a guy who would prepare me for love, I did not need Brian trying to prepare me for all of life. There are tutors for that.

"Brian, I really care about you and am so grateful for all you've done for me, but I'm just not in the right mindset to be dealing with this drama and I just gotta learn to manage things on my own."

"Well good fucking luck with that. Addictions don't just disappear overnight, Liz." And off he went, back to wherever he'd been before he crashed my party. Did he just call himself a drug? Yeah, "rational" my ass.

I looked out the window. He was gone. I took the biggest exhale of my life. The sun was down but I think if I were to go on the beach right now the whole damn ocean would have evaporated. The one inside me was.

Suddenly I felt the need to do something crazy. The roar of the waves from outside was creeping into my ears, getting louder the more I listened. It was like the ocean was playing the drums, setting a rhythm for me. I could feel it in my chest, maybe that's how our hearts beat. Rise and fall. Rise and fall. Before I knew what I was doing I was running out the door of the cabin and into the world. I was free.

DEATH

Chapter 27

AWAKE AGAIN

Present Day

Sometimes when I walk in my room it feels like I'm wading in a stagnant pool of algae, like the air is physically weighing me down as I walk. My nights are no more comforting, and I often find myself caught in nightmares, waking drenched in sweat and my heart pounding. These dreams usually have something to do with making the wrong move, making a decision that hurts everyone around me, and the guilt sticks with me even after I escape sleep.

So eventually, I stopped sleeping. I lie in bed, staying in the same position for hours on end, but I won't let my eyes close. I never want to leave my thoughts to their own devices. Sometimes I feel like I'm physically sinking into the mattress, like I no longer know where the sheets end, and my skin begins.

Mom complains she isn't getting much sleep either, presumably worrying about her daughter who lives a million miles away in the room downstairs. Twenty thousand leagues under the sea.

"The bends," or decompression sickness, happens when a person ascends from a pressurized environment too quickly. It causes nitrogen gas, which has dissolved in the body's tissues under pressure, to re-emerge in the form of bubbles that can go anywhere in the body, causing all sorts of problems. Symptoms can include fatigue, numbness, shortness of breath, even paralysis or death. The risk and severity of decompression sickness increases the longer and deeper the diver remains underwater, as well as with the speed in which the diver ascends.

Sometimes I think Brian was like a weight that was dragging me to the ocean floor. I would hack away at the rope tying me to him, and a couple times I almost broke free, but he always found a way to pull me back down again. The most messed up part is that when I finally managed to cut the rope completely, I rocketed up to the surface too quickly. Everything that happened after I got out of the hospital and split from him for good feels like a fever dream now. None of it should have happened.

My phone buzzed next to my pillow. I reached over and turned the screen to my face, unlocking it to find a single notification. My heart lightened as my eyes were drawn to the pink and purple colors of Instagram and the red dot attracted my finger. As soon as I tapped it, I wished I hadn't.

"Your friend has a recent post! Check it out here:"

I let out a sigh. I pressed on the post. The faces of two blonde girls in graduation robes filled the screen. Their smiles seemed to seep through the phone and shove their happiness in my face. Their dresses hugged their curves and their makeup was flawless. I couldn't look that pretty if I tried. And so, I almost never tried.

Chapter 28

EVERYTHING IS OKAY

8 Months ago

I didn't see Brian all summer after Ruby Beach, I'm not sure where he went. The only time I ran into him was at that Yale Summer Program he'd convinced me to do, but I did my best to ignore him there too. The rest of summer consisted of lazy days at the pool with Lucy like the old days, not prepping for classes with Brian like I had the last few summers. It's crazy how some chlorine, watermelon and a best friend can take your mind off things. We didn't even know what day it was most of the time.

Dylan was throwing an End of Summer Bash two weeks before school started, and thankfully for us, he was naive enough to make it an open house. The party started at seven, and I was driving myself. I'd planned before to wear a fun, universe-created outfit to the dinner, and had even separated my wardrobe into piles, but without Brian there, it all felt a little silly, and kind of pointless. Besides, Mom had recently bought me a new, red mini dress, that had just as recently been shrunk in the wash, and I had a feeling it would look rather "cute" on me.

As I pulled on the material though, a wave of guilt rippled through my body. I couldn't explain where it came from, but I had a pretty good idea of who brought it. Even when he wasn't there Brian still had power over me, had an influence on me. I had already chosen the dress, and I was determined to look sexy that night, but I couldn't stop myself from wishing I had landed on it randomly, like I actually deserved to wear it.

I'm not sure when I first heard that word "deserving" but ever since I did, I could never get it out of my head. It probably started in Kindergarten at the Catholic school I'd gone to despite thinking they'd given me the wrong necklace when they handed me a rosary on the first day. I was confused because none of the girls' names even started with "t". My family had never been religious so I'm not quite sure how I ended up there, but I did.

They teach you right off the bat there that even though you've probably heard "God loves everyone" there are actually very specific, documented ways of keeping his love. Basically, there are rules to follow if you don't want God to dump you. One of those rules was saying some prayer to every bead on my T necklace fifty times in order to deserve a good night's sleep, but my parents quickly confiscated those after a week of hearing my cultish chants every night. The other, equally important rule that they did encourage though, was to be a good person. Now that was a lot harder to do. It was so vague. So much uncertainty. There was no inflexible set of 10 rules to follow to make sure you were a good person.

I was nervous when I got into the car that night, it was the first time in a while I was going to drive alone, without Mom or Brian. I turned the radio on, to keep my worries in the water, even though Brian had warned me against the dangers of listening to music while driving. But I ignored this, you can't even hear music when you're drowning.

"Liz! You're here, my favorite Liz!" Dalia shouted as I parked my car next to hers.

"Dahlia, I'm the only Liz you know!" I shouted back, climbing out of the vehicle.

"Exactly, so wouldn't it be a problem if you weren't my

favorite?" she replied, pulling me in for a hug. I wonder where she told her mother she was this time.

"*Touché*, smarty pants," I giggled.

Tentatively, I made my way into the house. The place was far smaller than my own house and barely decorated at all unless you were counting the red Solo cup collections littered around the floor. I could picture a younger Dylan hanging out here, sitting at one of the leather bar stools and acting like an older man with a glass of red wine. He tried so hard to sound smart in AP Literature, but some kids just don't have it. Maybe he had just partied too much.

Brian had never let me go to parties when we were together, even though Mom was the kind of parent who would give me a fake ID for Christmas if I asked Santa for one. Brian told me I had an obsessive personality and partying, and stuff could really derail my life. I think what scared me more though, was my addiction to him. But still, parties always made me want to QuickStart an application for medical school just in case I absorbed too much "slackerness" in these places.

The ceiling hung low, and the walls were painted an olive shade of green with orange lights accenting each corner of the room. It was so dark it was hard to make anyone out.

"Liz! Over here!" Lucy called me over to where some of her theater friends were.

"Hey Loser," the brunette girl said to me, or maybe she was saying it to Lucy. I recognized her voice though, it was nonchalant. And then I recognized her. It was Ms. Rainbow Fish, Mary.

I'd seen Mary a few times over the summer when I was hanging at Lucy's house. Without judgy Brian around, I was able to be more relaxed around her, but I still was in awe of her effortless confidence. I'd continued highlighting my hair and was the blondest I'd ever been, I called the hair dye solution "confidence in a bottle" as I felt almost like a new person with my new look. But all my purchased confidence paled in comparison to what Mary seemed born with.

She looked surprised to see me.

"Liz! Is this your first time at one of Dylan's?"

"Yeah, it is, this place is crazy though." I rocked back and forth on my feet.

"OMG, I know." She looked over her shoulders in awe like she was taking it all in again, as well as a big sip of the Solo cup contents. "Lots of hot guys here. And even hotter girls."

Again, I marveled at how confident Mary was, so undeniably certain. I stopped saying "love you" to my girlfriends' freshman year because I was tired of having to convince myself that I didn't in fact, like girls that way. Mary could just say anything and nobody would question her.

"Someone said Mia was here." I told no one in particular, trying to start a conversation with anyone.

"OMG is that her name? The dork with the glasses bigger than her tits?"

I nearly spit out my drink. And then I nervously spun my head around to check that an angry four-foot-10 Mia wasn't anywhere in the vicinity.

"Don't worry," Mary said reassuringly, "the chick's probably balls deep in her favorite Pearson textbook right now. Oooh, what subject do you think turns her on the most? I'm thinking, medieval history. Oh, wait no, advanced mathematical theory."

I wished I could stick with a joke and run with it like that. But when you don't commit to a jump all the way, you end up tripping. Badly.

"Yeah, I've never seen that girl leave the library. Although, I've never actually been inside it myself." Mary continued. I saw Lucy steal a glance at me from Mary's side.

"You're going to have to change that, you know. You're going to be off in college next year." Lucy said.

"Don't remind me."

"You're not excited?" I asked.

"To get off this conveyor belt and jump on the next one? No, I'm not. I don't know, the whole concept of more school just feels so static, you know? My worst fear is dying and not being able to determine my last day between the day before it."

I'd never thought about this. If it were up to Brian, each day would be a carbon copy of the last. Like a train following its tracks. He had me walk right out of that ethics class when the professor brought up the trolley dilemma. Even his notion of "spontaneity" had a controlled, orderly way about it. You just couldn't look at it that way if you wanted to have any fun.

"So, are you a fan of these parties?" I asked, trying to change the subject.

"Eh, they're fine," Mary said, shrugging her shoulders. "Dylan always pulls through with the keg and honestly I'm a sucker for free alcohol."

"Oh, yeah this is great," Lucy chimed in. I wondered if Mary knew Lucy didn't drink yet.

"So, what do you want?" Mary asked me as she headed towards the counter of the makeshift card table bar.

I couldn't even think of alcohol when my mouth tasted like saltwater.

"I'll take two Truly's please, thanks Ted," Mary said to the bartender.

Ted, who I had a feeling did more than serve drinks to Mary based on the looks they were currently exchanging, handed the drinks to Mary, both of them.

"Aren't you gonna get something, don't tell me you're some straight edge," Mary teased.

"No, I, uh, definitely drink, like I love to drink. I'm not an alcoholic or any..." I paused, Mary's eyebrow was up and I could tell I was losing her.

"What do you want?" Mary asked.

"Umm," I glanced around the house, glad to not see Brian among the crowd with his judgy stare, "I'll have a Bud Light please."

Ted reached into an ice bucket and tossed one with a smile, though his eyes were on someone else, and it wasn't Mary either. I looked over my shoulder and saw Lucy talking to a boy I didn't recognize. Cute boys never start talking to me, Brian was all I had, and he was nothing to look at. But Lucy was different. She was pretty, but not in an intimidating way, the more I looked at her, the prettier she looked. Unlike me, she came by her blond hair honestly, and her hazel eyes shined bright against her light olive skin. It was her dimples though, that seemed to charm everyone. Her stomach was firm and flat too, like a waxy layer of an apple, whereas my stomach looked like a banana – only after it'd been chewed up and spit out after you realized nope, you still hate bananas. It was the consistency of mush. I was tempted to chug the whole Bud Light right there, beer stache and all.

The rest of the night went by in a blur, even though I had only actually had one drink. Mary on the other hand, probably couldn't count hers on one hand, or count at all by the end of the night. I finally felt like how you're supposed to feel when you're a teenager. Free.

It was 2:30 in the morning by the time Lucy, Mary and I came stumbling back into my house (Ted had dropped us off), and I half expected Mom to be sitting in one of the living room chairs, waiting for her to slowly spin around and flick on the light with a classic "well, well, well" like all the tv show moms when their kids got home late. But again, I reminded myself that even if Mom didn't have a strict bedtime of nine o'clock, she would never have acted like that. In fact, she probably would have wanted me to break curfew, she would have encouraged it. As much as she'd say she is a "cool mom" we both knew she just had a lame kid.

"Domino's." Mary announced as soon as we got to my room.

"What?" I turned to face her, unclear if she really wanted to play a game right now.

"I'm starving. Aren't you starving, Liz?"

Brian hated when people used that word, because chances are they weren't actually on the brink of death. And even if they were, they shouldn't be wasting energy by whining about it. If I wasn't so tipsy, I would have felt more inclined to answer that question as I always did, which was in the negative for body issues reasons.

But I was feeling that drink. Or at least I was convincing myself that's why I was acting like this. My body must've been trying to get on the same page too, because my head was aching and my stomach felt like it was about to rip in half. Banana split anyone? I cleared my throat.

"Yeah, I'm hungry too."

"Great, do you like pepperoni? I love it."

"Um, I..."

"Yeah, ok, I'm ordering DoorDash. One large pepperoni pie? You up for some garlic knots?" Mary asked.

∽

"I can't believe we got all of this for three people." I'm not sure I'd ever seen just how large a large Domino's was. It took up most of the floor space in my little room.

"I know right, you should've ordered double. I could do this in a minute with another drink." Mary giggled.

"No more drinks, Mary," I said, patting her on the back. I wasn't sure if she and I had bonded enough for it to be my job to take care of her, but it felt good for someone as independent as her to listen to my advice. Besides, if I didn't look after her, who would? Lucy didn't seem to be a fan of drunk Mary.

"Can I tell you something?" Mary said suddenly.

My mouth was half full of pizza and half full of garlic knots, but I nodded as I scanned the floor for the ranch container. Domino's was smart for not having the nutritional label come on their boxes of pies, but the ranch had the calories right there. 145 for half the container. This was my second one. What would Brian say?

"I'm so fucking wasted, Liz."

Lucy started laughing so hard a white stream of ranch was trailing down her chin. "No shit, Sherlock."

"Me too." I said, even though Lucy was eying me suspiciously now. I coated the rest of my slice in a tangy pool of Hidden Valley's finest. I knocked the lid over "accidentally" and the last of the ranch just happened to spill onto my plate.

"God, you're such a messy drunk," Mary said through laughs.

"I know," I said, but my eyes were cast down at my banana split of a stomach that was now oozing with vanilla ice cream. Some of the ranch had dripped onto my top.

"Fuck men!" Mary blurted out.

I raised an eyebrow as Mary stabbed her fork into the molten lava cakes our order had come with. She put the whole thing in her mouth at once. Lucy was looking at her with disgust, but I could see Mary's smile lines when she chewed. If she could look like a human and still be confident, why couldn't I? I slid the box to me and put another cake in my mouth. All fruits look the same when they're covered in chocolate.

"So," I said, "what led you to make such a statement?"

"I don't know, I mean maybe it's the vodka talking but I'm just so done with all these assholes."

"Same. Anyone in particular?" Lucy asked, grabbing another slice of pizza.

"You guys, I don't even remember the names of half the guys I've gotten with. And I was sober for a couple of them," Mary said laughing, until another piece of pizza was in her mouth and she had to focus on chewing.

Lucy looked at me and I looked at the cross on her chest and I knew what she was thinking.

"Do they still talk to you, like after you guys hook up?" I asked.

Mary didn't look so drunk anymore.

"Hold up. No one tries to drop me," she said, her voice raising. "It's the other way around. I'm not interested in relationships. I've got self-respect you know."

I nodded. If it were any other girl, I'd probably think the whole Irish goodbye was a way to protect her own feelings, you know, to leave before they can tell you to. But Mary, I could tell, was different. I genuinely don't think she'd ever done anything in her life she hadn't wanted to do at that moment. All those guys were probably left scrambling around their bedrooms looking for anything Mary had left behind like it was Cinderella and the glass stiletto.

I opened my mouth to say something, but there was nothing to say.

"Who needs guys when you have girlfriends?" Lucy asked.

"Here, here!" Mary cheered.

I again felt drunk even though the effects of the Bud Light had long since worn off. Was the cool Rainbow Fish including me as one of her friends? I ignored the fact that she was clearly intoxicated and smiled to myself. It wasn't that I'd never had a friend before—I had Lucy—but there was something exciting about befriending a person that embodied everything you were taught to be scared of, everything that was different, that made it feel so special. It was fascinating that she could live her life and I mine and together we'd be friends. Sometimes I just watched her because I was fascinated. It was nice to be the one on the outside of the aquarium tank sometimes.

"I'll get us some sleeping bags." Lucy stood up and walked over to my closet where she knew I kept them.

I hoped it was too dark in the room for them to see me smiling like an idiot. Lucy and I hadn't had a sleepover in a hot minute. Technically Lucy and I never invited each other to our houses, we just sort of showed up with a pillow and nothing else for you to do. But it had been a while and now it felt like I was suddenly so much warmer inside, even though my sleeping bag was practically thinner than my sheets.

∾

I opened my phone, afraid of the girl I was going to see in the photos we'd taken last night. Especially if she looked anything like the mess in the mirror this morning—my hair was all staticky from jumping around with Mary on the makeshift dance floor and I assumed my makeup was all smeared and faded off by now. My skirt had a stain on it from some mysterious drink Mary had spilled on me, so at this point I was just hoping I didn't look completely homeless.

When the pictures finally loaded, I was pleasantly surprised. The girl in the photos probably looked nothing like me, and not because her hair was all messed up or her skirt was dirty, but because she looked like she was having fun. The creases in her makeup were from smiling and her dirtied feet were from walking barefoot in the parking lot while carrying her tortuous heels.

I took off my dress and stood in my underwear. I looked down at my body. I knew that vodka burning fat was a myth, and that my ten-minute little dance party with Mary couldn't have whipped me into shape that quickly, but looking at myself, and those pictures from the party, I thought I was seeing the newest Barbie model. Of course, I didn't have any insane thigh gap or minuscule waist, and my stomach was nowhere near flat, but it was the 21st century after all, and surely a "Body Positivity Barbie" would sell easily.

Nonetheless, the girl in the photos liked her body, because it wasn't trying to be anyone else's. And for the first time in a very long time, after barely managing to pull up my pajama pants, I decided that it was time to change my wardrobe, not myself. I'd changed enough. Besides, Mary liked me the way I was. Wasn't that how it always turned out? The popular girl realizing the dorky, anxious kid was a lot more fun to chill with. The anxious girl just happy to chill for once.

⌇

The next two weeks before senior year started, Mary and I began spending more and more time together. We often got together without Lucy, which felt strange at first because I still couldn't help thinking Mary was Lucy's friend, not mine.

But here I was at the end of summer, with college applications looming and my last chance of getting a perfect ACT score a month away, spending any moments of my free time lounged out on Mary's old rope hammock. We would put chip bowls beneath it so all we had to do was reach our hand through the hammock's ropes for a snack. It was one of Mary's talents: finding new ways to be lazy. She told me it was technology.

One time I reached through the hammock with my foot and grabbed a chip between my toes and brought it to my mouth. I never would have done this with Lucy who would have been appalled. But Mary gagged in mock disgust then burst into laughter.

"You're so weird, Liz!" For a second I thought maybe I'd crossed the line, I often struggled with the boundary between funny and crazy.

"I know, I'm sorry," I said apologetically.

"No, that's what I love about you. I've never had a friend like you before. You're not stuck-up like so many of the other girls at school, and you're not a boring basic bitch either. Embrace your weird, Weirdo."

I laid back on the hammock, looked up at the cloudless blue sky, and let out a deep exhale.

Chapter 29

⥬⥬⥬

CAN'T TALK

I really think branding summer vacation as two and a half months was the biggest marketing ploy ever made. I mean, most of us spent the first four weeks catching up on sleep or getting a jump-start on the mountains of summer work we all wanted to get over with. And then of course the final four weeks were just a count-down to misery where you actually thought about school starting more than summer happening. And if you were like me, that dread kicked in probably around July. I feel that emotion a lot: dread. Dread and overwhelm. Sometimes the dread is over-whelming.

I was dreading Senior year, especially without Brian. I hadn't exactly thought this whole thing through; ditching my swim floats just in time for the wave of college applications and the impor-tance of first quarter grades. And what if everything he said about me was true, what if I really was lazy and unmotivated without him? Maybe all the time I'd spent at the pool with Lucy and lounging on Mary's hammock this summer had rubbed off on me and I was destined to be a sloth forever.

The first week of Senior year started out ok, but once my teachers started assigning homework I started struggling to keep my head above water. Without Brian's strict regimen, I didn't

212

know how to motivate myself or prioritize which task to do first. So instead, I did nothing. I came home from school and watched TV. I didn't even shower for a week until Mom saw my greasy hair and said she was unplugging the TV until I showered.

The Tuesday of the third week of school, the shit hit the fan. My English paper was due Wednesday, and I hadn't even started it. This wasn't me, or was it? The flighty feeling started in my stomach; I must've forgotten to clip one of those butterflies I thought I'd gotten rid of already. There was so much to do, and no structure to do it. It felt like I was one of those retro video games where you have to collect the stuff falling from the sky, but it keeps raining harder and harder. I guess when you try to put life in slo-mo it's bound to come up on x2 speed later. You can't cut corners. You end up falling miles behind.

I took out my laptop and shed the plastic skin of my textbook. No time for an outline, or to re-read the book or write a fucking book review: it was game time.

But maybe the team's only as good as the coach. I stared back at my blank computer screen, as my stomach tied itself in knots, trying to create a dam against the waves. My anxiety crept up like the tide and lunged like a tsunami. I almost wished Brian had just given me a checklist, like something straight out of the extra credit handbook, that would tell me exactly what to do to "go beyond." There was too much pressure trying to think of these details myself, like designing an obstacle was even harder than getting over it.

As much as it'd been ingrained in my mind that Brian had been the only reason I cared about school, there was still a part of me that liked making those teachers happy, that liked that feeling of working hard and getting a good grade to show for it. It wasn't like the runner's high I'd have on Brian's schedule, or at least what I would imagine one to feel like, because I wasn't running anymore. I'd be working toward a finish line I could see this time. You study and keep studying. You work hard enough for long enough and you don't even have the urge to check your phone again, and eventually you won't have to. They stop texting. Admittedly, it felt good to feel better than everyone else, more driven.

But senior year was my last year with my friends. There should be some sort of trade off, right? A 'B' would have to work. A 'B+' would be pushing it, practically a gateway drug to an 'A-' and perpetual perfectionism to be honest.

I ended up staying up till 4 am writing that paper, and every consecutive paragraph after 2 am got less and less coherent. I don't think I'd ever stayed up that late when I was with Brian. He always warned me about procrastination, saying that my eye bags were too purple already to afford any more lost sleep. How come none of my friends ever had to use concealer?

I came home after school and my mom had a feast of snacks spread out. She was clearly trying to have some "Bonding Time." Maybe she'd heard me up at 4am and wanted to give me a treat.

"Mom, this is nice. You uh didn't have to do all this though." I was referring to the display of cucumber sandwiches, toast, and fresh fruit that spanned across the table.

"Oh, nonsense. Why don't you eat something, you must be starving!"

I was.

I hadn't eaten bread since Brian said I should take a break from carbs a year ago. The smell of the buttered toast alone was enough to make my mouth start watering. Tentatively, I filled up my plate. I piled on sandwiches, strawberries, banana slices, muffins, scones, biscuits, anything Brian would have hated. I didn't even like pastries.

The first bite I took was of toast, and admittedly, I found myself quickly checking for any unignorably large blobs of butter before placing it into my mouth. Old habits die hard. The familiar taste flooded my system with memories of early morning school days and breakfast with my dad: the one meal he was always in charge of. The bananas reminded me of the milkshakes I used to get with friends, because if it was fruit flavored, it was pretty much negative calories.

And soon, to my surprise, the plate was reduced to a matter of crumbs. I was already craving more of Mom's signature sandwiches; the smooth spread of the herbed cream cheese paired with the crustless white bread made me never want to look at a piece of a whole grain carbless bagel thin again. But upon reaching for the platter, I noticed the increased distance that now separated me from it. I looked at Mom.

"So, why don't we catch up for a bit?" She offered with a smile, placing her napkin over her own, barely touched plate.

I didn't feel so hungry anymore, and for the first time since I left Brian, the guilt began to infiltrate my conscience. The conscience that I once could pinpoint as criticism from Brian now had no place to call home except my own self. How was I to know where to go, after expelling my very own compass?

Mr. Swanson's classroom looked like Shakespeare's basement if he had been a mad scientist and obsessed with cats. There were globes split in half resting on desks, play masks dangling from the walls, and not a single ballpoint pen in sight: only quill and ink. He once told us that when his beloved cat, Hester, passed away, he was going to use his auburn fur to make a feathered pen. The dude was weird.

The class wasn't huge, but the ceilings were high enough to create an echo every time that man spoke. Although Mr. Swanson wasn't exactly the speaking type. He had this thing he would do where he talked as if he was British (he was from New Jersey), but it only really sounded like that because he said everything in a proper sort of air. Opting for "fellows" and "great heavens" instead of "you guys are late again," that sort of thing. I was late a lot these days. I guess I wasn't used to using a watch because I always had Brian to keep me on track.

"Liz, the lesson is up here."

I pulled my head up from the desk. Lucy said his echoing voice reminded her of those old-timey black-and-white shows, where their voices were all granulated and stereoized. That's when we realized he looked exactly like Fred Mertz from I Love Lucy: from the shiny head and sharp nose right down to the ironed slacks, which really wasn't that far down because, like Fred, he wore his belt right below the nipple line.

This was the one class I had with Lucy this year.

"So, as I am sure all of you are aware, the deadline for your comparative essay on two Shakespearean plays is fast approaching."

I hadn't even taken either of my Shakespeare books out of the plastic wrap. I was hoping I could get a good price for them too if I kept it that way. It was weird how a breakup could shift your priorities. You kind of start to wonder if they were ever your own. I mean, Stanford? C'mon.

"I would hope that all of you have chosen which plays you'd like to focus on, yes?"

We all nodded simultaneously, even the kid dozing off next to me: good timing, I guess. Sometimes high school felt like being in a room full of bobble heads.

"Wonderful. Let's move on to last night's homework, shall we? It's one of my favorites. Now who can tell me, why might Shakespeare have spent so..." he paused to cough into his elbow. That was another thing, the man was always hacking up something. Lucy and I were waiting for the day a giant furball would land on his desk. "So much time depicting the hideous appearances of the three witches?"

Shit. I didn't remember anything about witches. I guess it would've been weird if I did though, judging that I never actually did the reading. I glanced at Lucy with my "what-the-fuck-are-we-talking-about?" face and she rolled her "one-of-these-days-it's-gonna-catch-up-to-you." eyes. Honestly, Mary was right, I kind of liked the thrill of it. Before senior year, I hadn't left an assignment incomplete more than 24 hours after it'd been assigned, even if it wasn't due for weeks. Brian made sure of it. All that time I was thinking I was the one with the willpower.

"The witches, there's three of them, and they basically are gross looking with beards and shit and creep Macbeth out," Lucy whispered.

I nodded. I recognized that character at least, only because his name was on the cover of the book.

"Yes, Lucy." I hadn't realized her hand was raised until now.

"I think Shakespeare was given too much credit for breaking into less traditional gender roles for these witches, because all their features are stereotypically masculine. I mean the beards, their ugliness, it all points to characteristics that take away femininity and ends up reinforcing that only gross, manly women could ever do things for themselves."

Mr. Swanson had a big smile on his face, and I could imagine the laugh track going off like Lucille Ball had just made one of her faces again. I didn't usually think of Lucy as being smart, and especially not smarter than me.

I told myself I could've come up with an even better explanation if I did the reading. But with all the re-reading and studying and memorizing Brian had made me do over the past five years, I think I'd done my fair share of work. Probably for the rest of my life.

And then Mr. Swanson handed our papers back, the one I stayed up until 4am finishing, and I almost thought he'd swapped mine for Lucy's. I got a D. She got an A. The world was falling apart.

I had my head slumped down on my desk for so long I could feel an ugly red indent already starting to form on my forehead. The class continued and new assignments were assigned but time seemed to be frozen. English was my thing. I was the kid the teacher would pull aside after class and tell me that my style was something they'd never seen before, that I had real talent. I won a regional poetry competition in the first grade. I was the goddamned Editor-in-Chief of the Washington Highlights Newspaper.

I guess I should have listened to Brian. He was always reminding me to stay humble. I never paid attention to what my teachers taught in English class because I was better than the formulaic way they taught you to write in middle school, with that "Firstly... secondly... in conclusion" nonsense. I knew better than to take advice from my "peer editors" when they told me "How about you start your essay with a question?" You should never start your essay with a question. But that had all been in middle school. Kids catch up. Brian said that was my big problem, you couldn't tell my 5th grade writing apart from my 10th. If you're not constantly working at being the best and practicing and perfecting, you risk becoming average. And if you're not doing that and you're not paying attention in class, well, I guess that means you get a D.

The bell rang and I packed up my things as quickly as I could. I didn't want to be in that room any longer. I watched the pretty girl in front of me toss her essay with a big old C on it into the trash on the way out and then she reached in her pocket and pulled out a little slip of paper. Dylan had slipped her his number. I watched them all on their phones, Nerdy Neal too, taking a picture of his A+ and sending it to his mom. They all had something. I made my way to the doorway. Mr. Swanson told me to stay behind.

"Hey, Liz, I wanted to ask you something."

I stared at the ground because I think if he said the letter D again, I'd just start crying right there.

"I think I'm going to switch things up in the classroom. I'm going to move you to the front, okay?"

"Okay." I mumbled. It couldn't be further from the truth.

After he told me that I moved my feet as fast as I could to get out the door. I ended up tripping on my laces. I felt like I was falling for an entire minute, waving my arms around, but there was nothing I could do but watch it happen. I was going down.

Fortunately, my newly acquired back rolls cushioned the fall. I took a moment there, crouched on the nasty linoleum floors with my palms surely coated in a mysterious dust that coated the halls like sand. I looked up at the sunlight pouring in from the window across the hallway. Suddenly Brian's head came into view like he had a halo.

"What's the weather like down there?" He said, towering over me, blocking my view of the outside window.

I cleared my throat. He smiled.

"Listen, if you quit this little rebel act now there's still time to save your transcript."

I shook my head, and I reached to pick up my stuff. Suddenly Brian's foot was hovering over my fingers.

"Don't tell me you're happier like this. I've been watching you Liz, I've never stopped. It kills me that you're throwing so much away here."

"You know Brian, somehow I still feel less of a failure now than I did all those years getting straight As with you." I said, though I only sort of meant it.

"It's not just about the grades, Liz."

I followed his eyes to my shirt. I guess it had scrunched up when I fell because part of my stomach was out. I quickly pulled the shirt down. Brian smirked. I'd just proved him right.

Brian was always right. He was right when he told me down in the beach cabin last summer that I'd be running back to him sooner or later. I had taken it as an insult at the time, like this whole idea of me being a pathetic needy girl who doesn't have any self-respect. But maybe it was just the truth. Not the loserness, but our unbreakable bond. The undeniable, unchangeable route of the future that would always bring me back to him.

The best way I could explain it would be like sleeping in your own bed again. You go off on an adventure in a whirlwind of swinging hammocks, musty dorm bunks, and pull-out beds in your parents' basement, and there's so much going on you almost can't feel that pea under the mattress. But then it all starts to add up: the back pain, the sleepless nights, they get to you. Brian was like that bed you wished you could live in, because no one could hurt you in it. A tornado could roll by and uproot the house, but your bed with its fluffy mattress wasn't going to move an inch. Brian was the pillows you could hide your head under and block out the noise of your parents not loving each other anymore, or the deafening silence when they finally stopped trying to. Brian was the thick duvet that if you crawled under completely, you became invisible to the night intruders coming to kidnap you or the monster hiding in the closet. Brian was that thin little sheet you wrapped around your naked, sweat soaked body in the sweltering summers without any AC, because it didn't matter how overheated you were, you still needed something to bundle up with. To hold you, so you could let go and go to sleep.

I wasn't pathetic for taking him back, I was just tired.

"Brian listen, you're just..."

"I promise I'm going to be more chill, Liz, I swear. I keep my promises. I'll stay in my lane. You'll have more balance, not just work all the time. I got carried away; I'll admit it. I just see all your potential and I love you so much I feel like I have to make sure you're everything you're meant to be. I'm like this because I care about you. All I've ever done is because I want to see you succeed. But I know all the pressure I put on you wasn't sustainable; you've taught me that, Liz."

I pictured a world where Brian and I hung out and did work and then got to watch TV and have an ice cream cone every once in a while. It didn't sound terrible.

"Just let me help you." Brian was offering to pull me out of the water. It was up to my throat; everyone could see it now. This wasn't in my head: there was a D on my paper. There were rolls all over my body. I was flailing.

"I promise it's going to be different. I've changed," Brian continued to plead with me. I couldn't deny it was comforting to hear. The world was so competitive these days it felt good to know at least one person was on my side.

"Really? You promise you'll ease up?"

"Really. Just let me back in, we'll make this work."

I'd be lying if I said I couldn't hear all the Tina Turner and Rihannas of the world yelling down at me to leave him, that this wasn't love. That no one could make you happier than freedom could. But I'd had my taste of freedom, heck I ate a whole damn plate of it. I looked down at my stomach. Turns out freedom doesn't taste quite so good when the "free you" is someone you hate.

"Brian?"

"Yeah?"

"I want you back in my life." I held my breath, I didn't know what I'd just stepped into.

"If that's what you want, I'm here. And Liz..."

"Yeah?"

"Everything's gonna be okay. You can count on me. I promise I'm never gonna hurt you again."

I nodded. I just hoped he would stick to his word, I just hoped it was even possible for him to stick to his word.

And just like that I was back to where I'd started. Back to the exhausting runs and painfully specific routines and schedules and perpetual productivity. But at least I knew where I was and where I was going, and my heart was back in my chest.

$\backsim$

I stared up at the ceiling, its cracked paint, dusty fan, and recessed lighting looked like a beautiful painting above my head. The holes that littered the surface from previous light fixtures created constellations in the dark room and caused my eyes to dart along the trails they followed, most of them ending in a spider web.

I was normally cold in the mornings, as if sleep was the ocean, and emerging from it was like stepping out without a towel. My hair would be in knots, and I could barely see over the puffy bags that seeped into my eyes. I often scared myself in the mirror, not just once, but twice: first when I stepped in the bathroom, thinking Chucky had climbed through the window, his evil eyes and crooked teeth staring into my soul, and second, and even more terrifying, was when I realized it was only me.

But today was different, not to say I didn't look like a 1980s serial-killing-doll—I most definitely did—but that's not what I was thinking about. I wasn't thinking at all.

For the first time since school started back up, my heart wasn't pounding, and my chest wasn't sinking as I imagined the day in front of me. There was no agonizing, gut-wrenching sensation of dread that so often filled my newly awakened body. My arms weren't filled with goosebumps, because Brian was back. My mind wasn't racing, because Brian kept me perfectly still. Brian was facing the hurricane, and I was basking in the draft.

Chapter 30

CLAMPING THE VOCAL CORDS

"So, how was school today? I'm sure it's been more fun now that you've made that new best friend of yours, what's her name? Molly?" I'd been home from school for 5 minutes and she was already aggravating me.

"Her name's Mary, and who says she's my best friend?" It wasn't that she wasn't my best friend, but it felt weird having anyone but Lucy's name fill that title.

"You told me. That day after she slept over after the party this summer."

"Of course I did."

"Yeah well, I'm glad you did, I'm your mom, I like to know these things. I saw on your phone you have a missed call from Lucy; you should call her back. Maybe she's calling to tell you about some new party tonight."

She probably wasn't—parties were more Mary's thing. But who knows, maybe being in the play with her was making Lucy wild.

"Liz, it seems like you're working too hard again with all your schoolwork. Is everything ok?"

"I'm not in middle school anymore. Grades matter, Mom."

"I know, but having a life matters too. Trust me, you're only young once."

She sounded like she was winding up for one of her lectures on how I should be living my life.

"Hey, listen, you've got your first appointment with the new therapist tomorrow, we can't be late."

"What happened to the old one?" I asked, watching my mom flip through a cookbook like it was a deck of cards. I couldn't imagine she was really looking at all the recipes. She was probably just looking at the pictures.

"She wasn't working." I watched her reach the end of "Family Style" and grab the next Barefoot Contessa book from the cabinet. I heard the pages flip through until the back of the book's hard cover hit the marble countertop. I watched her reach into the cabinet to unwrap her newly arrived "How Easy is That?" as I left the room.

Chapter 31

SPASMS AND MORE SPASMS

Brian was over again. He was always over these days. After my Lazy Summer, I was behind on my college applications, and he had me on a regimen of writing one essay a day. Even if I wasn't sure I was going to apply to a school, I had to write all the essays for every college on my initial broad list, just in case.

He was looking at the stack of Post-it notes on my desk; and I couldn't tell what was bothering him because they were neatly placed at a perfect right angle to the desk on the top left corner where they belonged.

"What are those for?"

"Um, I don't know, I use them all the time for to-do lists, essay ideas, reminders, lunch box notes," I joked with a smile.

"Hmmm ... ok, where did you get them?"

I felt a shiver go through my body; I didn't like where this was heading. It was strange, I never used to be this intimidated by Brian. It seemed like the more I pushed him away over the summer, the stronger he got, like while I was hanging at the pool with Lucy, he was at some boot camp all summer and came back a Marine drill sergeant. I wondered what would happen if I ghosted him for a year. I had always had a thing for Dwayne Johnson. But I would never risk leaving him again: you push too hard, and you tear a muscle.

"Well, I'm waiting?" he said in his disapproving tone.

"I got them from school, in the Newspaper office. I was using them to make notes on some of the articles and then I took a stack home because I thought they'd come in handy with my homework too. And there are literally cases and cases of these things in the Newspaper room supply closet."

"So, when you call Lucy at all hours of the night"—Brian's face warmed up—"do you use the school phone as well?"

"Why would I do that?" I asked, sensing water begin to pool at my ankles.

"Well, I just assumed that you steal all your school resources for personal use." Brian finished with a chuckle, but it was clearly fake. It was the kind of laugh you could make in a mirror; and it wouldn't reflect it back. It was that fake.

"I didn't *steal* them. They were sitting on the editors' desks, and even if I did, what would these cost like twenty-five cents?!" I replied defensively, though part of me was still holding onto the idea that this was all a joke.

"Just stop it, Liz."

"Stop what?!"

"Stop making excuses for yourself. You did something wrong, and then to make it even worse, you won't even admit it to me. You probably haven't even admitted it to yourself."

"For fuck's sake, it's a Post-it!" I yelled back, as if those sticky squares of paper could ruin someone's life.

"Right, well it's a Post-it now. Next week it will be a stapler, then a charger, and in a month Liz, I honestly wouldn't be surprised if all our computers suddenly disappeared!"

"They're not going to disappear."

"You can lie to me all you want Liz but stop fucking lying to yourself. You're stupid enough to believe it." I rolled my eyes, if he thought I was stupid what does that say about his teaching? I'd learned everything from him after all.

"And what exactly have I tricked myself into believing?" I asked, though my voice had lost the conviction it previously had, and my question was far from rhetorical.

"That you're a good person."

"You can't just say that." I finally replied. I hoped I was right too, I knew there had to be some unspoken rules that you can't just tell your loved one she's a bad person. But was lying to me better?

"Actually, I can say that because it's the truth. And you know it's the truth; that's why you hate hearing me say it. You stole supplies from school, you had no intent on returning, and you tried to hide it from me."

"Brian you are overreacting! Everyone steals Post-its from their office or school!" I yelled back, though I was aware my choice of words had changed.

"So that makes it ok? If all your friends just randomly decided they wanted to rob a bank, would you go along with it? Don't you want to be better than the people around you?"

I paused, letting his words seep into me like a sponge as I tried my best to keep the water out. There had been a time when I wanted to be the best, to be above my classmates. I remembered the way I would purposely order some fancy salad after all the other kids asked for chicken fingers at a restaurant. I had thrived on feeling superior, even if it meant eating rabbit food for the night. Maybe Brian was right, maybe I really was a bad person.

"What do you want me to do now anyway?" I finally asked, my eyes carefully finding Brian's commanding expression. "I mean, I can't exactly put the Post-its back, I'm pretty sure people would notice half the stack missing and a bunch of ugly scribbles like every other one."

"Well, it seems like to me the only thing you can do is confess. Unless you're willing to live with the guilt every time you walk in the office."

"That's ridiculous! I'm pretty sure Mr. Swanson would think

I'm crazy just by trying to have a conversation about sticky notes for more than a minute."

"Liz, I thought we were done with the excuses."

"This isn't an excuse, I thought I was trying to keep my new position, not get fired!"

"So now you're saying your title is more important to you than taking accountability for your actions?" Brian asked, his quiet tone seeming to scream in my ear.

I didn't know how to respond. Everything I said in defense was only used to attack me harder. That was the thing about fighting with Brian, the more I tried to protect myself, the worse I was bound to be hurt.

"Whatever, it's your life Liz. Do what you want."

"That's all you're gonna say? You don't get to argue with me and make me feel stupid and then suddenly decide you don't care anymore, I mean I was the one who never cared in the first place!" I yelled back, confused as to why I was willingly restarting the argument.

"I'm not gonna sit here and argue with someone who doesn't want my advice." Brian returned, making his monotone words sound even colder in response to my fiery ones.

"It's not that I don't want your advice, it's just not the advice I want to hear."

"So, it sounds to me like you're just seeking reassurance. You're not completely sure you're doing the right thing, but you know that uncomfortable, uncertain, sticky feeling will all go away if I approve it. But guess what Liz, I'm not going to do it!"

Brian's statement left me dumbfounded. I had never really put my needs into words, but Brian, who seemed to know me better than I knew myself, had done it in three sentences.

I remembered all the tantrums I'd throw as a toddler, when I'd hold up two dresses to my mom, and pray to God she'd choose the one with the frilly pink sleeves. Most of the time she picked the right one, but there were two, maybe three times where she hadn't. It would throw my entire day off. My anxiety would crumble me onto the floor and my frustration would send kicks so hard to the floor my toes would bleed.

"Please just tell me I'm doing the right thing." I asked again, this time with tears threatening to ruin yet another dress. But my request was met with silence.

"Please just say it." Silence.

"Please!" My voice was getting shaky now, and I could feel the anxiety building, the numbness that somehow coexisted with the throbbing, flighty sensation coursing through my blood. I asked him again. I pleaded. He was so cold I feared my tears might turn to ice.

"Liz, I'm not going to tell you a lie to make you feel better."

His tone was definite. More certain than my mother's when she would point to a dress with a shaking finger.

"Fine, then tell me the truth."

"You need to admit that you've been stealing from the school; it's the right thing to do, Liz, and deep inside, I think you know that."

"Yeah, I know," I finally replied. I mean, I knew he was right, and I also knew that if I told anyone else about this, they would tell me I was crazy. They would say I was being stupid, but stupid things are not the same as the wrong thing. No one would tell me I was being a bad person by confessing to something that practically everyone does. Brian was right about another thing too: it felt good to be above other people, as bad as that seemed.

෴

"Well, go ahead. I'm all ears." Mr. Swanson looked at me expectantly. We were the only ones in the Newspaper office.

I took a deep breath, while my stomach tied itself into knots. I knew what I was about to say was going to sound crazy, and I really did not want to say it. But I also knew I had to, this was a test for me, and I wasn't about to fail.

"I stole from the school," I blurted out, hoping it would be better to exaggerate it and then explain to him. I knew Brian would have approved; "no avoiding it" was the last thing he'd said to me that morning.

"Excuse me?" Mr. Swanson said, his face going from playful to stern in a matter of seconds.

I'd hoped he wouldn't believe me, that he'd tell me to "stop joking around and get back to work." I couldn't speak; I just stood there looking down at my shoes.

"Liz, are you aware that stealing is a crime?" He believed me. "I mean this is serious; you can get in real trouble for this. What did you take?"

"A Post-it." I finally said, feeling my cheeks flush a deep crimson. I knew my words were not going to be received well. "I mean, it wasn't just a single Post-it note, that would be silly I guess, I mean it's still technically stealing I guess, but um, no. I stole the whole pack. Yeah, um it wasn't opened or anything." I mumbled at the end. It felt like I was trying to defend my need to confess. It didn't feel like me, it felt like Brian. I hadn't decided if that was good or not yet.

"Is this supposed to be some kind of joke, Liz?"

"So, you don't care that I stole from the school? From the Newspaper?" I inquired, my shaking starting to lessen to a mere foot bouncing.

"It was a pack of Post-its for heaven's sake!"

"So, you aren't mad?" I asked. I didn't know why exactly I wanted to hear him say it, but I knew it would make me feel better. Some waves could shrink with just a few words.

"Liz, listen to me. I don't really care about the Post-its, take as many as you like. What confuses me though, is why you felt the need to come into my office and get me all worked up about stolen property, when you were only talking about a stack of paper that cost ten cents? If you're trying to prove to me that you have integrity and whatnot, well, I'm afraid this is not the way to do it."

He paused, and I didn't say anything. He took a deep breath and combed his hands through his thinning blond hair. "I mean, this isn't rational behavior, Liz. Are you ok? Is everything alright at home? If you want someone to talk to I can ask around..." He trailed off, glancing down at his own feet as mine were now completely still, frozen even. I wanted to punch that old person's gray spot right off his face. I knew what "talk to someone" meant; that someone being with a clipboard and good writing stamina.

I didn't say a word. I couldn't even make eye contact with him. I hadn't ever gotten into much trouble before, the kind where the kid gets told off by their teacher or a similar authority figure. I mean Lucy and I would get into arguments, like the time I threw her cupcake in the trash after I saw how dirty the birthday boy's hands were who handed it to her, but it was like fighting with a sister. And sure, my mom would get mad at me, pretty much every other day, but it's different when it's someone you're not related to, or someone you feel related to. What you did had to have been so terrible that they felt comfortable yelling at another person's child.

An icky, cramp-like feeling began to form in my stomach, and even if I wanted to speak I couldn't, for fear I might spit out one of the angry moths that were scaling my throat at this point. Their wings, flapping against my pharynx like a bird trapped under the covers, caused my heart to race with the same velocity. I was afraid I was going to faint, but what scared me even more, was what would happen if I didn't. How could I remain in this room another minute? It was suffocating. I had never been put in time out, in that notorious corner of shame, but I imagined this is what it felt like.

I ran out of Mr. Swanson's office as fast as I could and of course Brian was there to greet me. I could hardly even acknowledge him. It wasn't that I was mad at myself for listening to his orders, it was infuriating that he had the audacity to even think he could tell me what to do. Because I would do it. Which gave him no right to say it in the first place.

"Liz, I'm glad you confessed. I know you're sorry."

"Yeah, sorry I let myself be guilted into doing something literally crazy!"

"Liz, you know what selfish people think about those of us who actually have integrity? CRAZY! It's all a mind game, getting the audience to root for the villain. There's a reason people normalize 'cutting yourself some slack' and not 'working until you drop.' It's 'cuz we're all a bunch of lazy fat-asses! And seriously, you of all people could use practice in admitting shit."

"What's that supposed to mean?"

"Nothing," Brian responded.

I scoffed at his pettiness. "Fine. Be quiet now. But for your information, I have no problem confessing to things, as long as they're actually worth confessing."

"So, I'm assuming the reason for your parent's divorce didn't make the cut?" Brian asked, with a mocking voice.

"Look who's quiet now," he added.

"How dare you, how fucking dare you bring that up?! I told you my fears about that in confidence!"

"Yes, and if I recall correctly, you were the one who told me not to lie to you, and not do the whole 'it's not your fault' spiel. And I didn't, because I know, and deep down I think you know too, that your dad wouldn't have walked out if he hadn't run out of love for you." Brian whispered, his voice softening.

I was crying now, but as bad as his words hurt, I knew it was good for me to hear, it was how I would heal.

"Liz?"

"Mhm," I answered through muffled sobs.

"I'm only looking out for you; I'm always looking out for you, and I just want what's best for you. I love you."

I didn't know what to say. All I knew at that moment was that I needed him. Not the kind of need stemming from protection or even possessiveness, it was the kind of need I would have listed among shelter, water and food. I hadn't known Brian my whole life, but I knew I wouldn't be able to live if he left. I wanted to tell him that we were bad for each other, that he was too controlling, and I was too easily controlled: but instead, I said, "Stay with me."

"Don't worry Liz. I'm not going anywhere."

After a long day of exams and in-class essays, I couldn't be more excited to kick back, relax, and watch some good old Bachelor when I got home from school. I'd probably watched every episode of that show starting at the age of eight, and I remembered saying to my mother once, on the season finale, "I don't like boys." Of course, being the hyper liberal accepting "hip mom" that she branded herself as, Margaret had told me, "That's okay sweetie, it's totally normal to love girls too." To which my 8-year-old self responded, while simultaneously drooling over the shirtless Travis Stork walking across her screen, "Um, no, I like men."

Margaret was probably disappointed. It wouldn't have topped Larissa Martin down the block with the kid who thought he was a cat, but it would have given her some lesbian leverage on all her parenting Facebook groups.

I was just about to turn the TV on when Brian walked into my room, uninvited. So much for my relaxing afternoon.

"Ok, you still remember that routine I taught you? The one about getting ready and being productive and everything? Well, I think we should add to that, make sure we aren't catching ourselves slacking." I didn't answer him at first, but the presumption of his words was bringing other words to my head I knew would only make things worse if I let them free.

"Well, since you're pretending not to hear me, I'll just go straight ahead with my ideas."

"Isn't that what you always do anyway?"

Ignoring my remark, Brian continued, "I think it would be wise to do a scan, you know of your room, every time you leave it. To make sure everything is in place and that you're not leaving anything behind that you need."

"You want me to do this every time I leave my room?" I complained, not hiding my exasperation.

"You know what Liz, forget what I said. Do whatever you want." Brian sighed, which sounded like ocean waves in my ears.

All my life that's all I'd ever thought I wanted him to say to me. But now that he did, it sounded more like a challenge. I'm not so sure I even know what I want. And I wouldn't know how to get it if I did.

"Wait!" I called, debating whether I was actually going to agree with him without at least complaining first, "You know what, I think that could be helpful. I mean, I feel like I'm forgetting something every time I leave the house."

<h1 style="text-align:center">Chapter 32</h1>

DIFFICULTY BREATHING

As I walked into the pearly white bathroom, with the spotless counter I had spent an hour cleaning off the other day, I caught a glimpse of myself in the glass shower doors. Brian had made me cover the mirror that was above the sink with a towel, citing reflective surfaces as the root to all vanity. The walls of the shower were made of chunky glass that were just transparent enough to make me uncomfortable using them. I couldn't see the details of my face, but the outline of my body was perfectly visible.

I was wearing a shorter shirt that day, probably one of Lucy's. I could clearly see the rolls of my stomach protruding from the back and I rubbed my midsection, pretending to wince as the imaginary baby danced around inside of me. I wasn't pregnant, but I had always enjoyed acting like it. When I was little, anytime I would get full at a restaurant I would ask my mom for advice because "Baby Tommy was being feisty in there."

Being pregnant didn't seem so exciting anymore. It's not that I didn't want to have kids one day. I did; I just didn't want to have them with Brian. The problem was that I never wanted to leave Brian either.

"You aren't pregnant, are you?" Brian's voice sounded from

behind me. I didn't like it when Brian came into the bathroom with me.

"Um no, I'm not."

"Okay, but um your stomach is…"

I tried to suck in as much as I could, my belly was normally covered when the lights were on.

"Yeah, I mean it's where I carry most of my weight, I think. I'm pretty sure a doctor told me that."

"Did they also tell you that 300,000 Americans die from obesity every year?" Brian asked, unfazed by his own frankness.

"Brian, I'm not like obese obese. I mean, the people that develop serious health problems are like those sisters on 'My 500 Pound Life' or whatever. Do I look 500 pounds to you?" I questioned back, genuinely curious to hear his answer.

"No, obviously not. But I also doubt those sisters were born weighing anything near 500 pounds either. It's a progression."

"Yeah, I get what you're saying, but your body type is like 80% dependent on genetics."

"Do you know what else is entirely genetic?"

"What?"

"Your hair. Its texture, color, and growth speed all come from your DNA."

"Okay, and?"

"And let's say you were born with the greasiest, frizziest, ugliest color hair. Would you just shrug your shoulders and pretend like there's nothing you can do about it?"

"No, obviously I would like to try to dye it or treat it with something, I don't know. I heard that keratin stuff works really well, and clearly, I like to highlight my own hair."

"Exactly. Just because something originally isn't in your control, doesn't mean you can't learn to control it."

"It's not like I haven't tried." I whispered back, my eyes falling back to the floor. I stared at the stained carpet, and I pictured myself back in middle school, doing sit up after sit up in the early hours of the night. If it wasn't for all the fat I had on my back, I probably would have bruised my spine from all the times I collapsed on that hardwood floor. I thought back to the bathroom I was just in and imagined myself leaned over the toilet, as if guilt could really be thrown up. I had done everything I could to control it, from liquid diets to intermittent fasting to buying Ritalin off my ADHD friends. There's a point in life when you can't keep fighting the current; you'll die before you make it to shore. If you're far enough away, no one will see you take off your life preserver.

"I'm not saying you haven't Liz, I just think you were going about it the wrong way."

"And what's that mean?"

"It means you tried to buy a clean wig instead of showering your hair every day. Your hair is constantly growing; you can't expect one temporary action to fix it forever. It's not about a single hairstyle, it's about…"

"The lifestyle."

"Exactly."

"I think we should make a plan then. I mean in the past it was like a new diet or fad every week and I never followed through with anything. I need something to follow."

"You need some rules."

Rules, I loved rules. I've loved rules since being a good person meant following the ten golden ones that were written on my preschool door. Don't break any of them all week and at the Friday morning meeting you'd get a sticker to rub in everyone else's face over the weekend.

"Right. But I can't, like, eat the same thing every day or do the same workout. I'll never stick with that."

"I know. It's fine if you have options, just as long as none of those options are Oreos and Coke."

"What about Diet Coke?" I said with a laugh, though I wasn't really a fan of carbonated drinks.

"Yeah, that's fine."

"Wait really? I was kidding, isn't that super bad for you, like even more unhealthy than regular Coke?"

"I mean sure, but it's 150 calories less than it. People get so caught up these days on what they're putting inside their bodies, when they should really be paying attention to how it makes them look on the outside. Didn't you tell me that once?" Brian asked.

"So, tell me," he continued, "what did you eat after school today before I got here?"

"Um, well, normally I'd just eat an apple and some popcorn. But my mom made chocolate chip banana bread, so I had a couple slices of that. And then there was an open bag of potato chips in the pantry. And an open bag of Oreos. I wasn't really hungry after a little bit, but I kinda just kept eating. But I think that's fine. I mean, it's not like I'm gonna be pigging out like this every day."

"Right."

"And, I'd have to eat like four thousand calories over the regular to even gain a pound. Um, I'm pretty sure I read that somewhere." All he had to do was tell me it was all fine and I hadn't just ruined all my progress.

"And you think you ate less than four thousand?"

My heart began to beat faster. "I mean, yeah. I just had a couple snacks."

"You might wanna round up just in case. But if that's all you ate, you should be fine." I was almost certain he knew it wasn't.

Apparently, I had underestimated Lucy's relationship with this soccer jock, and by that, I mean, the fact that one indeed existed. I put the pieces together as soon as she started to blow off our weekly Top Chef competitions with the cafeteria microwave, or our pregnancy pranks in the girls' bathrooms. She told me it was on account of them being too immature, which thoroughly pissed me off because I'd been thinking that since middle school. It's like when the little sibling finally "spills the beans on Santa" to the older one, when really, they've just been keeping the secret alive for them that whole time.

I told her not to worry about me, and to go have fun with Ocean Eyes. We started calling him that once he showed up at Lucy's and I looked through the peephole and thought the house had turned into a cruise ship. She did worry though. Leaving me alone on Friday nights, eating lunch in the bathroom like elementary school. She offered to invite me along with her and Ashton, but that was just Lucy being Lucy.

As sensitive as she could be, it kinda gave her this hyper-empathy, before the word "empath" was a thing and all. They were "just hanging out" and hadn't even kissed yet, but the girl was glowing. I mean smiling ear-to-ear full of happiness. I could never tell her that while her life was looking like some Happily Ever After movie with Prince Charming "just a friend," mine was headed down towards a disappointing spin-off. C-list actors and everything.

It turned out I never needed to say anything for Lucy to see the dark cloud that had begun to follow me around school. Lucy had never liked Brian, even when he was just a harmless twerp in grade school, she told me not to trust him. We were good with each other like that, picking up on the small things before they got too big to ignore. If only I didn't ignore her warnings.

Chapter 33

CHEST PAIN

Brian was over, helping me get ready for Dalia's New Year's Eve party. I'd submitted all my college applications early. Most of them weren't due until the first week of January, but since Brian had made sure I'd written all my essays in advance, as soon as I received the deferral from my Duke early decision application on December 15, I hit "send" on the remaining nineteen regular decision applications. The application process was officially behind me, but the waiting for decisions made me more anxious as there was nothing I could do now but wait.

I quickly started separating my clothing into piles. One for tops, one for bottoms, one for undergarments and so on. Beginning with the first pile of blouses and t-shirts, I closed my eyes and pulled out a random article of clothing, almost like a claw machine. Only instead of a stuffed animal, I extracted an old white t-shirt mom had given me. I'd never intended to adopt this whole system as a routine, but Brian was right, you get in a habit of doing something, then not doing it seems even more stressful than it was when you decided to make a routine to deal with it.

I may have worn some questionable ensembles to school, but at least it didn't take forever to pick out my outfits anymore. I moved on to the underwear. And then the bras, which didn't end up working out that great, given I had selected a neon pink one with my already partially see-through top. But, with Brian on the watch, the embarrassing combo would have to do. That is, until I saw the black denim mini skirt that would bring the whole outfit together.

Mary had convinced me to buy it one day on one of our mall trips. It normally would have been too revealing for my typical attire, but there was something about the way the fabric hugged my thighs, and the seams felt like velvet on my hips. The skirt was so short I could flash anyone in an instant, but at the same time, the skirt was so tight it wouldn't be able to move an inch anyway. It always paired well with pink.

Conscious of my company, I carefully pictured the skirt in the pile. It was on top of my black dress pants and the bottom of it was tucked under some ripped jeans. I pictured the texture of the velvet between my fingers, the scratchy Velcro clasp in the back. Before Brian could question my hesitance, I reached into the pile, carefully keeping my hand outstretched, so I could touch a number of pants without seeming too obvious in picking up a specific piece. The only issue, I soon found out, was that I had positioned my hand directly above my desired article. This meant that when I fully extended my fingers, only my palm was touching the velvet. I hoped Brian wouldn't notice the sudden twitch of my hand that placed the skirt rather than the black pants or jeans in my grasp. He didn't say a word.

I quickly threw on the outfit, nearly breaking the clip on my bra. The skirt felt scratchier than I remembered. Even though it had become a size too big for me recently, the skirt still felt tight against my hips. It wasn't as if the fabric was "hugging my curves" but rather attacking them, attempting to form me into a 2D shape that my body desperately wanted to escape. My shirt squished me together, untying and re-tying the knots in my stomach. It felt like I was shrinking, and soon the clothes would fall to the floor, as the carrot nose and striped scarves did when the spring passed across front lawns. Only guilty men truly knew how it felt, to be eaten from the inside.

"Ta-da," I said as I twirled around.

"Big deal," Brian mumbled, "It's just clothes."

"What?!" I demanded.

"Nothing. I mean you look great."

Bile began to form in my throat as I realized that even Brian thought I was crazy. I mean, he was right, who got this stressed out about clothes? Maybe all this time this was just one more way for him to have power over me. I suddenly felt lost in the dust of the other's ability to face the world. Lost without a trail from those that blazed ahead on the street without worrying they would step on a crack and kill their mother. Lost in the beams of light that streamed from TV screens of people who could watch the news and not feel like throwing up. Lost in a world where others swam, while I drowned. How utterly incompetent I was, breathing water instead of air.

Who knows, maybe I was just reading into everything.

∽

Brian started walking home with me after school. He said I shouldn't drive anymore because I was such a bad driver, and besides, I could use the extra 7,000 steps.

"So, how was lunch? You didn't seem to need me once you sat down at Mary's table, did you even notice that I left the cafeteria?"

"Aww, come on now Brian, you should have stayed! You're welcome to hang out with us next time you know," I offered, feeling bad I'd ditched him in the cafeteria, although I'd be lying if I said I always liked having Brian around when I was with a friend. He used to follow me and Lucy around, but in an annoying way where he'd always tap my shoulder and disappear when Lucy was in sight and then distract me while I was trying to listen to her. He was like a pesky horsefly, always buzzing around my head when Lucy wasn't looking. Normally you duck under water when those flies are on your trail, but not with Brian. He wasn't afraid of water even though he made me be.

He'd get mad when I tried to ignore him or got embarrassed by him, and Lucy would yell at me when I couldn't recite the story she'd just told me. Even then she could probably tell I was a bad friend. But at least she never minded my "quirkiness." That's what she called it when I'd be writing essays for "fun," refusing to play the silent game because that's when Brian distracted me the most or tiptoeing around sidewalk cracks, so he didn't come prancing out of the bushes telling me my grandma was in a wheelchair now. I guess that's the thing about dry drowning, you look pretty silly when no one else can see the water.

"Oh, that's okay, I don't really like Mary anyway. She's got a very strong personality," Brian answered with a smile. I knew what he meant, Mary didn't give a shit. Ever. The last time I'd seen her worried about something was when she couldn't find one of her nails that had fallen off in Biology class.

"I'm sure you guys will warm up to each other."

"Well, I guess if you like her, she can't be all that crazy," Brian offered. I could tell he was trying to be positive.

"So, what did you have for lunch?" he asked as we walked in my front door.

"Um, a burrito. I just got the same as Mary."

"What was in it?" Brian inquired further.

"I'll tell you in a second, just let me focus here." I concentrated on the door in front of me. I turned the lock clockwise, but I sneezed right when it would have made the clicking sound. It couldn't be turned any further, it had to be locked. I unlocked it, turned it to the right again. I heard the click. I tried to open it, then jiggled it, and jiggled it again, just in case I had imagined the first time.

"Come on."

I rolled my eyes, finally walking away from the door. "Ok, all done. Sorry about that."

"Don't feel bad, you were doing the right thing."

"Yeah. Well, um, about the burrito, I don't remember much of what was in it, but there was definitely chicken." I glanced at a displeased Brian, "but I didn't eat any of it, I just kind of played around with it." His anger scared me, more so what it led to.

"If you didn't taste it, how did you know there was chicken in it?"

"Well, I had one bite I guess, but that was it." I could hear my voice taking on that special flighty sort of tone it did, like I was getting backed into a corner. When your back hits the wall you have to stop thinking about how to escape and instead about what option leaves you the least hurt.

"In the future..."

"What?"

"Don't even try it at all, fake it if you have to. The thing about unpackaged food is that there could be any number of calories in a single bite, there's only ever gonna be zero if you never open your mouth. Ignorance is the thief of control, Liz."

"Okay, well, I still need lunch, I just wanted to make it here, so I knew what was going into it."

"Not today."

"What? You said skipping meals slows down your metabolism."

"But you had lunch already."

"What? You're counting a bite of a burrito as lunch?!"

"For all I know that could've been at least three hundred calories."

"But that's not fair, because it also could have been like 20 calories. And, if I'd known I wasn't gonna get anything when I got home, then I definitely would have eaten more than that!"

"And risk having a 900-calorie lunch?"

"You take everything to the extreme, Brian!"

"I do it because I care about you, Liz. Love is black or white, whoever tells you it's a spectrum is in a fantasy relationship. I do everything for you Liz, so sorry if that's too 'extreme' for you."

I took a step back. He was right. All the times I had looked up at those models on the billboards and asked myself what they were eating to look like that? I understood now. There wasn't room in those tight little skirts of theirs for a bite of anything that couldn't be counted, that couldn't be calculated into their algorithm of slim beauty.

"You're not a kid Liz; I can't force you to do anything. If you want to go in the kitchen, be my guest. Just don't come slumping back to me once you step on the scale."

"Ok fine, I'll wait 'til dinner." I said, trying to hide my disappointment.

"You can have water. And there are some Splenda packets in the kitchen, you can have as many of those as you want because there's no calories and…"

"Zero times anything is still zero." I finished for him.

"Exactly." Brian said contentedly. "Now, I'm not saying you can never have snacks. Ok, so your house number is 2 Pine Street, so what is 2 in military time?"

"2 a.m."

"Yes sir."

"So, I'm supposed to stay awake until 2 in the morning to eat a snack?!"

"Hey, I didn't make the rules, it was kinda the universe on this one. On the bright side, you'll be less likely to binge at that hour. And since you're gonna be exercising more, hopefully you will be wanting to sleep more than snack." Brian exclaimed, clearly proud of his new plan.

Brian and I had two very different outlooks, without a doubt, but there were times I saw a glimpse of myself in his sporadic behavior. Normally I might have been thoroughly pissed off at Brian for holding all my beloved snacks hostage all day, but it was the time of their release that made me giggle. The winding, irrelevant but relevant, tangled, but also perfectly laid out path that led to an answer, was all something that I admired.

I often used the same technique in school. Nearly every subject except math could be mastered through the art of memorization. It wouldn't always get you an A on its own, but it would make sure you passed. My friends would sometimes ask me how I did it, but I never really explained, because honestly, I would probably sound a lot like Phil Dunphy on Modern Family who used elaborate word associations to remember things. It was like having a secret language only you could speak. For example, in Spanish class: a random food unit in Spanish? No problem. How do you say "dough?" Well, dough is often associated with pizza or bread, or other popular carbs. What happens when you eat too many carbs? You get fat. Women have a higher percentage of body fat than men. In Spanish, "a" is usually associated with feminine nouns. Being fat means you weigh more. Another way to categorize this is through their mass. Put 'mass' and 'a' together and take away one of the 's', you have masa. La masa. The dough.

With practice, this path could be followed in less than ten seconds. It was the perfect way to remember something, without really remembering anything. All you had to do was play a game of association in your mind. Common sense and clues that formed a spider web, that no matter which way you went, you'd end up in the center eventually. It was nice to follow a path. I tried making a trail of breadcrumbs in the ocean once, but they got soggy and sank. That, or seagulls ate them.

248

I stared down at the dice in front of me. It used to just be one die, but Brian and I had agreed back in January, upon starting a new year, I would add a second one. Sunday meant run day. The five and the three looking up at me meant I would be going eight miles today. Only once, in the past nine months had I been forced to run six miles, and I wanted to give up the whole time.

The main reason I quit sports was because of my anxiety, the crushing dread and racing heart that made me feel like I would faint before the game even started. Once I was on the field it was fine, but walking to it felt like the moment before jumping out of a plane. It was anxiety fueled entirely by anticipation. I would have a cramp before I even started running.

Standing in front of the mirror, I positioned the headband just between the base of my ponytail and the top of my forehead, already decorated with beads of sweat. I wrapped my Apple watch around my right wrist, this time having to make it one notch tighter. I patted down my leggings, checking that they were still there, and then moved on to tying my shoes. I yanked at the laces in frustration as I glared down at my ankles. After all my hard work, after all the weight I had lost, they were still fat and chubby.

I still had cankles. Brian always told me they looked fine and said to stop complaining about them. But he also never told me to stop my constant calf raises while we waited in lines, or to take out the ankle weights I slept with at night—even though they made the bruises hurt even more. Brian said if I started repaying for my mistakes now, maybe I wouldn't burn so much in Hell. Maybe I'd just make it out golden brown like a marshmallow.

Leaving the house after locking the door, re-locking it and jiggling the handle twice, I stepped onto the dirty sidewalk. Brian wasn't with me, I could pretend I had rolled snake eyes, or in our language, a rest day. Just thinking about that guilt though, made my stomach tie in a knot, perhaps it was creating my noose. Immediately I started sprinting down the street. I was running on seven almonds and a slice of watermelon, but I was running in the right direction.

I enjoyed Sundays, for the most part. They were definitely better than the Peloton that left indents on my butt, or the Saturday swims that left my hair in dreads from the chlorine. Running was like going to a movie theater, it was an illusion of an escape. When my feet were darting from one to the other as I bobbed along the sidewalk, there wasn't enough energy in my body for my brain to think. It was freeing. I felt like Maria Von Trapp frolicking down the hills of Austria: like I could do anything I wanted. Movies give you a euphoric feeling of wonder, yet everyone would be pretty mad if you left the theater halfway through. I glanced at my watch, I still had six miles to go. I was tired and out of breath, but I didn't want any popcorn to be thrown at me.

I was always a little paranoid on runs, but that day I was particularly conscious of people looking at me. I had a terrible feeling I was going to wipe out on the black ice that sprung up in patches along the path. I tried to make sure I always got a good footing on the slippery parts, because I was not in the mood to end up like that famous lady who fell down the snowy hill right after claiming the "perfect conditions." Although it was one of my favorite clips.

The only thing that really ramped up my anxiety was the fact I couldn't stop running until the run was over. Everyone knows it's harder to start running again once you've taken a break, so I had decided, with Brian's approval, I would always keep moving. Slowing down was fine, but I never took a definite stop. This was the first run since it snowed the other day, and the icy sections proved hazardous. So, when Lucy called, I let the phone ring in my leggings pocket, too scared to get distracted or even take my eyes off the ground in front of me.

It wasn't until I hit mile four, the halfway mark, that I decided to pull up some of my texts. In the last ten minutes I had received twelve missed calls and a text from Lucy was on my home screen: "WHERE ARE YOU?!"

And that's when I remembered: I was supposed to drive Lucy

to the mall to get a gift for Mary and then drive straight to Mary's 18th birthday bash. Lucy's car had broken down last week and I'd promised to drive her. Fuck.

An old therapist once told me that stress and anxiety were like one big storm: a tornado that would only suck up more things you cared about if you didn't calm it down. She said the last thing you want to do in an emergency is panic. Two years ago, I would have said that was the stupidest thing I'd ever heard. When a person is in danger, their fight or flight system is supposed to be triggered, and there isn't anything calm about either of those options. In my own experience, the calmer I was, the more time it would take me to make a decision, I would analyze my choices, perhaps a pro-con list would be created. Whereas if my heart was beating faster than my mind could keep up with, I tended to make a decision quicker, I didn't allow myself time to overthink it.

But reflecting on it now, I knew the lady with the pointy nose and never-ending closet of cardigans had been right, because panic could give you an immediate direction, but who knows where you would end up. Without even slowing down my pace, I turned around and headed home, to finish my run.

When I felt the vibration on my wrist signaling the sixth mile, I nearly stopped to check that my watch wasn't malfunctioning. I had never run two miles that quickly, nor felt like I had so much more energy left after completing a run. Lucy's message had come at the perfect time; everything seemed to when I followed the rules. By the time I reached my house, I knew I could probably still have run more, but that wouldn't have been allowed either.

Brian was waiting for me on the front steps. "How was your run?"

Ignoring him, I went inside and checked my phone again. This time I had a text from the birthday girl herself. She wanted to know why me and Lucy hadn't shown up yet.

My heart was beating faster than ever now, and I was desperate to get to Lucy. I checked my watch; I was supposed to have picked up Lucy over an hour ago. Her family only had one busted car, so I was her only ride.

With half my body out the door, as if on cue, Brian didn't hesitate to remind me to scan the house for anything I may have forgotten, like we had earlier established I would always do.

"Do you have a gift?" he asked.

I didn't, but I figured my temporary gift for Mary could just be getting Lucy to her party and I'd buy her a real gift later.

"You can't go empty-handed, Liz, what kind of friend shows up without a gift on a girl's 18th birthday?"

"But I don't have time to get anything now, Lucy needs me to pick her up. Trust me, I'll just say I ordered something online, and it got delayed in shipping," I answered him, annoyed that it felt like he was purposely trying to delay me.

"I'm not the one you should be convincing to trust you, it's yourself. What kind of friend would you be if you didn't bring something to at least make up for your lateness? This is a very special moment in your friend's life. Liz, she needs to see she has friends who care about her."

"Well, what am I supposed to bring her?"

"I don't know, but I'm sure there's something in this house she might like. You should probably scan it. Left to right of course."

The tornado was picking up speed.

✌

My head was spinning, a minute ago I was all set to leave and now my hands were covering my eyes. What should I do? Who should I listen to: myself, who had only ever gotten into trouble, or Brian who always saved me from it? Was it even worth it to distinguish between the two? My mind had become the tornado, whirling around in circles like the ones you made in science class, and all I wanted to do was pour the water out of that little glass and down the sink. But Brian knew as well as I did, that there is a reason for everything. The more I let this tornado terrorize me, the deeper I would dig myself into the ground, and the more time I would waste. The only way to make the right decision was to stay calm, and everyone knew, the stillest part of a storm, is in the eye of the tornado. The only problem was that I didn't exactly know how to get there.

"Your rules are your directions, Liz. Block everything else out."

And that's exactly what I did. It was like I was back in second grade with the red noise-canceling headphones the teacher only let "special" kids use. I was aware of the chaos around me, but if I couldn't hear it, none of it was real. Starting along the right side of the bedroom I scanned the floors, following the lines of the wood.

"Usually, the smallest things are the most special." Brian called out from behind.

I bent down on my knees and walked to the edge of my bed, examining it along the side. Books, and hairbrushes, and earrings, none of which was what I was looking for. I moved on to the bathroom, opening the double cabinet doors in front of me. At first glance, none of the toothbrush or mouthwash bottles seemed to call out, but that didn't fool me. Starting at the top of the shelf I grabbed the container of flossers. I imagined Mary in her party gown, drink in hand and jumping on the dance floor. I pictured her asking to clean her teeth. It felt just as real as the phone vibrating in my pocket. Not important. I moved on to the second shelf. I did the same with the Q-tips, picturing my friend being overjoyed to get to clean out some ear wax now that she was finally an adult. Not probable. On to the hair ties, and then the lip balm, even my old retainers that were somehow not thrown away yet.

There was only one shelf left, but I knew I wouldn't be getting to it anytime soon once a bright green package caught my eye from the top. The small rectangular object was wedged next to the corner of the cabinet, right up against the hinge, which was probably why I had failed to spot it the first time. Upon further inspection, I recognized it to be an old gum pack. Its corners were faded to the point that they were white instead of green, though the leaves on the front indicated it was mint, Mary's favorite.

When I opened the package, I was pleasantly surprised to find more than half of it still full, and those that were left weren't even mushy. This was one item I could picture my friend liking; only it wasn't gift material. What defines something as gift material? The price? The sentiment.

The only issue was that the gum rested on the right of the top shelf, and I had already made my way down to the bottom one, meaning I would have to redo, or rather rethink, every item that existed on the middle shelf. Brian had always made it clear: skipping wasn't allowed. Glancing down at my watch, my eyes widened in disbelief. Thirty minutes had already gone by. It didn't feel true. Perhaps time stood still in the eye of a storm, I would have to look that up later.

I started back on the second shelf, determined to go through each item as quickly as I could. However, I soon found that the more I tried to rush the process, the less certain I felt in my decisions. It was like trying to run through water; you're better off putting your head under and committing to it. At one point I really did start to question whether or not Mary would like my old toothbrush manual as a gift. It was like when you repeat a word over and over again until it just sounds like nonsense, and then you wonder if it ever sounded normal.

I had received thirty-two more messages by the time I made it out of the bathroom. One of them was a voice message from Lucy. I pressed the play button.

"Hey Liz," she was on the verge of tears, or at least she must've been because I hardly recognized the voice at first, "I'm sure you're busy, but at least respond to me. This isn't fair. You promised me you'd take me, you know I don't have another ride." I hung up. I hated that she thought I was choosing Brian over her. I hated it even more that I was. But the thing is with him, you can't pick and choose. You get all of him or none of him. I've seen where the latter's gotten me.

My mind felt seconds away from developing a crushing headache, and my legs felt just about ready to collapse from beneath me. I had discovered early on that if I could walk around, it took less focus on the actual thinking part of the ritual, and so pacing around the room became customary. Perhaps this was what my therapist had always been referring to when she accused me of "ruminating."

My phone began to vibrate again, my shaky pocket sending a wave that spread through my body like a fire, while my mind tried desperately to douse it out with orders. Sometimes I imagined myself in a plane crash, with the wings and tail aflame and suitcases flying everywhere. I could hear the sounds of children wailing on all sides and the desperate gasps of air from the mouths of young mothers who were just starting to realize they may not still be one when they got off the plane. I could taste the stale coffee breath steaming along the aisle from business class, as boring, rich white dudes turned into hysterical, sweaty babies, shuffling around the aircraft looking for someone to bother like a flock of headless chickens with black cards in their beaks. I could even feel the heat of the flames, inching closer with every second that passed. I wanted to scream but the smoke around me forced silence, though the rapid beating of my heart proved loud enough. Nothing was worse than that fluttering sensation, the kind of anxiety that made you want to throw up but at the same time stuff your face with food to try and push down that jumpy feeling in your stomach.

It was only after I'd met Brian that I found an escape to the recurring nightmare. I had to turn off the lights. Of course, that in itself wouldn't make the fire go out or the plane suddenly elevate back into the sky, but it would do one thing: it would turn on the aisle lights. It was like the yellow brick road, nothing else mattered but following it. That was the way out of the plane. That path led me to the kitchen.

As soon as I entered the fluorescent-lighted room though, the sheer multitude of tasks ahead dawned on me. This was the first time I really noticed just how many cabinets and drawers and random appliances littered the space. I didn't even know where to begin because many things were stacked on top of each other. How on earth was I supposed to start on the left? I squinted at the countertop, and specifically its corner. While the granite edge stuck out over the compartment of dish soaps and cleaning products at the top, at the base of the cabinet the countertop was more indented than the protruding bottom of the storage space. It felt like the aisle lights were starting to dim and the brick road was looking more and more off-white than yellow.

"Trying to figure out where to start scanning the kitchen?" Brian called out to me.

"Yes! Help!" I yelled back at him, my heart beginning to beat faster and faster as I squeezed my eyes shut. The aisle lights only turned on when the plane was practically pitch-black inside.

"Well, you remember the rule where you must always start on the left? And how breaking even just this once, would set an extremely bad precedent to the point you'd be too lazy to ever go about it this way again?"

"Duh? Why do you think I've been trying to figure out where to start at first: the countertop or the cabinet?"

"Well, the only thing I was thinking, is that you seemed to have completely forgotten about the rug you were standing on!"

Brian yelled, clearly more excited than he was angry that I had given him an opportunity to correct me.

I grudgingly looked down, and sure enough, my feet were standing upon a large, rectangular carpet. It was dark blue, almost navy, one of those shag rugs. The kind my dog would always mistake for grass. So, if this rug was anything like my old, white-turned-yellow one, I was probably standing on a whole bunch of pee. It was also the kind of rug that if you dropped anything ranging from a safety pin to an AirPods case, there was a chance you'd have to get on your knees to sift through it. The only redeeming quality was that the rug was certainly further to the left than the confounding cabinets were, which meant I would be dealing with it first.

"Don't just skim that rug though, you never know what kind of things you'll find in there." Brian shouted over my shoulder.

I crouched onto the ground and knelt down on the carpet. To my surprise, it was much rougher than I had expected on my bare knees, and I was certain the activity of scuttling over to the furthest left corner would leave a red mark. However, that wasn't my biggest concern at the moment, compared to the whole half hour I spent staring at that countertop, my phone buzzing the entire time.

Looking at the first tassel of the rug, I searched around its base for anything that would stand out. As Brian had always taught me, I would look first in front of the tassel, then the bottom, then the sides and then directly on top. After this quick inspection I moved onto the next square inch of the rug beneath me. As I scanned, my thoughts drifted to a memory from preschool.

Kate and I were having our first playdate because she just joined my school, and it was one of those double hangouts where our moms were also drinking grape juice and talking about us on the couch. Kate was cool, from what I could tell, and she liked to play with my building tiles, the kind that stick to each other so you can build cool towers. She helped hold up the blocks so I could add another floor to the castle I was making. She told me she liked to pretend to be a princess, and I said I did too, and that I had a whole bin full of Disney costumes. I guess I shouldn't have mentioned that though, because then Kate asked if she could see it. I wasn't stupid, I knew she'd asked to try the costumes on too. I pictured her stretching out my purple dress and making the wigs all knotty, but for some reason it felt weird to tell her no. Instead, I said, "it's over in that corner, just don't touch the Rapunzel stuff."

"Are you sure you really checked that first one?"

"Yeah, why?" I questioned, already on to my ninth.

"Well, you don't have to, but it might be a good idea to check it twice. You wouldn't want to miss anything."

I moved back and stared at the start of the rug, and all the progress I had made. If I went back now, I would have to start all over. Even worse, what would stop him from suggesting I do a third check, or even a fourth, when I was halfway through with the rug? My heart pounding as I sat there, crouched into a ball on the rug hugging my knees.

I'd pretty much forgotten Kate was still over at the costume bin by the time I finished my block palace. It was as tall as I was, but I don't think I could fit inside of it. I'd remembered to add the doors this time, which was hard because it made the bottom less sturdy. If you're going to make a tall tower, you have to make it strong.

I was just about ready to present my castle to my mom and her friend when I saw a purple plastic heel step on the rug in front of me. It was the Rapunzel shoes. She wasn't allowed to wear those.

"Hey!" I said. "I told you not to touch the Rapunzel stuff."

"Oh, I'm sorry," she said, giving me those puppy dog eyes. But if she was sorry, she would start taking the shoes off. I saw her mom take a picture of her in my dress-up clothes, standing in front of my castle.

I don't know what happened but soon I was pushing over my plastic tower. Not on Kate but the floor. It made a big "Bam!" when it hit the floor and all the metallic blocks scattered across the rug like marbles.

"Woah, Liz," Mom said, suddenly remembering I existed. "Clean that up honey."

I was too mad that if I did try to pick up one of the pieces, I might throw it at the TV or something.

"Liz, come on, can you please clean up your mess?" Mom said again.

"Liz sweetie, if you clean up your toys then we'll have some room to play with the dress up." Kate's mom suddenly chirped in. I wanted to knock her grape juice right out of her hand.

Suddenly though, before I could make any moves—which I hadn't even decided what they were going to be yet—that little princess Kate started cleaning up the blocks.

The moms went crazy.

All I heard was, "My sweet Katie this..." and "what a helper that..." and then my mom goes...

"And it wasn't even her mess to clean up. What a good girl!"

"Kate, you are such a good girl. So good," Kate's mom said after Mom.

I just stood there watching her. And she wasn't even very good at cleaning! She picked up each block individually, just showing off right in front of my face. And she never took off the shoes either. I dug my heels into the carpet.

I returned to the rightest part of the rug, settling for a triple check this time around. I wasn't about to lose a friend over my own laziness.

"Just keep going Liz, if you don't pull through on this one thing, everything will be sacrificed." Brian's voice echoed behind me. I thought of the thinner arms that were under me, sifting through the carpet, and the new confidence I felt from my over-achievement and recognition at school.

There was so much at stake, all resting upon a fluffy blue rug covered with dog pee.

I'm not sure when exactly I started screaming because I had first placed my hands over my ears. But I could see it on Mom's face, those red cheeks of hers that came out whenever I was being bad in front of company. I hated seeing her like that. I ran out of the room as quickly as I could and went upstairs to the bathroom. I sat in the bathtub because I was crying so much, I didn't want to risk flooding the whole house.

"I'm not a bad person," I said, rocking back and forth in the dry tub. "I'm not a bad person, I'm not a bad person, I'm not a bad person." I said it again and again and again. Mom came bursting through the door in a couple of minutes and hugged me, but I just kept on saying it. "I'm not a bad person." I'm not sure if I was saying this inside my head or out of it.

"I know, sweetie. I know you're not a bad person." Mom told me, her red cheeks changing to watery eyes.

Somehow, I just couldn't believe her. I could see from Kate's mom that every parent seems to think their kid's a princess.

"I'm not a bad person."

I didn't want to double check the carpet for this mysterious perfect gift, but at the same time, being a good friend meant you had to make sacrifices. I went slower this time, squinting my eyes at each spot that seemed even the slightest bit off color. Even as I focused on each tassel, I kept my peripheral view open, to make sure nothing was hanging with the rest of the rug. It wasn't until the fifth one that I actually found something. It was only a paperclip, but the fact that I'd skipped over it the first time, made the whole double-checking thing seem all the more important. Ultimately, I decided to remove the paperclip and place it in a drawer on my desk, as I figured I might need it someday, so I'd hate to throw it away. I did the same thing with the following thumbtack, button, and sewing thread that turned up on the other side of the rug, questioning first though, if any of them could make an acceptable birthday gift. They never were, but instead of this comforting my anxieties, it only perpetuated them: what was I missing? If I knew what I was looking for I wouldn't have to search with such scrutiny, but because it could be anything, it meant I had to inspect everything. And for this reason, when I did finally make my way to the other side of the rug, I felt no better at all. It was like I had swam the length of the ocean but found no land.

Chapter 34

AIRWAY SHUT OFF

The thing about abuse is you feel like you don't have any other options which for someone who hates choices like me, normally, yay! But the abuser gets in your head, making you think if he were gone, you'd only hurt yourself more, that the pain was pain but at least he was inflicting it for you. What a gentleman, right? He's keeping you in line, so you don't fall off the sidewalk and into traffic. You want to leave, but your bones are broken either way. Save yourself the money and skip out on the crutches. You're not going anywhere. I wasn't going anywhere.

It started slowly, the physical stuff. Sure, you could say Brian had been verbally and mentally abusing me since middle school, but senior year is when it crossed the line, though you could even argue all the forced exercise was a form of physical abuse too. I can't remember when it all started, but soon after we got back together in the beginning of senior year, Brian's punishments for my laziness became physical. Too tired to finish re-writing that English essay a fourth time because you found a single spelling error and therefore had to start from the beginning again? A kick in the shin. Get caught taking a shortcut home from school? A slap in the face. Nothing super violent, never any blood, but just enough pain to not want to bear it again.

My heart was pounding, and it felt like I was struggling to breathe. As if this time, my lungs were filled with sand. My hands were clenched in fists.

"You spent half the day in the bathroom." I punched my head.

"Your teachers are disappointed." I punched my head again, harder.

"You were so lazy today."

I punched my head so hard my knuckles were turning red. Sometimes if an abuser is really manipulative, he gets in your head and makes you do the dirty work for him.

～

"Get up honey. You have to go on your run now." I didn't reply. My ears were still ringing.

"Don't be lazy, Liz. It's time. It's Sunday, you have to," Brian repeated.

I couldn't even answer him if I wanted to. The combined noise of my racing heart and pounding head made it impossible to even think of speaking. I doubted she would even hear the words come out.

"You're gonna mess up the whole day. Just get it over with and then you can relax!"

I was silent. My body was curled into a ball on the floor, squeezing myself so tight, tears were trying to escape out the corners of my eyes. I hadn't realized when I'd started, but at some point, I had begun to rock back and forth on the carpeted floor. My movement became faster and stronger with each second, and soon I imagined myself creating a forcefield from the friction that kept my hair all staticky. And for a little while, it worked.

That is, until my phone began to ring in my pocket. It was Margaret.

"Liz?" Mom asked, as if she was uncertain whether her daughter or Brian would be the one to pick up.

"Yeah." I answered, somehow finding my voice again. I was even sitting up now, fearing my words would come out muffled otherwise.

"I'm at CVS. I thought I'd pick up your meds, but the pharmacist told me they didn't have any because you hadn't picked up the Remeron in three months."

"And?"

"And I'm just wondering what's going on sweetie. Why aren't you taking your meds?"

"Because I don't need them."

"Ok well Liz, that's a conversation we can have with your psychiatrist, but honey you can't just suddenly stop taking prescribed drugs, I mean there are serious side effects to this sort of thing."

"I feel fine. Actually, lately I've been feeling my best." I bluffed. "Maybe it was the meds that were messing with my head."

"Where is this coming from?" Margaret raised her voice. "It's really not that big a deal to take these, it's nothing to be embarrassed of."

"Mom. Listen to me. I decided I didn't need them anymore because I was starting to feel happy again, I mean, genuinely, genuinely happy."

"Okay, but that feeling isn't going to be permanent, and when the shoe drops..."

"God Mom, I just wanted to know if this happy feeling was real or if it was synthetically made in a lab and packaged into a pill. I don't want to have to depend on anything but myself to feel good again. Is it that wrong of me to want that? It's all you've ever wanted for me."

Margaret was silent for a moment. I hoped she would believe

me and let it go. I knew it wouldn't have gone over well if I told her the truth. How Brian told me each pill was two to five calories more than I was allowed, or how I deserved to face my mind without "cheating" assistance.

"Liz?" her mother finally asked.

"Yeah."

"Do you want this, or is this just a new rule of yours? Or should I say of..."

"I do, Mom, it's just me. Stop trying to make excuses for me, what if it's all always just been me?" I hated when she blamed things on Brian. She never understood him. He just wanted me to be happy.

Carefully, I placed a hand over the growing purple lump on my temple, as if my mother could see through the speaker.

⌇

Lines of sunshine flowed into the room from the border space between the windows and their shades. I could spot little dust motes dancing in its rays, playful and free. Their movement reminded me of the astronauts I had seen in space, calmly floating with no control whatsoever. I wished there wasn't any gravity on Earth. Then I wouldn't have to stumble to the bathroom on blistered feet, and sore quads. Even my swollen head would finally be at rest, aimlessly floating without having to think about where or why.

I could hear the vague thumping sound of a basketball on concrete outside my window, and I imagined a skinny little boy smacking it down each time, determined to make the team this year.

Like any other day, I began by going to the bathroom or rather entering the bathroom. The only problem was that once I got there, I didn't have to "go." Except, at the same time, I had to go—it was part of the routine. I stayed another minute on the seat and tried to concentrate on something, anything, leaving my body. It was just another day, and I knew this was going to throw me off if I prolonged it. And yet, nothing happened.

I tried watching tiny water drops trickle down the glass, predicting which one of them would win the race to the windowsill. I tried listening to the distant rain that vaguely resembled the sound of peeing. And still, nothing. Perhaps it was the weeks of fiber-less meal plans, or the lack of water breaks I allowed myself, but something or another had definitely caught up to me. Or rather, I had caught myself up. And so, I sat.

With places to go and piles of homework to finish, I remained glued to the seat. Because if I had learned anything from Brian, it was that you must never skip a step. Ever. So, I stared up at the clock, ticking away the already too little amount of time I had to get ready for school. And even though I was doing the right thing, my heart began to quicken. My feet began to grow numb from the coldness of the bathroom tile.

I was going to miss school at this point. And the school secretary would call my mom. Margaret would then come storming upstairs looking for me and I would have to explain that I wasn't at school because I was determined to use the bathroom. And Margaret would call me crazy. And I would feel so sorry for my mother, as she would be right, the amount of willpower I withheld to do the next right thing was crazy for an average lazy woman. Clearly my mother didn't have enough self-respect to at least suffer the tiniest bit to set herself up for success later. It was pathetic, truly. And I would feel bad for her, that she, of all people, had clearly let herself go. And I hoped Brian would agree it counted when a single teardrop made a gentle splash into the toilet water.

I came out of the bathroom clad only in a pajama top, underwear, and a pool of sweat. Brian, who was now walking me to school as well as home, was exasperated, "Liz! Let's hurry this up!"

"Actually," I said tentatively, "I think you need to leave."

"Excuse me?"

"I said," my voice threatened to falter, "I need you to leave."

"You sure about that?"

"Y-yes."

"Okay, well before I go, let's just get one thing straight. You may be smart, and you may be doing well in school, Liz. But you are nothing without me!" And before I could respond, he was gone.

I had expected him to fight back; to list all the reasons I needed him, to beg. Maybe get violent. Instead, he just left. And somehow, we both knew, that's what would scare me the most.

The basketball sound started up again, each thud hitting the cement like a metronome. The birds were chirping a sweet melody, and the drizzle of rain laid out a beat against the pavement. Perhaps the orchestra played every day, and my lock checking, house cleaning, and lengthy morning routines had distracted me from it, but maybe, just maybe, there was a chance it was performing just for me today.

And so, with the music behind me for comfort, I began to get ready for school. I brushed my hair because it was knotty from tossing and turning all night. I brushed my teeth so my breath wouldn't stink. And finally, I changed out of my pajamas, because, well, I kind of had to. On my way out, I glanced in the mirror, and for the first time in a very long time, I saw myself.

And then I did something I definitely didn't have to do, and I raised up my middle finger and whispered, "I want to live without you Brian."

~

Brian hadn't even suggested it, but I knew it was the right thing to do. I am getting better at that now.

"Come in," Mr. Swanson's voice sounded from the office.

"Hey, so um I wanted to tell you something." I started, this time finding confidence in my voice.

"Go ahead. You can take a seat," he said, while his eyes remained fixed on the screen in front of him.

"Okay well, I was thinking about the article I'm writing on the new Principal."

"Yes, what about it?"

"Well, I just wanted to make sure you like it beforehand."

"If you're happy with it, I'm sure I'll like it too."

"Well, it's not so much about that, I was hoping you could just check my dates and everything."

"Liz, I don't have time to fact check your work, we have student editors for that." My dates were right, I checked them against the event calendar 30 times, they were right.

"Well, I just wouldn't want to give any false information, so if you could just take a quick look..." I started pushing my laptop towards his side of the desk. All he had to do was look at the damn thing. I just needed him to look at it. All the student editors had gone home for the day, he was my only hope.

"If you upload it to the app, one of the editors will check it later. I'm busy now and it isn't my job to check your dates." I could tell he was mad. He had a bad way of hiding it. But I was too anxious, and I had an even worse way of hiding that.

"You, you don't even have to read it, just look at it and then tell me it's good." I was getting desperate now. Why couldn't the old geezer just tell me it was fine. Hell, I'd take a thumbs up.

"Liz, what is going on? This doesn't even make sense; what you're asking me to do."

"Right, I realize that now. But since I'm already here and everything's pulled up, you may as well just look at it."

"Liz, this is a problem."

"Right, well that's exactly why I came to you. I wanted to

screen out any problems before we go to press." I quipped back with a smile, but I could tell Mr. Swanson was on his last straw.

Instead of losing his temper, he just sighed and looked at me with concern. "I can see this role is too stressful for you. I should have known back when you came into my office confessing about those silly Post-it notes. Why don't you take a step back and take a break? Get some rest, focus on your health. Enjoy what's left of your senior year. I'm sure Mia would be happy to take over as Editor-in-Chief."

I wasn't expecting that.

"Oh no, that's okay. I don't ever take breaks."

"I'm not asking you, Liz."

And I definitely wasn't expecting that.

∽

Putting on my sneakers, I decided a run would help ease my anxiety. That, and it was Sunday. Sun rhymes with run. It was also March, which meant that the month was odd, which meant it came first on the x-axis rather than the y. Because you always plot the x coordinate first. And every math kid knows, nine times out of ten, you can bank on the time variable being the x-axis. Which meant during January, March, May, July, September, and November, I would be tracking my runs based on time intervals rather than distance goals. And according to the number rolled on the die, I was only running for forty minutes. Brian didn't always like to torture me. He was just spontaneous with his rewards and punishments like that. It kept me on my toes, literally.

After I finished checking the lock not once, not twice, but four times, I stepped outside. I still hadn't seen Brian, but I was sure he'd show up sooner or later.

The cold air hit my skin like a whip to the face, and goosebumps started to cover my body in a matter of seconds. As bad as it felt to admit, I usually liked timed runs better, because there was no reason to go very fast at all. However, today felt like one where if I wasn't running quickly, I'd be freezing.

After jogging to the train station, which was roughly five minutes from my house, I pressed start on the timer. All I had to do now was run. The only issue I soon discovered, was that the faster pace I kept, the harder the wind pushed back against me, reddening my nose to the point of numbness. My only hope was that my legs would get sore enough that I stopped thinking about the rest of my body.

I focused my mind on the people around me. Babies in strollers seeing the world for the first time and older people paving their way with their canes. No one waved or smiled at me as I passed them. Runners tended to be the only ones to acknowledge other runners, and even that was usually a clever distraction to speed up and get in front of the other.

Finally, the familiar voice of the Spotify ad lady sounded through my AirPods, this time reciting some crap for Uber Eats. But that's not what I was concerned about. Instead, the advertisement, which recycled roughly every half hour because I didn't have a premium account, meant I was allowed a sneak peek at the timer. As I had assumed, I had a little less than ten minutes left. That was always my favorite part of the run. One of the first things Brian taught me was that you could do anything for 600 seconds.

My Apple Watch buzzed. I looked down. An email from Duke. Today was when they were releasing their decisions. I pulled my phone out of my pocket, clicked on the link to the portal, and "Congratulations!" was the first word I saw and the only one I needed to see. My heart soared. My dream school. All my hard work was paying off.

Huffing on the sidewalk I quickly exited the app. The timer would be going off any minute now. As I put my phone back in my pocket a Grammarly ad came bursting through my AirPods, forcing me to adjust the volume. But at the same time, I noticed something very, very wrong.

The timer, which at this point should have displayed less than a minute, no longer appeared on my phone screen. My heart began to beat faster than it had the entire run; I must have somehow turned the timer off when I checked my email. All the excitement and relief from the Duke news had evaporated. Suddenly the cold seemed a whole lot colder, and the burn in my legs, which dared not stop moving until their job was completed, began to intensify.

Most people spend 47% of their waking hours thinking. Around half of those thoughts are repeated ones. Also called over-thinking. Most people don't have rules that dictate every minute of their lives and schedules in the form of sticky notes so numerous they paint a wallpaper. Because if they did, they wouldn't have to think at all. Unless of course, even those rules weren't specific enough. Because I soon discovered, any line can become a blurry one if you squint hard enough.

The overhead lights had been off for a while, and now only the occasional flickering of my nightstand lamp remained to remind me of the rest that I did not yet deserve. Brian's words battled each other in my mind. On one side, I pictured him screaming at me to keep running, no matter what, until that beautifully obnoxious timer went off. On the other hand, I imagined all the times Brian had told me to only check the time during the ads, and if no timer was there, I was done. And after the Duke email, an advertisement had started playing. At the forefront of all his teachings, the rejection of laziness always found a seat. Maybe I should've kept on running after all, he certainly couldn't be mad about that.

Carefully, I removed the covers that clung my body to the bed and stood up in my pajamas to face the window. It was dark out; I could only make out the orangish glow of the street lamps on my block. I started to pace back and forth across my room, trying with all my weary-eyed attention to envision the phone in my sweaty palm earlier in the day. I needed to convince myself I had done the right thing.

I could picture the blue sky and the chilly air making my hair stand on end as I adjusted my jacket and re-tied my laces. But with each new detail that came to me, the clarity of the event seemed further pulled from my memory. Because any information that was once forgotten could just as easily have had a fabricated counterpart.

Over and over my feet paddled across the sea of carpeted floor and each time I felt closer to sinking. In fact, I had reimagined myself back on the sidewalk so many times I started to question whether I had even started the timer in the first place. The more and more I tried to grasp a hold on that memory, that mundane moment in time, the less it seemed real. This, of course, led me down a whole other spiral, because then there was the chance I never went on a run at all, and the even more daunting thought that I would need to get outside and go on one right at that moment. And there would be no one to stop me; I had lost the ability to do it myself a while ago.

Suddenly, a knock on the door interrupted my thoughts. And a second, more forceful one, brought me back to reality.

"Is everything okay?" Mom asked. Her eyes were squinting as they adjusted to the light, but I could make out creases that formed an expression of concern. "I've been hearing a bunch of thudding all night, what's going on in here?"

I could feel the saltiness of the freshwater creep into my eyes as I tried my best to twist my face into a convincing smile. I even tried to laugh a bit, to show how stupid her worry was, but I only ended up inhaling more of the ocean.

"Everything's fine." It wasn't, but I couldn't just tell her that. Brian was in the bathroom. It's crazy how obvious a lie can seem to the person who's telling it compared to the ignorant person they're talking to who's standing just three feet away and nodding their head.

"Are you sure, honey? You look like you're hurting. This is supposed to be such a happy day for you, I don't know what's going on." Mom questioned one more time, shifting her eyes from my face to my bruised legs. The way she said it was something I hadn't heard in a while, it wasn't how she normally would ask. Usually, I could picture the checklist in her hand whenever she wanted to "see how I was doing." She was reaching out, offering to pull me back in from wherever I had drifted, a lifeboat of sorts. And of course I had to stab a goddamn needle into it.

But what could I have done? Brian would never have let me accept help so easily. He would tell me that other people could never understand this special thing we had, this painful, perfect torture that was love and success and pride all wrapped into one.

In a final, gasping breath, I told her "Everything is fine." And, not wanting to miss any more sleep, she went back to bed. Maybe if she had been wearing her glasses like she normally did, she would have noticed that the second time I spoke, my eyes had been filled with water.

Defeated and hopeless, I crawled back in bed, with even the dawning lights of morning failing to bring me enjoyment from the edges of the window shades. Never again would I be granted a guiltless escape route.

∽

I looked down at my breakfast. The measly bowl of cereal Brian suggested I eat every day had reached an all-time level of disappointment. The milk leveled off at an inch, and the Cheerios barely covered its surface. If I wanted to, I could put a piece of cereal on each of my fingers and only have two left to spoon down the milk. But of course, I would never do that, because then my meal would be over in 30 seconds. With the mastered skills I had acquired over the last couple of months, I could effectively turn those seconds into minutes.

Step one: The very first lesson I learned was to always separate my food. I could effectively double the quantity of food on my plate by eating each ingredient on its own. A single PB&J sandwich could be turned into a three-course meal; four if you peeled off the crust first.

Step two: never ever use a spoon. They're terrible at separating practically anything. Their volume control was minimal and if you try to get a smaller bite using the back of the spoon, the contents are so smeared you can barely taste it: the worst possible outcome. On the other hand, you can keep your diamond earrings, because a fork, that was this girl's best friend. I could eat my rice one grain at a time if I wanted to. I could squash my quarter of a banana into endless pudding. I could even chop up a cracker, spit some water onto it, and eat the paste one lick at a time. The opportunities were endless.

And of course, it would be out of the question to ever add food to my plate, so I regularly added water to my meals to increase their volume. Water, H_2O, didn't have carbon, which meant it was the only consumable product not containing calories. Thus, I opted to treat myself with a pint of watered-down cereal milk over the traditional two inches of two percent.

Brian didn't seem to agree. Trailing me after I refilled my pink Stanley cup in the school water fountain, Brian asked, "Thirsty much?"

"What, you've got a problem with water now?" Brian could be impossible sometimes.

"Yeah, I mean you seem to drink a lot of it," he remarked.

"Water? Well, that's because I like it."

"Right but just because we like something doesn't mean you can just have as much of it as you want."

I didn't understand why he was getting worked up. Water had always helped keep me full and gave me something to occupy my time. Margaret used to love preaching "moderation is key" but balance was hard when you didn't know what would tilt the scale and what wouldn't.

I remembered being a little second grader asking my mom to buy every piece of candy in the store. Margaret said my teeth would rot. "After how many pieces?" I recalled asking. Margaret, not wanting to give me a complex, had replied saying, "It would take a lot of candy I suppose but even before you ate half the store you'd be so sick you wouldn't want to even look at another Hershey bar." I disagreed. That was the other thing, I could never get tired of candy. I also could never get tired of sleeping. Or watching TV. Or painting. Which also meant that at any moment all my teeth could fall out, I could forget to wake up, become blind, or go insane from lead poisoning; because I would never see it coming before it was too late. Just like the frog who wants to stay in the warm bath.

"I mean, I would even argue that when you like something too much, the best thing to do for yourself is to take a break from it. Maybe save it as a reward, only for when you truly deserve it." Brian continued.

He wasn't completely wrong; I did enjoy the way ice cold water felt like raindrops racing down my body. How one glass could gaslight my stomach into believing something had in fact been consumed in the last 12 hours. I'd always been fascinated by the idea of infinity, a limitless entity you never have to worry about depleting. It was for that reason I'd decided I would never live in California. In California, you could turn the tap on, and the water might not come on. Or even worse, it could run out.

Another reason I loved Seattle. Water was the only thing in the world you could never have too much of, right?

Wrong.

"You're gonna accidentally overdose one day," Brian's voice broke through my thoughts again.

"Excuse me?"

"You know, when you have too much of something."

"Brian, you monitor literally everything that goes in my body. How would that happen?"

"Not water."

I raised an eyebrow.

"I don't monitor how much water you drink."

"Ok, but like why would you? It's literally calorie-less."

"Maybe, maybe," Brian rattled on. "But water intoxication is a serious problem. It'll leave you with permanent brain damage or dead."

"I think you're thinking of alcohol poisoning."

"Nope. Look it up."

I rolled my eyes, but I made no move towards my phone. Brian never bluffed when it came to him being right about something. It wasn't that I really thought I drank four liters of water every hour, it was just that there was a possibility that one day I might. And if one day I might, then that meant every day I would have to monitor myself.

I started by just allowing myself one sip of water after each meal, and half a glass of water after runs. I knew there was water in the milk in my cereal but that didn't count. I thought I was doing a pretty good job, but Brian wasn't satisfied.

"Given you've already been drinking like a fucking camel for the last month, I suggest you start trying to get all the excess water out of your system that you've been storing."

"Ok, well I'm not exactly in the mood to sit on the toilet trying to pee all day." I said. Been there, done that.

"No, no, no that would be silly, and unnecessarily slow. Instead, Liz, I want you to sweat it out."

I glanced outside through the window; the blazing sun was already painting the sidewalks a bright shade of orange and the puddles that once filled the road's potholes had been reduced to patches of wet gravel. A late spring heat wave had reached the city the day before.

"And I suggest you get started soon too, cause the pavement's only getting hotter out there."

Sure enough, within minutes, my sneakers were pounding against the pavement. It felt wrong. Running wasn't supposed to feel like it'd be the last thing you do before collapsing. It wasn't supposed to hurt so bad you'd be willing to intentionally trip on the raised part of the concrete sidewalk just to catch a breath with a scraped knee. And yet, with each moment my sneaker connected with the sizzling ground beneath me, I felt like breaking down. My body had so little energy left that even the fundamental ability to produce a cooling sweat had been stripped from me. Any moment I could be overcome with heat stroke, dehydration, or shock. But at any moment, Brian could be watching me; so, I continued to run. My legs were in a rhythm: bending back and forth like clockwork. Sometimes I wondered if that's what Brian wanted me to be: a machine. He was always praising them, reminding me that "machines don't stop working when they're 'tired.'"

It wasn't clear to me what had happened first: developing a

throbbing pressure in my head or being pulled up by strangers from the sidewalk. Words spilled out of my mouth like I was throwing up gibberish or maybe it was just vomit. Though I could have sworn I heard myself yell out "SpongeBob." The admittingly sponge-y-shaped lady behind the ice cream counter where the strange people had brought me to, began to scramble around the shop for some Gatorade. Her manager, who had recently appeared in the hallway clad in sweat stains bigger than the ones I was sporting, was wearing a much angrier expression. I turned what little was left of my attention to where the man's eyes were focused. I wondered if the fact my sweat-soaked torso was pressed up against the glass of the ice cream display may have contributed to his unsettled state.

I had wanted to tell the lady unboxing the big box of Gatorade there was no need to go through all that work, that the average bottle of red Gatorade contained 150 calories. There was already a spilled Styrofoam cup of water on the floor, which I could only have imagined was initially offered to me with little success. You had to admit, it was kind of amusing, or maybe it was just sad. Even when strangers turned to SpongeBob, and my legs turned to jelly, Brian's voice never left my mind.

They say you hear God's voice before you die.

I could feel the bright, orange rays of light descending on the tops of my eyelids before I opened them. The air around me, I could tell, was cold, though my body felt warm and at rest. When I went to move my arms, I found they were stuck in place. That is, if they were even attached to me at all. I could only see directly above me, so the orangish air freshener smelling particles obstructing my view seemed to encompass the entirety of my surroundings. For the first time in a very long time, I felt completely rested. As if I was entering an eternal sleep.

Only I couldn't be in heaven. Because in heaven, I would be able to move my body. I wouldn't need to of course, but my body would be so perfect I would probably be wanting to show it off. Looking down at my relaxed chest, I could say definitively that I was not in heaven. It didn't matter that I could count all twelve of my ribs. My thoughts were confirmed when the nurse arrived with two cups of sugar free Jell-O, each with the "NOW ONLY 10 CALORIES" label wrapped around the plastic like a pageant queen wearing her sash. Food didn't have calories in heaven. Everyone knew that. It was the first thing Brian would always remind me of when I felt like quitting and exchanging that piece of spinach for a Hostess treat. "There are Twinkies at the end of the tunnel," he had said. Coming so close to death like this, I made a mental reminder to ask about what was on the menu in the downstairs department. Just in case.

"How are you feeling honey? I was hoping you'd perk up after I put the IV in," the nurse asked. I hadn't even seen her coming over. I started to say I felt ready to leave, but when the woman with the clipboard appeared at my side, I was thrown off guard. Her dark caramel skin shined like bronze beneath the hospital lights. Her light blue scrubs clung to her body like saran wrap, and I couldn't help but stare at her backside when the woman turned. For the first time in my life, I wished my own body could fill out clothes like that.

I didn't notice Brian coming before he arrived at my bedside. He always seemed to catch me off guard, when my life was seeming just a little too easy. Or not hard enough. And now that I took a moment to think about it, I noticed my body had been feeling much better recently. My tongue, usually coated in a white-ish film that somehow managed to dry my mouth out more, now felt soft and moist against the roof of my mouth. My legs actually felt like a part of my body, not like wooden attachments on a puppet. Brian would pull the strings when I ran.

Admittedly, there were sometimes when Brian made my life a little less difficult. But today was not one of those days.

"Pull the IV out of your arm."

"No." I said, surprised by my firm tone.

"What makes you think you can just get away with disobeying me all of a sudden? Is it this hospital? Because I hope you remember how convincing I can be."

I hadn't forgotten.

"Take it out now," he seemed to be pleading rather than demanding. It had never occurred to me, that Brian too, didn't always know the right thing to do. I wondered why he didn't just rip the IV out himself. He was close enough now. But he wanted me to do it. He wanted me to do it, and I wasn't going to. Because maybe, after all this time, it was him who was nothing without me.

He left the hospital before I could tell him it was over. But he wouldn't have left if he hadn't figured it out himself.

Chapter 35

UNCONSCIOUS

As soon as I got home, I started packing up my bedroom and moved my things to the basement guestroom. I didn't think about doing it before I did it, it just felt right. There were too many reminders of Brian up in my old bedroom, too many triggers. I didn't want to see that bathroom mirror. The girl in that mirror belonged to my old room, to Brian. The girl in that mirror wasn't Liz anymore. I needed a fresh start.

When Mom drove me home from the hospital, the car was silent. No podcasts this time, just white knuckles on the wheel. We stopped at Target on the way for some "retail therapy," and got me new comfy bedding for the guestroom to make it feel more homey.

"Guestroom" is a euphemism; it was a partially finished basement which meant it had thin gray carpet covering a concrete floor in an open space area that contained a Queen bed, white wooden nightstand, and mahogany dresser—all mismatched pieces from my parents' bachelor days. The cinderblock walls were painted a pale yellow and were cold to the touch. I repurposed a storage closet for all my clothes on hangers, shoving the original contents into an unfinished storage room where I was sure a family of mice lived. My mom had tried to brighten the room up with some colorful floral curtains, but there was no mistaking the room for what it was: a damp, draughty, dark cellar.

The "nicest" part of the basement was the bathroom. When my parents first bought the house, they put a laundry room on the second floor, converting the original basement laundry room into a large bathroom, twice the size of my old bathroom upstairs.

I kind of loved the basement, it reminded me of a little cave all to myself. Even with all the lights on, the room was still dark. I had to stand in the doorway for a couple of minutes until my eyes could adjust to it. I crawled into the queen bed filled with my new grey and pink throw pillows and fuzzy, cheap white blankets. The pink duvet was lumpy inside its cover as I didn't have the energy to fix it. Every once in a while, while curled up, a giant blob of stuffing would fall on my face. On the flip side, it made for good cuddling potential. The duvet blob hugged me, and I let myself fall into the mattress. I pulled the covers over my head and stared up at the ceiling through a small hole in the sheet. It was a perfect cocoon.

I could hear Mom's voice above me, talking on the phone with someone, and the noise in the kitchen, but with just enough concealment I couldn't make out a word she was saying.

I wished I had these covers when I'd been with Brian. Hearing his voice all day could really take the spirit out of me. I didn't miss him at all, I swear I really didn't. It's just that he'd been a part of my life for so long it's hard to believe he wasn't going to be in it anymore. But things with him had gotten too noisy, he was too overbearing. Brian was the sort of guy who never knew when to pick his battles because he just wanted to fight all of them. "I'm fighting for you," he would always say, and yet I'd be the one ending up with the bruises. It didn't matter that he'd make it up to me later with praise and band-aids. Scars are scars. I am better off without him. I am better off without him. I'd made the right decision in ending our relationship. The right one. I said it over-and-over again until I could believe it: it was a trick I'd learned from him. Only it's kind of hard to believe it when you're lying in bed next to a moldy box of pizza for company.

I'd be lying if I didn't admit I felt a little lost without him. Imagine all your life you have this guy making you feel like you're on this special little island of love and perfection where nothing can go wrong, and then all of a sudden, he leaves, and you realize that island is just a crappy raft, and you're actually stuck in the middle of the ocean. It was sort of like that. He had been right when he said I'd like the world a lot better when it was only big enough for the two of us. But I had to go off and chase my Flynn Rider of freedom.

"Liz, we need to talk."

For a second, I'd forgotten my mother was on my bed. I sat up beside her, keeping my eyes on my lap.

"Liz, I'm so sorry baby." She was crying now; I could hear it in her voice. I pictured that collage of freckles on her face, all getting washed away. I hoped they wouldn't stain the new duvet.

"I should have seen the signs. I should have realized things had gone too far. I can... I can see now the pain this has caused you." She was looking at my legs, probably the bruises, possibly their thinness.

"It's fine, really." I clenched my jaw; I wanted to be anywhere but here.

"Look at me Liz, please." I felt her hand take mine. I looked up.

"Oh, Liz." Her voice sounded like it was ready to pack up and leave her throat, the way her words seemed to cause her physical pain. I guess she saw me crumble before I even knew it was coming. My cheeks get hot from warm tears racing down them and that's when it hit: I was sad. No amount of puppeteering or "dissociating" could stop that from being the truth. And in that moment, I let myself show it. I didn't exactly have a choice, even ice queens melt watching their mother look at them like that. Like they wish they could save themselves and look away.

"Mom." The word felt foreign in my mouth. "I don't think

I'm okay anymore." I barely finished the sentence before she grabbed me into a hug. My snot clung to her faux cashmere and her fingers grabbed my back. We didn't move; we couldn't afford to break the tension that compressed us, so we weren't trembling anymore. This is what safety feels like. Not weighing your food so you stay skinny. Not forcing yourself to write essays so you can get straight As. Safety is embracing sadness and realizing you're still okay. I guess I hadn't allowed myself to feel it, I'd been too preoccupied with Brian.

"I think I just need to listen."

"What?" I lifted my face from her soggy shoulder, leaving behind a trail of snot on her sweater.

"God, there were so many times, Liz, where you were trying to tell me something, that something wasn't right, and I just blew you off." Her shoulders started to shake, like just saying it out loud made her all the more guilty. "And, and I just played those stupid podcasts at you and threw you into those therapists' offices and hoped you'd come out fixed. When all you really needed was for someone to be there for you, to believe you."

She wasn't wrong. I had tried to explain to her why I wore a leather jacket to Christmas or why I had to check the oven "just to be sure." Her response had always been, "Why are you being so difficult?" or "then just don't listen," when I'd tell her what Brian wanted me to do. I'd tried once to say I needed to go on a run because it was Sunday and the dice told me so and otherwise Brian would make me feel guiltier than if I'd committed murder, and she had looked at me like I was crazy; after that I just told her the weather was perfect for a run instead.

I knew this was the time to tell her it wasn't her fault, that there was nothing she could have done to stop this. But I'd been keeping it all inside of me for so long, if I didn't start talking, I was sure to start crying.

"I'm lost, Mom." I couldn't look her in the face, though it was more of a collection of wet eyes and droopy wrinkle lines at this point. I told her how Brian had become my whole world, and she nodded like she understood but I knew she couldn't really understand. "And that world just kept getting smaller and smaller, closing in on me with those walls decorated with to-do lists and time-stamped routines and orders." The best analogy was to describe it like the trash compactor Luke and Princess Leia get trapped in in the original Star Wars movie. That made her smile at least—a sad smile.

I expected her to ask why I hadn't left. Why I came back to him again and again. Maybe she would have if her eyes weren't pouring out as many tears as they were. You wouldn't want to inhale all that water.

"I tried to resist, you know, establish some boundaries. He said I was being lazy, Mom, that he was the only one who was looking out for my potential. He made me feel so special sometimes, like I was better than all these other people who laughed and ate ice cream and loved themselves." I stopped so I could catch my breath, my chin was quivering as it always did when I was about to start crying again. She was silent.

"And do you know what the worst part is?"

"What?" She asked so quietly I could barely hear it. I could tell it pained her to listen to me hurting even if she didn't understand what I was trying to tell her. I knew if it was Dad in her place, he'd buy me a new house before he dared step inside his sad, sobby one.

"I don't even know who I am anymore." The words came out before I'd strung them together in my head.

"Oh, Lizzy. This, this, this ... asshole, doesn't define you, honey." She was looking right into my eyes this time.

"I mean, all this time it's like he's been slowly turning me into his little robot. Do I actually care about being honest and confessing my mistakes? Am I a hard worker or am I just scared of him hurting me?" Saying it out loud made it so much more real. So much sadder.

"Liz, even if you're a little lost right now, I know you. I know my daughter, and you are all those things. All on your own. Trust me."

I wanted to.

"You and I, Liz, we're gonna get that girl back." She was pointing at the mirror now, trying to convince me she recognized her daughter in the frame. It's interesting what parents could make themselves believe the "real you" is.

"Do you like your hair that short?"

My mouth moved to say yes. Because you are supposed to say "yes" to be agreeable. And Brian had said a pixie cut would reduce wind resistance when I ran.

"I look like a lesbian."

I heard her laugh, saying, "Well, that wouldn't be the worst thing in the world." I hadn't realized I'd said my comment out loud. All these years I'd been talking in my head, but Brian had said to keep it there.

"Hey, hey, Liz, calm down. It's gonna be okay, you made the break, you're over this now. Nothing's gonna happen."

Famous last words, I thought to myself.

"We're going to get through this." Her voice finally found some solid ground. Her hand was still wrapped around my fist, gripping it like her steering wheel. I released my fingers, and I watched as the pale red replaced the whites of her knuckles. It was kind of satisfying. Not in the same way that finishing a seven-mile run in the heat was, but it got the job done, and minus all the sweat. She was right, things would be all right, even if they didn't feel "just right" just yet.

⌁

I had to make a few things right before anything could feel right. First on my list was apologizing to Mary. I called her number and Mom placed her hand on my knee as I held my breath. She answered on the fourth ring and I just started talking.

"Listen Mary, I know I've been flakey, and I feel really bad about missing your birthday and all. But it wasn't part of the plan or anything, I mean I had every intention of being there."

Mary was silent on the other end of the line. I knew none of it made sense, but I tried anyway to explain how Brian made me go on a run, and next thing I knew he had me searching around the house for old gum and then the rug has a million tassels; it sounded even crazier saying it all out loud. Couldn't she understand that he would've been so mad at me, and he would have never let it go, you make one mistake with him, and he holds it over your head for weeks. I told her things would be different now that we'd split. I'd never choose Brian over my friends again.

"But you were my best friend, Liz. Shouldn't that count for something?"

"I know, but that's what I'm trying to tell you. I was at my house trying to find a gift for you and I was just so worried about everything being perfect..." I could tell I was losing her; justifying Brian's orders used to come more easily to me.

"What I needed Liz, was you. I mean this wasn't like the time I asked you to help me with my bio homework and you flaked, or the time you showed up at the closing bow of my play and I had to pretend I didn't notice for Lucy's sake. This was like a big moment for me, the first time my parents ever threw a party just for me, and all my friends were supposed to be there. Then you don't show up and Lucy arrives in a panic over an hour late, what the hell? I know you have issues, and I'm glad you're not going to listen to that brainwasher anymore, but I think it would just be too hard for me to have you around. I know it wasn't personal, maybe, if that's what you're trying to say, but it still happened. I, uh, don't think I'm ready to just invite you back into my life. I mean first you, then Daniel, I just don't think I can take being let down like that again."

I didn't bother asking who Daniel was, it would only show how shitty of a friend I was. "Oh, okay" was all I could mutter. In other words, Mary was breaking up with me. It's not you, it's me, but it's actually always gonna be you and you should've known that before you got into all of this.

"I really care about you Liz, I just..."

"No, I get it. And I'm sorry."

"Thanks Liz. I'm proud of you, for doing this, you didn't deserve any of this." But didn't she just explain how much of a shitty person I was?

"Goodbye Liz."

"Goodbye Mary." Our call ended. And that's when the conversation really hit me, that I'd never be getting my friend back. So much for embracing my weirdness; apparently, I was just too screwed up for Mary. Strike two for me.

I guess the whole time I was with Brian, after Mary and I stopped hanging out, some part of me never thought I had really lost her, or Lucy for that matter. Like once I explained to her that I was actually doing everything that day for her, it would somehow make up for everything I'd done, and it'd all be okay again. But that wasn't how it worked, I could see that now.

I looked across at my mother, who was looking at the floor, playing with her hands. I couldn't help but wonder if she wasn't my mother, would she still be here? After all the times I pushed her away for the sake of pleasing Brian. I couldn't just be this heartless monster and then break up with my boyfriend and expect everyone to take me back with open arms. I didn't forgive my dad when he tried that act on me, so I don't know why I expected a different response. You may be a victim, but that doesn't mean you're innocent. It can't exempt you from the hurt you caused. We are all victims. And as much as Brian did to try to bury the feeling and outrun it, we were all guilty on some level.

"She'll come around; she just needs some time."

I looked up at my mom, this time seeing some hope behind her eyes.

"She just needs to be away from you for a while. She's still hurting."

"I know."

"It's for the best honey. You know what I always say: hurt people hurt people."

I nodded, even though she seemed to think she came up with that phrase herself. I wondered who ever rammed their knuckles into Brian's head. They must've gotten to him good.

Chapter 36

NOTHINGNESS

What they don't tell you about leaving a toxic relationship is that it's not just an emotional feeling. Your body's gotten accustomed to that person being there too. It's like you start going through withdrawal. Pain imprints harder on the body than love, or at least I think someone told me that once. It was like all of a sudden, the only thing I felt was sadness, making up for all those years of feeling nothing at all.

I couldn't go back to school. I knew I'd see Brian there and I was avoiding him. Mom told the school I was recovering from "a hospitalization," a vague but true excuse that bought me some time. By April, I'd been home a month and Mom and I barely spoke, even after that big heart to heart when I got back from the hospital. She spent her time mostly out of the house, because she couldn't stand being in a house with so much silence, so much stifling stillness. I spent all my time in my basement room, only coming upstairs for another helping of ice cream from the freezer, or to retrieve the newspaper from the deck. Mom said she refused to clean up my messes anymore, and the mess was always building. My Domino's stack was still going strong: the Leaning Tower of Pizza.

Eventually, Mom said she couldn't keep lying to the school

and I had to go back. I wasn't sure how to do school without Brian. Last time I tried, in September, I got a D on my English paper and couldn't finish any homework. I knew going back without him now, with AP exams around the corner, that things would be even worse than September. But I had no idea about the storm that awaited.

I'd had a few "tornado moments" before, and Lucy had her fair share of downpours, but April 10th, my third day back at school after five weeks at home, was the kind of storm the Doctors-who-make-you-feel-better don't sugarcoat: panic attack, is what I later learned to name them. Art History had so far been a pretty chill class. Besides the whole me hating art and history, the elective course had at times been interesting, especially if our homework was to read a picture book. I didn't like reading normal books. It didn't happen all the time, but sometimes when I read, the words looked like gibberish so I would have to go back and read them again. And again. And again. Starting at the beginning each time. Or I'd read the whole chapter and then not be able to tell you a single thing that happened because I just read the words. So as boring as Frankenhaler and Vasari were, they beat a textbook any day of the week. Except today.

"With the gallery packet I am handing out today, I request that all of you take Post-it notes and write comments on each of the paintings for next class." Easy enough. And it would've been if it wasn't for goddam Caroline Shillings. That girl was the queen of stupid; pointless questions and it drove me crazy. Every test she'd ask if, "it's okay that I wrote out the full date right, not just with the slashes?" Or "would you rather us write King Louis the 14th or King Louis 14 in Roman numerals?" There were kids in that class who wrote Van Gogh as "Vango" and still got full credit. The class was chill. That Caroline girl, not so much. So, I guess I should have seen it coming when she raised that shaky hand of hers and asked, "Um, this might be a stupid question," (that would normally be when the teacher said, "no such thing" if it had been any other kid) "but what color Post-its should we use?"

The old man let out one of his loud sighs and told the class "Just pick your favorite color."

Fuck me.

Lucy was in Art History with me; it was our only class together. She invited me over, promising we could work on homework together. It's sad that she still felt she needed to bribe me with homework; she didn't realize that now that I wasn't with Brian, I didn't care about my GPA anymore. I'd already been accepted by my dream college. But I was happy to spend time with her. Since breaking up with Brian, I tried to spend as much time distracting myself with friends, TV, or my phone. And Lucy was kind of my only friend left. Plus, she said she had a ton of Post-it notes at home, and after my last incident with the "stolen" Post-its, I was happy to use her supply.

I got to Lucy's house first; she had Bible study after school. Her family always kept the back door unlocked (another thing Brian couldn't comprehend about Lucy) so I let myself in and went up to Lucy's room. She had one of those catalog bedrooms, where the bed was always made and the floor always shining. I dropped my backpack on the floor and walked over to her desk. There it was: the motherload of Post-it notes, her mom must have bought out the whole shelf at Target. I stared down at the rainbow array of Post-its in front of me. Their crisp edges and smooth faces sneered at me. Some of them were the same color, just a different shade. There had to be at least thirteen options. Give me two and I couldn't tell you which I liked better. I mean how do you really know? Back in preschool I tried asking Doctor-who-makes-you-feel-better once, and she just told me to listen to my gut. I asked her what language it spoke?

There are colors and foods and books and people you like more than others, and then there is your "favorite." The thing that trumps everything else on your imaginary scale that somehow measures quality, taste, aesthetic, memory, connection, and happiness all at once. And then of course your gut would put its two cents in. What currency? I'll never know.

Brian would've had a method for choosing a color, there was no doubt about it. But I wasn't doing things the "Brian Way" anymore. Or at least I was trying not to, but this would be difficult. Give me any calculus question and I'll answer it for you. Give me a trivia question and I'll tell you that it was Gary Gilmore, a murderer on death row in the 1970s who was the first to coin the term "just do it!" But ask me if I prefer Nike or Adidas, and now I'm on the chopping block. The thing about choices was that the smaller and less important they seemed, the more they were bound to come back and haunt you. The world goes around with causes and effects, everything happens for a reason—unless you're thinking like Lucy, 'cause then no, I do not think God is that reason. It wasn't your grandma's "time to go," it was her being determined to buy those Nike slides you said you liked six years ago but she only remembered it now, as her little gray head could barely see that semi-truck above that steering wheel.

"It's not that deep" my ass. Just ask the butterfly who created that tornado?"

My hands were shaking now, hovering over the laid-out Post-its hoping that if my gut couldn't speak English, it could at least direct my body to the right stack. "If you're with us tonight, show us a sign." Only my dog wasn't here to knock over a candle in my room and send Lucy running back to her pastor daddy. I wanted to scream. I wanted to fucking curse out whatever God or universal power had cursed me with a defective gut. I wanted to scream at my mom for believing the pediatrician when they said "she'll grow out of it" when I put the "Would you Rather" cards in the fireplace. Balls of sweat were forming on my forehead. I wanted to know what kind of twisted measuring system had been created, where the color of a frick-ing Post-it note felt like the weight of the world on my back. My heartrate rose some more. I wanted to know why it had to all be on my back? 'Cause I was ready to drop it now. Let down that world that always let me down. And that's what I did.

I ripped up every single one of those Post-its, after I had

broken apart some of the stacks first of course. I wasn't Superman. I noticed more sticky notes on her bedroom wall, more pastel and neon pieces of paper screaming at me for being so messed up. I tore those to shreds too. The room was covered in rainbow confetti in no time. I sat down in the middle of the pile, some of the pieces with the adhesive side sticking to my butt. I grabbed a handful and threw it in the air, letting it fall like candy erupting from a piñata. Happy birthday to me. Just don't ask what I'm wishing for.

When Lucy came in and saw me sitting in my pitiful pile of Post-its, she didn't say anything. She just bent down and started picking up the pieces of paper and putting them into her wastepaper basket. I didn't even help, I just sat there, still stunned by my own bizarre behavior. Still being the same little brat that let the other kid clean up her messes.

It turns out you can't just go back to living your normal life once you've spent a day making snow angels in a pile of Post-it note pieces. Or in Lucy's case, the same thing goes if your "friend" of two months decides to ghost you the week before Prom.

"I just don't get it. I thought things were going well. This probably sounds stupid but I kind of thought he might ask me to Prom. That would be our chance to really take our relationship to the next level. But I guess he's going with someone else."

"Hey, Lucy, you didn't do anything wrong. You just can never trust those guys; they can switch up so fast."

"But he was different, Liz. Like he actually cared about me. And I cared about him. And now he's probably not gonna even show up to the dance and summer will start and he never even fucking said goodbye Liz."

"That's fucked up. I know how much you were looking forward to it."

She was crying now, doing her soft little sniffles I used to hear once a week in elementary school. We weren't the hugging type, but we held each other close that night. And the night after that. We didn't go to class, cuz fuck school. Crazy what a pack of backpacks and Post-its can do to a person.

The final day to register for the prom was Friday. Lucy waited by her door all day because she "didn't even care if he was gonna stop by or not." He didn't. We got ice cream from the DQ in town. Lucy's pick of flavor of course and ate it right on her floor.

∿

Lucy found the Post-its in the trash two weeks after our drown-your-feelings-in-ice-cream night. I had come over to hang out instead of doing homework; of course, I had already dropped out of Art History anyway. She didn't say anything at first, just sat on the floor looking at me with those hurt puppy eyes. She looked the same way the day she had to put her dog down because he bit one too many ankles. Or at least how she looked on FaceTime (I couldn't be there because it'd been exam week. And besides, her dog had never liked me.)

That's when I saw what the Post-it pieces were: each of them was orange, scruffy bits of paper, but when you put the seven of them together you could see their message. The chicken scratch writing spelled out in black ink read: "Stick with me at Prom?" Surprisingly, even though the notes were ripped to pieces, each word was intact, except for the heart at the end, which was split in two. I would've called that a half-assed proposal if I hadn't remembered that leaving notes at each other's houses had been their cute little messaging system since the first time he left his number stuck to her window.

I could tell Lucy was crushed. At the time she had said that she still had fun, going to the dance with me as a placeholder, even though my dress completely clashed with hers. As lame as she always claimed those school functions to be and the people like Queen Aubrey who actually cared about them, I think she secretly liked getting all made up. I think she probably felt stupid putting lipstick on for me. I was no Ashton. And as much as she could say she'd rather die than be Aubrey, Lucy could never be Aubrey.

What should have scared me the most was the fact that Lucy had stopped crying. Even her flushed cheeks weren't the kind of red I was used to. I should've picked up on those signs.

"How could you?" Lucy's eyes were staring into mine now, daring me to look away.

I didn't answer. We normally didn't have confrontations like this; the silent treatment morphing into ignoring the issue, then moving on had always been our MO.

"You just couldn't stand me having something you didn't, could you?" That's when I realized she thought I had done it on purpose. Ripped up the note inviting her into her dream night just so she wouldn't leave me eating ice cream alone on the floor. My heart sank.

Part of me wanted to remind her we had fun at Prom, us two against the judging world of tight skirts and tipsy guys behind our pointing fingers and hand-covered whispers. We figured out the snack table was pretty much abandoned once the punch bowl came out, so all the bored fundraiser moms were dishing out their "famous" Tollhouse cookies and Rice-Krispy prom crowns to anyone who had ears to listen and a mouth to eat. And then we hid in the bathroom during the ceremony. Ashton had been named king, but he was nowhere to be seen. Lucy's head had been on a swivel all night for him. Even if they had gone together to the dance though, she probably wouldn't want to dance with him after his nomination. That's what I could never understand about her. If a guy half as hot as Ashton even looked in my direction, I'd steal the CCTV footage and make it my profile picture. I'm not sure Lucy even told anyone besides me she was talking to him. And she barely told me. She deserved for everyone to know and be jealous of her and hate her the way we hated everyone.

"You don't even have an excuse, do you? I mean, honestly, at this point I should have expected this."

I wanted to tell her it wasn't like that, that I had ripped up all the Post-its because my gut was apparently mute. Every time she asked me what I wanted to do? I felt like my body was covered in fire ants. That I actually didn't like Taco Bell's beef burritos but my eenie-meeny-miny-moe's seemed to have some fan favorites on that drive-thru menu. But I couldn't tell her all this. It was like at the end of the movie, Tom Ripley style, where you're screaming at the guy to just tell the fucking truth and stop burying himself deeper. But that's what Lucy and I did. We buried shit. We buried her dead ankle-snapping dog in the back of her old yard and now we were burying our friendship. I tried to ring the bell in the coffin.

"Okay, but just the other day you told me Ashton wasn't even that great. Remember that toe cheese conversation you guys had? I mean…"

"It's not about him, Liz! It's not like we were even dating!" I hung my head.

"I know."

"All my life I've been telling myself that good things will come for me, that all this praying and confessing and hymning is gonna pay off some day. That God is listening to my honest words and not the fat check your dad left you and your mom when he ran off. That one day I'm gonna be rewarded for all the shitty times I had to watch you get a new phone when my family could barely afford to share one. Watch you get 'A's on all your tests even though you never even had to study while I'm sitting here cramming my brains out for a lousy B-. And then that time finally comes, and I start getting closer to the guy of my dreams who I've had a crush on since Freshman year, who actually likes me for who I am, who doesn't want to rush things because he gets along with God too. And now everything is ruined. You just couldn't stand that could you? You needed to have everything, you needed me to sit on the floor with you and confirm that no, there wasn't any ocean water in your throat. Did you know dry drowning isn't even a real thing? I looked it up. And then I had to pretend to care about your daddy not loving you and all your embarrassing quirks like dressing like a fucking homeless person. Well, you know what Liz? It's a pretty damn hard thing to do! And I've tried, Liz, for 15 fucking years I tried to understand where you were coming from, that you know, 'oh maybe she was just kidding when she asked who Ashton was?' That you respect my religious views on the inside but it's hard to express yourself. You dared judged my religion, when meanwhile you were following your little cult leader pretty religiously. I've had it. I'm done trying."

I was staring into a dark corner now, because that way it felt like my eyes were closed. Losing Mary was one thing, our friendship had barely started before it ended, but Lucy—Lucy couldn't be done with me too. I didn't know when it started, but my body was shaking now. The kind of pulsating vibrations you get when you're all mad and you think your veins are gonna pop. Except I wasn't mad. Or maybe I was, at myself, at Lucy's crappy friend in the sky, or whoever said that 15 years of friendship won't just dissipate in a day. Turns out they can.

Chapter 37

GOD, ARE YOU LISTENING?

Present Day

I scrolled further down on the feed as if there was anything that could make me smile the way Lucy made me. Reels of trending workouts and food vlogs took over the stream and I scrolled faster. Every once in a while, I'd see a funny video of a toddler tripping on something or a dog playing the piano. I tried to smile at them, I had even started to laugh at one, but you feel kind of stupid laughing alone. I used to tell jokes all the time just to hear Lucy's laugh.

Although it was actually kind of silent, her little cackle, which is what made it so funny. I'd say something witty and then she'd just roll over and start hacking up a fur-ball trying to catch her breath, while I would just keep piling on more zingers. I don't think there's a better feeling in the world than that. And Lucy seemed to like it too. I'd sent Lucy a long, rambling, possibly incoherent apology text after our falling out, but she never replied.

Her words back in April still played over and over in my head, four months later. "You did this on purpose." I was starting to wonder if I did. Had I read it and then spontaneously decided to turn my best friend's life upside down into a pile of confetti? The things she had said, the reasons she told me I did it, weren't untrue. It felt terrible being the one all alone, especially because being single never felt embarrassing when you had another single bestie around your arm. If Lucy, this incredible, secure, stubborn girl could be single and unbothered, then how terrible could it really be? It turns out, way more terrible than you would have imagined once she leaves you in the dust for some backpack-wearing hot shot. Now being single isn't cute or as Lucy said, "a statement" anymore; now it was just plain pathetic.

I recalled how Lucy had acted, once she told me what I'd done. Like I made her sick to look at, like all my weird quirks she had no problem ignoring in the past now seemed like "irreconcilable differences." That's what my parent's divorce settlement claimed. We lived like two strangers. Lucy went back to class; I stayed in bed. For the rest of the year, I never set foot in Washington High again. Word got out that I'd sabotaged Lucy's proposal; I never got confirmation, but I suspect Mary was the source as Lucy is way too private a person for gossip and the only person I could imagine her telling was Mary. But it didn't matter who spread it, it was out there and even Mom heard about it from a friend. I just couldn't show my face in school; I couldn't even bear to look at Mom.

I'd already missed five weeks following my hospital visit, so missing the final five weeks of school got me an "incomplete" on my transcript which meant I couldn't graduate. Duke rescinded their offer, and I didn't try to appeal as I could barely make it to the front door, let alone move across the country. Maybe a part of me wanted to prove to Lucy that my life wasn't as great as she thought it was, that privilege can only launch you so far before you fuck up so bad, bury yourself so deep, people can't even see the color of your skin because you're so covered in mud. Credit cards look like plastic garbage from far away. Of course, now my "Daddy" had proved her right, he'd "made a few calls" and gotten me into Franklin College without my even asking. I couldn't escape my privilege even if I tried.

I scrolled down to the next clip, but I should've just put my phone down. Soon enough I found myself engulfed in the blazing forest fires taking over Tucson. Trees swayed in the wind like they were rag dolls ready to give up trying to stop their stitches from tearing. The red-hot spools of fire took up most of the image in one big spewing blob of ash and debris threatening to block out the sun in the sky. Even with my phone on the lowest volume you could still hear screaming. Shrieking and crying and the silence that was plain disbelief. I stared at the video. I watched it again. I was supposed to be concerned by what I saw, or at least thinking about people who lived there: some of my family even. My stepsister in Arizona had asthma, surely the smoke couldn't be good for her. But my body gave me nothing. Completely and utterly nothing. Everyone always says that tears "relieve the body of what it can't express out loud," but my eyes were just as barren as the rest of me. It was like I was hovering outside my own body, looking in: trapped inside like a puppet who had lost its goddamn strings. That, or I was just a really, really shitty person.

Suddenly I got the urge to clear my throat. I could feel Brian's words trying to take over again, and instead I took a deep breath. The butterflies still flapped but I didn't clear my throat. Maybe the water would drown them. Liz, you're not a bad person I told myself. I said it again and again because it turns out people weren't lying when they say you start to believe what's repeated to you. I'm a funny person. I'm smart. I do care about my friends. I do want to go to college. I'm my own person.

I smiled, and I guess deep down I knew I wasn't completely gone. All the times I'd crack jokes to myself or silently correct Lucy's grammar when I was supposed to be listening to Brian, that was me. Brian may have been an actor, but he was no damn comedian.

I glanced around the cluttered bathroom and searched for the brush I had stopped using many months before. I eventually found it next to my pink makeup bag, filled with expired foundation, dried-up mascara, and unopened wipes. I picked up the wooden handle and placed it at the top of my roots, and then to the tips of my hair, as I remembered Mom said it would hurt less starting there.

She was wrong. I was barely able to move the bristles an inch before they were entangled by the jungle of knots that had seized my scalp, and I lowered my wrist in defeat. Thankfully, I remembered there had been a hair detangler spray in the cabinet. The spray made the brush work more smoothly, though each stroke felt like my hair was ripping out. After working from top to bottom and bottom to top across most of my scalp, I gave it a rest and looked again at the girl in the mirror, only this time I looked a little more familiar. Baby steps, I told myself. I could practically hear Brian's voice in my ear telling me to do it differently, but instead of listening to him, I laughed at him and continued.

Going upstairs for breakfast, I tried my best to evade Mom's pressing figure, but she approached me as I went into the kitchen. Immediately, I wished I'd been wearing my hoodie, I didn't exactly know why, but I didn't want my mother seeing my hair.

"Liz, do I see some freshly brushed hair?" Mom started, reaching out to feel the silky hair that had once been tough with knots. Too late.

"Um yeah, I brushed it." I said, gently removing Mom's hand from my hair.

"Why?"

I couldn't help myself from smiling. I mean it was funny,

wasn't it? That my mother would be asking an 18-year-old why she brushed her hair? But then again, why had I?

"I, I'm going to take the spot at Franklin." I blurted out without thinking about what I was committing to.

As soon as those words left my lips, a smile formed on Mom's. Her eyes beamed down at me and I hated that she felt she had made this happen, but I admitted to myself, it was nice to see her happy again.

I'd never actually considered the idea of moving out, I had thought about it, and told my parents I would do it, but I never really pictured it happening. Besides, I had lived in that house my whole life. Those walls had held me together while they squeezed Dad out and outstretched a hand to Lucy, through the second-floor window with a brick ledge beneath it that she'd use as a step stool.

"Wow, Liz, I'm so happy! This is going to be so good for us, for you!"

I nodded as she went on to tell me about how amazing the school would be for me and how much purpose it would give me which I knew Mom thought I needed. I just kept nodding along, as the anxiety I thought I could bury under my covers began to rise, and my heart took flight. Next thing I know she's telling me she's found a new therapist. I swear she's gone through these people faster than Emily Gilmore has her maids.

I hadn't seen Mom this happy since Brian, and I had compulsively cleaned and scrubbed down every corner of the house eight years ago because he thought he saw a "cancer bug." There were times I felt like she liked Brian more than me.

Brinnnng! Brinnnng! Mom's phone went off like a smoke alarm. I never understood why old people kept their volume so high up, I mean it was only bound to startle them.

Brinnnng! Brinnnng!

"Well, are you gonna pick it up or just let it yell at us till its voice gets hoarse?"

"Oh, right yeah. I just didn't want to ruin, you know, the moment," Mom said sheepishly.

"Moment's past."

"I see."

She reached across to the kitchen table where her little iPhone 8 was rattling itself silly, but she paused when she saw the caller.

"Who is it?" I asked suspiciously.

"Um...it's Lucy."

"What?! Why is she calling you, maybe she has the wrong number? Wait, how do you even have her contact?" The phone must have read the room because it finally quit the buzzing.

"Well, she and I talk sometimes."

I didn't know what to say. I felt like I was back in elementary when Mom and her friend plotted on me and her own son becoming "more than friends" on our playdates. I still remembered how it stung when Robert told me "I don't really like you this yea'w, maybe next yea'w." Turns out, Mom had told her friend, who told her son, that I had a thing for the guy. How humiliating, the whole class still thought his name was Wilbert.

"Ok, am I missing something here? Since when? Lucy and I haven't even spoken to each other since April."

"Well, that's when she started calling me."

"Okay, well why did she start calling you, I mean did she need to return something of mine?"

"She was worried about you when you didn't go back to school, so she started calling to check in on you. To make sure you were okay. But sometimes we'd start reminiscing, and she'd tell me about all the fun memories she had with you, and I mean, I loved listening to them because, at that time, you weren't really talking to me either. We both had lost you."

I nodded my head, trying to ignore the guilt that was bubbling up from my stomach.

"You know, she actually told me about this abusive relationship you were in before you did. How you slowly grew more distant from her the more time you spent with that bully. I should've told you my feelings about it from the start, but I was so scared I'd push too hard and end up losing you entirely."

I didn't know what to make of any of this. I wanted to be angry at both of them—for knowing Brian was abusive but leaving me alone with him anyway, for having secret conversations about me all summer—but I was too angry at myself for hurting them more than they'd hurt me. I slunk back down to the basement and buried myself under my covers.

⁓

The day before I was set to leave for Franklin, I was packing up my things in a daze. It didn't feel real. None of this was happening the way I'd planned it for the last 14 years of my life. I was so stuck in my own head about it all I almost didn't hear the doorbell ring. I almost didn't recognize the girl on my doorstep.

Summer looked good on Lucy, with her lightened hair and tan legs and a smile you just couldn't help but return. Except I couldn't tell her everything I needed to with a smile. And I knew we didn't talk about these sorts of things but there are some things you just have to say to your best friend. You can't risk them not knowing it.

"I'm sorry, Lucy." She started to reach her hand out, but I kept going. "We don't have to ignore it anymore," I said. "This shit I've been pulling. You deserve better. I mean, all those times where I just left you waiting at the mall, not coming to your play, ruining your prom, I just felt like…" I could feel the tears coming. "I just felt like I could get all the time back, you know, that when I was with Brian the clock kind of froze. I guess because he sucks all the life out of the room. And I thought I was not missing out on it…life. But I was. And you were the one who was always there for me, and I guess I took you for granted, I thought you'd always be there, and I guess that's why I treated you so badly. There's no excuse for that. I'm so sorry."

I looked at the silver cross she always wore around her neck. "I'm so, so sorry," I repeated.

Lucy didn't say anything, just came up onto the top step and hugged me. We hugged for so long it felt like we were making up for all those times where we'd turn the other way in the hall, where she'd leave my calls ringing, where I'd prioritized Brian over her, we were getting all of it back. And I guess we never really lost each other like I thought we had; after all, she'd been checking in on me all summer with Mom, making sure I was okay while giving me time and space to recover. Time stood still but now life was coming back to me. When we finally released each other, my face was dry, and the sun was soaking up all the tears on Lucy's shoulder.

"Hey, Liz,"

That was the first thing she'd said this whole time. We never needed a lot of words. I held my breath.

"It's the last day of summer. Do you want to go swimming?"

Chapter 38

LOW TIDE

The first thing I noticed was she didn't have a clipboard, not even a pen in sight. I hoped this lady had some sort of photographic memory, because there was a whole catalog of things that needed to be added to my "things that make my mind unique" sheet. Those surveys were made by the Harvard kids with a fetish for all shades of loser. They were probably just jealous I got to check off 10+ hours of sleep. And at least compared to the last one, this Dr-who-makes-you-feel-better was slightly less anorexic looking, so yeah, I guess I felt a bit better. But still, this whole idea of Mom dropping one therapist after a week and recruiting a new one was bonkers. I mean, you keep losing jobs and blaming the boss like that and people start to turn their heads at the common denominator. But hey, if she thought these prissy fake doctors were the ones not trying hard enough to fix me up again, go ahead. They weren't even legally allowed to tell her if I genuinely confessed my worries to them or flipped my middle finger and ate Cheetos the whole time, only one of those being a true story.

"My name's Linda." Not a doctor.

"I'm Liz."

"Nice to meet you! I'd love it if we could just talk today, Liz.

No interrogations, just some getting to know each other. Do you have any questions for me?"

I let my silence answer.

"It's nothing to be embarrassed of Liz. I've got it too."

I raised an eyebrow. I hadn't really looked at what she was wearing until now. She was kind of a hippy. Doc Martens, hair clips, and a beanie. But who was I to judge someone by their attire?

"What exactly do you have?" I asked.

"It's called obsessive compulsive disorder."

All I heard was the obsessive part and I started to scoot back into my seat. She had a blanket around her chair, and it was starting to look eerily like Norman Bates' outro in Lucy and my beloved film, "Psycho." She was probably a vegan too; she really wouldn't hurt a fly. I couldn't remember what it was they said Norman had, that made him dress up as his dead mother for half the day and then go about killing innocent people, but "disorder" was definitely part of it.

"You may have heard of it as abbreviated to O.C.D."

Oh... so clean germaphobe neat freak. Not a psycho serial killer. Wait did she say we both had this?

"I think you might have to read over those Yale Health surveys again, I'm pretty sure I checked off 'Occasionally' for hand-washing after bathroom use."

I saw her wince and scoot back in her own seat now.

"And besides, you just shook my hand, shouldn't you have been wearing gloves or something?"

"Liz," she began, a smile returning to her face. "You're thinking of the stereotypical OCD. There are many different forms. I happened to have the contamination fear, but that was just my personal obsession within the disorder. And about the gloves, it's funny you said that because that's something I used to do a couple of years ago."

"Really?! No offense, but that's pretty crazy."

Her eyebrow went up this time. I forgot, I was one to talk.

She probably had a Post-it stack locked and loaded in her perfectly organized desk behind her.

"Well, I didn't want to continue living like that, and I tried doing some exposures. I worked with my therapist and slowly built up to shaking hands. Now, I make it a point to shake every new client's hand. It's sort of like a check-in for me. To remind myself of where I can't go back to."

I nodded my head. I still wasn't sure how this related to me at all.

"Decision anxiety and guilt are common OCD themes, Liz. Many people resort to rules, or routines, or mental ruminating when faced with a choice."

"Oh."

"OCD is made of two parts, Liz. Your obsessions, which are what you fear happening and spend a lot of the day thinking about. For me, it was the fear that I was going to get sick and die. And then your compulsions, which are basically the things you do to try and prevent that bad thing from happening, i.e. the gloves."

In all my life I had never thought there was a real definition for what I was. I thought everyone was just better at hiding their anxiety every time the lunch lady listed out the options. Does everyone have this anxiety and hide it? Did you think something was wrong with your brain? Like the "right" answer wasn't obvious, but only you had this? I never heard anyone talking about this, it was never on an episode of Grey's Anatomy.

"It's gonna be a little difficult for you Liz, since you've been living with this disorder undiagnosed for so many years. You probably just see it as part of your identity at this point."

She wasn't wrong. Sometimes I felt like Lucy had only ever been my friend because I was the kind of kid that would let her boss me around, and like it. That was just Lucy. Wasn't it?

"My first piece of homework for you is to start to disassociate yourself from your disorder. Start thinking about what thoughts are OCD and what are your own. Now, I've found that a really helpful strategy for doing this is to give OCD a name. A persona almost." Her hands were grasping the air like there was something in it, maybe this OCD person, who knows? At least she wasn't talking with her hand like the other therapists did, like they thought you were so dumb you needed them to mime out their words for you.

I nodded along, although I wasn't too keen on this mention of "homework."

"With my younger patients, we normally call the OCD 'Mr. O.,' or 'The Bully,' and I have them draw pictures of their OCD as this person or monster, to give it a face and a personality and to really separate them from the healthy part of their mind."

I didn't say anything.

"It seems to me like you've just been white knuckling this disease for the past few months to try and pretend it's not there, Liz. And I wish it was as easy as that. But we can't just keep suppressing it, it just makes it stronger. We need to do the opposite and acknowledge its presence. What do you say, what can we name your OCD?"

"I don't know. It's not like it's a separate person, it's just my brain," I said, still skeptical of this exercise.

"I hear what you're saying, but please give this a try, I think you'll find it freeing and enlightening," she said patiently and nonjudgmentally.

"Ok," she continued when I stared at her blankly, "it's your brain, you say.... Hmm. brain, brain, ah! What about 'Brian' as a name for your OCD?"

"Sure, Brian." I knew I didn't really have a choice. Not like I wanted to have one anyway.

"Okay. So, Liz, tell me about Brian."

Epilogue

To avoid getting "the bends," deep sea divers must ascend slowly, making multiple stops along the way to decompress and gradually reduce the excess pressure in the body before moving on to the next decompression stop. Move too quickly or skip the stops and you're in trouble. After I'd disastrously cut the rope too quickly before, Linda the hippy therapist taught me how to let go slowly, how to gradually wean myself off my dependence on Brian.

I'm not gonna lie and say there aren't still times I think about Brian. People will tell you that trauma can be cured, and that one day you'll be fixed: my mom being the biggest sucker in believing that scam. But what really happens is that it's just not that loud anymore. The thoughts: not my life.

My daughter wakes me up screaming every morning when her binky falls on the ground and gets covered with dog fur. My husband keeps me up all night talking on work calls because he insists that his mind is clearer in bed. The city never sleeps, there are bus horns and train engines competing to be the loudest, and yet things are quieter for me now. I still hear him in the back of my head every now and then when I'm folding laundry, and he tells me it's gotta be "just right" or to run that extra mile because I want to be alive for my daughter's wedding. But I have too many people who need me now. My daughter is my world; my husband keeps it turning.

I don't listen to Brian anymore. I hear him, but I don't listen. I don't give him that power anymore. And it works. His voice gets quieter and quieter like an elephant turning into the mouse it's terrified of. I picture him shrinking every day that I eat those donuts my daughter made with her kindergarten class. But as he always said, unless it was 0 to begin with, it will never be 0. And some days are harder than others. But generally, it's like an asymptote. Always approaching that silence, but never completely getting there. And I've come to accept that. "Dr." Linda (who actually does make me feel better) told me it builds character. I like to believe in that. I would like to think that in all Brian's efforts to ruin my life and everything I have to live for, I ended up gaining something from it. Trauma quirks, if you will.

⌇

"They're adorable together, don't you think?"

"Our kids, or the budding bromance between Ashton and my husband going on over there." The two of them in charge of the barbeque and in an animated conversation about grilling technique.

"Our kids, dummy. Gosh, look at Molly, she's a real beauty Liz."

I pulled up my sunglasses so I could get a better view of the two little kids, giving each other sunblock tattoos next to the diving board. Molly's strawberry blonde hair and dark, chestnut eyes glimmered in the sunlight, and her toothy smile twinkled. It was weird having a mini version of you, who had your same features, but looked completely different. I wasn't one to live vicariously through my child, but I could tell Molly would grow up to be prettier than I had ever been. It made me happy for her. I hoped there would be many things that Molly wouldn't inherit from me.

"Oh, look Liz, they're getting noodles."

I looked across the pool at the two children, laughing and fumbling through the stack of noodles in the bin. Their giggles seemed to make ripples in the water; it was contagious.

"Eenie meenie miney moe." The squeaky voices and familiar tune caught my attention. I looked back over at Molly and Mikey. I hadn't been watching to see who had sorted them, but the noodles were laid out in two piles: one red and one blue. Molly was moving her pointed finger between each one. I held my breath. I may have gotten rid of Brian, but he wasn't dead. You'd be stupid to think Pennywise wouldn't come back just because you faced your childhood fears. Same with Freddy and the nightmares. Some things just don't die.

I could see Brian flicking that little innocent finger, reminding me that no one was safe from his touch. It was like the Jaws music had started to play in the background, and that fin was circling around and around the one thing I loved the most. I guess Jaws 2 wasn't that unrealistic: your monsters don't just follow you, but you pass them down to your kids. We all become our parents, right?

I stared at the pool and felt as if my eyes could overfill it with tears in a heartbeat. Lucy was saying something to me, but I wasn't listening, I couldn't do anything but watch it happen.

I could tell her just to pick and tell her that she can stop looking for gold halos and the direction towards being a good person because God isn't real anyway. At least not the God who judges you and punishes you. But I needed her to stop on her own, it was my only hope.

But Molly didn't put her finger down. It stood there shakily pointing at the red pile of pool noodles like she'd seen a ghost. Maybe she had. I looked at her face, was she trying to understand if a red seahorse was her destiny? I held my breath but resisted the urge to clear my throat. The water had cleared out of my lungs but now it was right in front of me.

I didn't realize my eyes were closed until I opened them, and the light flooded my face. I saw Molly's concentrated face dissipate and the innocence returned like the color in your skin after you've been pinching it for too long. She threw her hands up in the air and grabbed a noodle with a smile. She laughed and the two of them jumped into the pool with a splash. I stared at her seahorse. I'd never been one for choosing things, but blue was my new favorite color.

Resources

International OCD Foundation (IOCDF)
Aim to ensure no-one with OCD and related disorders suffers alone. IOCDF provides a community for help, healing and hope.
Website: https://www.iocdf.org

NOCD
Clinical resource for effectively treating OCD.
Website: https://www.treatmyocd.com

Promly
A Gen Z co-created social enterprise that aims to unify via empowerment, connectedness and providing holistic support and education.
Website: https://www.promly.org

A portion of the proceeds from this book will go towards supporting the International OCD Foundation's mission to ensure no-one affected by OCD and related disorders suffers alone. Their community provides help, healing, and hope.

<h1 style="text-align:center">Acknowledgments</h1>

Above anything else, I am grateful to be growing up in this time, where neurodiversity is something we are no longer afraid to acknowledge, talk about, and write about.

My heart goes out to all the past generations of anxious minds that were called crazy and all of those "crazy people" who probably had a lot of great things to share with the world. As much as I hate to glamorize OCD, the attention-to-detail and over-analyzing specialties it has given me have allowed me to become a more insightful person. And with insight, comes empathy. We all just want to understand the world we see, even if it doesn't understand us.

I can't talk about empathy without mentioning my mother. This book is as much mine as it is hers. Every time the sheer number of words behind my cursor would send me into a spiral of overwhelm, my mom would come to the rescue. She helped me organize and cut and wrestle this mass of rambling pages into a meaningful manuscript and reminded me—without reassuring me—that no matter what my brain said, it didn't have to be perfect.

She stayed by my side as my unofficial editor throughout each year of high school despite me telling her she'd "never get what having OCD was like" and "teenagers aren't supposed to spend this much time with their moms." It wasn't till my junior year, my third year into writing, that I realized she wasn't trying to get anything. She simply wanted to be there right alongside me. Every case of OCD is unique, and no podcast, book, or even therapist can tell you how your kid is feeling better than they can tell you themselves. Thank you, Mom, for letting me be the one to tell my own story.

In terms of my literary pursuit, I can thank no one more than my elementary school teachers—mainly just for putting up with me. I was the sort of kid who wanted to impress adults, which meant "writing books" for them that were two words away from being the story we just read in class. Or reading books like "Watership Down" in third grade, which, who knows? Maybe I was Richard Adams' target audience for it because I really did think it was just about bunnies. My first real piece of writing though, in first grade, was a "special moment" story in "Ms. Jenny" Seeds' class. She said to write about a seed, not the whole watermelon. It's funny because I don't remember what moment I wrote about, but the day she read my story to the class was one moment I will never forget. She said as long as I could come up with ideas, I should keep on writing. Thank you, Ms. Jenny, for making writing something special to me.

I wouldn't have been able to write anything meaningful, however, if I didn't have support from teachers like Ms. McAllister. I'm not sure she remembers me, but I hope she knows what an impact she had on my life. Sixth grade was possibly the peak of my OCD, and Ms. McAllister didn't hesitate to become my makeshift teacher/therapist on campus, to the point where she would write out my homework on stickers to stick in my organizer because writing was too triggering. She would go on my Google Classroom account and turn in assignments for me, so I didn't spend my entire day writing essays when she asked for a sentence. Any other teacher would've just seen a defiant kid trying to be difficult. But she saw something in me worth helping, and when my true writing could be extracted from all the compulsive junk I was producing, Ms. McAllister made sure I knew it was something to be proud of. Thank you for doing way more than your paycheck.

I also want to thank one of my current teachers, Ms. Muttick, who is a writer herself. Ms. Muttick agreed to be my advisor during the later stages of my writing. She gave me valuable insights into what did and didn't make sense to a reader that didn't have the exact same mind as me, and she also gave me confidence to keep my authentic voice in my work.

The same goes to my publisher, Marina Aris, who took me on even though I was a seventeen-year-old girl with anxiety you could physically sense in our introductory Zoom call. She reminded me constantly to stay true to who I was and not be influenced by what I thought would sell or what I thought people wanted me to write. She just wanted me to write. But we talked a lot too, and I've gained an incredible amount of insight into the publishing world because of her. Thank you.

On a more random note, I would like to thank someone I have never met in person or virtually: Lena Dunham. Before I started watching Girls, I'd only ever seen OCD portrayed in the form of Danny Tanner with the dustpan or some other neat freak on my screen. I know I am not alone when I say the episode about Hannah's OCD is the most genuine depiction of the illness I have ever seen. The rumination, the misery, and the pure overwhelm of OCD was clear from Lena's outstanding acting and incredible screenwriting. I'd never felt more seen by anyone else before, and again, Lena and I have never met.

Finally, I could not have even fathomed writing this book if I did not have a support system in place in the other parts of my life. I want to thank all my high school friends, and especially Jamie Rosenbloom and Riley Algazy, who read my work and assured me I wasn't completely "delulu" about this dream of mine. Thank you for being my friend even when I showed up to school wearing ten pairs of socks and disappeared at lunch to eat in my mom's car where things felt safer. Thank you for helping me when I graduated to picking out my own clothes and eating in the school cafeteria that I'm still convinced may have been the tiniest bit contaminated. I knew these were real friends when they would yell at me in the kindest way possible to get out of my head because this was our school dance, and I was going to miss it. Thank you for reeling me back in, time and time again.

And thank you to my family, who have put up with me for seventeen years. It's not easy living with someone with OCD. If something wasn't just right for me, it was hell for everyone else. I'm not proud of it, but my family still never made me feel like a burden. Their love was always stronger than their frustration. And their anger was never at me; it was always this terrible disease that stole away their daughter and sister and then was glamorized as a neatness fixation in the media. But despite all the tearful moments and times they had to see me at my worst, my family was also the thing that motivated me to get better. The laughter as we played improv games together, the "Always Sunny" marathons we'd watch, the stupid humor of everything we did together as a family made life seem a whole lot lighter. Learning to take myself less seriously made me take recovery a whole lot more seriously. I am infinitely grateful to all of you.

About the Author

Sarah Marine is a teen writer, student, and registered EMT. She also writes poetry and contributes articles to her school newspaper. You'll probably find her re-watching Gilmore Girls (she's proudly Team Jess). Sarah writes for The Mental Notes Journal, a digital publication founded by her sister, and for Promly, a social media platform dedicated to helping teens make meaningful connections. She finds writing an invaluable way to process her thoughts and distinguish her voice. Sarah has called Seattle, London, and now the Garden State home. Someday, she hopes to keep telling stories, helping others, and making her mark one page at a time.

sarahmarine.com